A LADY
IN ATTENDANCE

Center Point
Large Print

Also by Rachel Fordham and available from Center Point Large Print:

The Hope of Azure Springs
Yours Truly, Thomas
A Life Once Dreamed

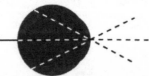

This Large Print Book carries the Seal of Approval of N.A.V.H.

A
LADY
IN
ATTENDANCE

RACHEL FORDHAM

CENTER POINT LARGE PRINT
THORNDIKE, MAINE

This Center Point Large Print edition
is published in the year 2021 by arrangement with
Revell, a division of Baker Publishing Group.

This is a work of historical reconstruction; the appearances
of certain historical figures are therefore inevitable.
All other characters, however, are products of the author's
imagination, and any resemblance to actual persons,
living or dead, is coincidental.

The text of this Large Print edition is unabridged.
In other aspects, this book may vary
from the original edition.
Printed in the United States of America
on permanent paper.
Set in 16-point Times New Roman type.

ISBN: 978-1-63808-009-1

The Library of Congress has cataloged this record
under Library of Congress Control Number: 2021936981

For everyone who made our time
in Buffalo, New York,
four years we'll never forget
and
for our friends at the PFD
who are now family.

To love at all is to be vulnerable.
C. S. Lewis

A LADY
IN ATTENDANCE

PROLOGUE

House of Refuge, Hudson, New York, 1893

The coarse gray fabric of Hazel's newly donned uniform felt uncomfortable and foreign against her skin. She scratched her neck, trying in vain to force the itch away, but it was no use. These drab clothes would likely never feel comfortable, nor would these dark walls and tall fences ever feel like home.

"You'll get used to it," said the girl on her right. She looked to be fifteen, maybe sixteen, and despite the dreary location wore a cheerful smile on her pale face. "It ain't so bad here."

The girl on Hazel's left snickered but nodded. Both girls had been assigned to scrub the dining hall's floor with her and had readily begun answering her questions.

"It ain't no castle with a moat, but they feed us three times a day, and that's more than I ate before bein' sent to the reformatory," the girl on her right said.

"It's prison," Hazel whispered, unsure why they were keeping their voices so low. "It won't get better. Not until we get out."

"Won't be all better when you get out. People don't trust no one that's lived behind bars.

11

Once a convict, always a convict. Even if they talk about us being trained and tutored for a better life, you'll still be stained. Your five-year sentence might as well be a lifetime one. Enjoy the food and roof over your head while you got it." The younger inmate pushed her stringy hair from her face with her wet hand and stared at her with large doe-like eyes. "It's better here'n where I came from. Better'n where most of us come from."

Hazel wanted to argue, to tell these girls that life outside the reformatory's walls *was* better. That freedom of any kind was better than iron fences. But she held back, knowing the world she had come from differed from their world. She'd had money and a family name. She cringed, remembering how her world had rejected her, the pain of her sentencing, and the stoop of her parents' shoulders. The truth was, she wasn't sure where she'd be at this very moment if she were not here as a committed prisoner of the House of Refuge.

With her eyes on the dirty water and a heaviness in her heart, she spoke. "Tell me what it's like living here." She had been in such a daze when she arrived, she hardly heard the matron's instructions. "I do wish to get through this time unscathed if I can—and perhaps somehow to have a future."

"There's a lady who comes by often. She runs

a club or somethin', and she's changed it around here," the inmate on her left said. She was older and less enthusiastic than her counterpart. "She's helping us learn skills so we can leave changed. They's teaching us to sew and cook, and they preach. But you gotta work hard too. You gotta listen and follow directions. If you do, you'll get by."

Hazel forced a smile despite the nausea assaulting her stomach. Menial labor held no appeal, yet these women spoke as though it were a gift. She chided her ungrateful heart and forced herself to listen despite her innate desire to argue and fight against her lot.

"What you gotta know is that this building's got three floors, and you move up or down dependin' on if you work hard and learn or if you don't. They even got cottages inside the gates for those who are doin' the best."

Hazel managed to weakly say, "I hope you get to live there soon."

"We all hope for that. The hardened women move to the first floor, and there are rooms that women have to go to all by themselves. I never wanna go there." She was old enough that there were creases near her eyes and lines on her forehead that didn't leave, even when her face relaxed. She picked up her brush and began scrubbing the floor again. With her head bent, she talked faster. "They have us pray every day, and preachers come and talk to us. I been hearin' their words since coming. They talk of picking a direction to run in and stayin' on a path. I don't understand it all, but I figure if I listen to them, I'll avoid the first floor, and maybe I could have a life that's better'n what I've known. I gotta hope." Her cheeks turned red. "I ain't touched the bottle in months now. What you in for?"

"I'm sure she's here for running about with some married man," the young inmate said with a giggle. "It's always men or drink."

"Nah, it's always being desperate that brings us here," the more seasoned inmate said.

"I don't know desperation—not like you've known it." Hazel took a slow breath as she wrestled with what to tell these women about her past. She had so much regret, heartache, and hurt she could share, but instead, she simply said, "I was accused of burglary."

"Burglary?" The younger woman's voice jumped up an octave. "What did you steal?"

The words assaulted her, and she opened her mouth, ready to defend herself, then shut it. They assumed her guilty. Like everyone else, they believed she'd stolen and brought this fate on herself. She swallowed the pain, knowing that she was not completely innocent, nor was she guilty. But saying as much would do no good. "It matters little," she said. "I'm here now, and I suppose all that matters is if I move upstairs or down."

CHAPTER
ONE

Amherst, New York, 1898

"Have you worked as a lady in attendance before?"

Hazel forced her eyes to remain on the man opposite her and made herself appear confident and at ease. It was no easy task, considering how long it had been since she'd been in such close proximity to a man who wasn't a guard. Nothing about Doctor Watts was overly intimidating, yet her heart raced as she searched for an adequate response.

Her eyes betrayed her and darted away, landing on a painting above his head. A lush, green landscape. Peaceful, serene, calm. Something her life hadn't been in a long time, not since before—

"I wish I could tell you I had years of experience, but the truth is that I've never spent one day, not even one moment, as a lady in attendance. From what I understand, not many women have." She sighed, worried her chances at a dignified job were over with the confession. Since leaving the reformatory, she'd already faced a slew of rejections and disappointments. Leaning forward, she said, "I have spent time in the medical field and know how to care for patients."

She winced, knowing she was stretching the truth—a habit she'd fought to leave behind. Her uncle *was* a doctor, and she had spent a summer in his home. That counted toward medical exposure, did it not?

"You're correct. It's quite new." His soft but steady voice interrupted her thoughts. "I try to keep up on what's working in dentistry, and there has been much success found in hiring help. It will not be long before it is the normal way of doing things." His words came slowly, as though speaking to her made him uneasy. Even his posture screamed of nervousness—his long fingers wringing together in his lap and the way he shifted about in his seat. "You say you've been involved in the medical community. That will help." He nodded his head, a small smile pulling at the corners of his mouth, and with it her hope grew. "I don't see the need to interview anyone else. Nursing experience is better than nothing at all. You may begin tomorrow."

Thrilled by his words, she grinned. A real, legitimate job—her first!

"Thank you," she said, rising from her seat so quickly the chair nearly overturned. "You won't be sorry. I can learn quickly, and I'll work hard. I'll work so hard. Oh, thank you. To work here is more than I could have hoped for."

"Just one more thing." His cheeks took on a slight pink hue similar to the shade of dress she'd often worn as a girl. The uneasiness she'd sensed in him multiplied tenfold.

"Yes?"

He shook his head and turned away. "Never mind. It's nothing. I look forward to having your help."

"Do you have a concern?"

"Well, yes. I suppose I do." He stood on his long legs and paced behind his desk. "I've never worked with anyone other than my father before he died. Since then, it's just been me and my patients. I . . . well, I'm not sure how exactly to go about it. We'll be in close proximity and . . ."

"Yes?" she said when he paused, unsure what it was he was afraid of. She'd given him no reason to suspect she had a shameful past, had she? "What is it?"

"It's just . . . I don't want things to get uncomfortable. That's all." From the looks of it, he was already distressed over the matter. He cleared his throat. "I see the advantages of hiring help, but I've heard stories. I need not go into what I've heard, but . . . there are potential problems with having a woman in the office."

"Problems?"

Sweat beaded on his forehead. He pulled a handkerchief from his pocket and wiped it. "There will be no . . . no extra affection given to patients . . . you know what I'm saying, what I mean?"

"I understand, and I assure you it won't be a problem."

"And . . . and, well, my father told me that . . . he said I ought to always be honest from the start." The pink in his cheeks deepened. "I feel it important to say that I have every intention of remaining unattached. We will be professional in our relationship, keeping firm boundaries. Never overstepping the lines of propriety." He wiped again at his perspiring forehead. "I apologize for my bluntness."

Hazel bit hard on her bottom lip so she wouldn't laugh. She needed this job and couldn't lose it on account of one ill-timed guffaw. Little did he know she was the last person he needed to worry about. All the romantic ambitions she'd held long ago had been put to rest and replaced by much simpler dreams. Now she craved a future unblemished by the past, enough bread to eat, and to be reconciled with her family. Beyond that, she dared not hope.

She politely put her hand out to him. It dangled in the air only a moment before he took it, his large hand enveloping her much smaller one. "You needn't worry on that account. I have no motives other than working."

He seemed to relax. "I'm sorry, it's just I've had a whole slew of ladies stopping in about the position, and most of them are young. The way they spoke and giggled unnerved me. Some even had mothers with them asking after my personal affairs. It has left me with my guard up."

"Please, be at ease." Hazel smiled, still delighted with the prospect of real work. "I'm twenty-five, well past my youthful years." She swallowed, knowing she ought to say so much more about her past, but voicing it was not an option. Her past, her identity, and especially her years behind those iron gates could not be mentioned, not if she wanted to remain employed and off the streets. "I assure you, ours will be a most proper arrangement."

"I believe we'll work well together," he said in his soft way. "Let me show you around the office."

"What shall I call you?" she asked before they'd gotten very far. "Should I call you Doctor Watts at all times?"

He ran a hand through his dark hair. "I suppose you could call me Gilbert when it's just the two of us. First names wouldn't be crossing any lines, considering we will be colleagues in a sense. But *Doctor Watts* would be more appropriate when we are working around patients. Does that suit you?"

"Any name will do. I simply wondered what you would prefer." *Gilbert,* she said in her mind. They were hardly acquainted, yet she already felt that his name fit him. It seemed like a gentle, friendly name.

"And I will introduce you as my lady in attendance, Miss McDowell."

She flinched at the pseudonym, looked toward the door, and for a moment thought of running away from the shame she felt, hating herself for the lie. Regret once again swept over her, churning inside until she feared she would be sick. Life outside the reformatory walls was supposed to be fresh and new, but already she'd soiled it with a falsehood. She blinked quickly, trying to still the rush of emotion. She'd lied, it was true, but what options did she have? In two other towns she'd asked after work and been swiftly rejected when she told them her story. "Call me Hazel whenever you'd like. I prefer it."

"Very well, Hazel. Here is where our patients come in and wait if we are busy." He motioned around the small front room that consisted of four wooden chairs set against a scuffed cream-colored wall. In truth, the room would have been forgettable if not for the vibrant paintings that added luscious colors, warm and rich, to the small space.

Without intending to, Hazel sighed. "I was so nervous waiting to meet with you that I didn't notice the paintings before. They're exquisite."

Gilbert looked from Hazel to the paintings. "Thank you. I'm glad you find them pleasing."

He motioned for her to follow. "You'll greet our patients, and when I am ready, you'll bring them back." They stepped past the front counter and walked to the back of the office. "I have one chair here that reclines, and it's where we do our actual work. In this next room, I have a cot, so if someone needs time to recover before leaving, they may rest there. Your job will be seeing to patients before and after they come to me. I like to help everyone be comfortable, but I'll work faster if you can help me with that. You'll also hand me instruments as necessary."

"I can do all that." She pointed toward a door. "What's down the hall?"

"That's the room where I make bridges and dentures. I call it my art room." His gaze stayed on the door at the end of the hall, giving her a moment to study him. He reminded her of someone, but she couldn't peg down who. She'd guess he was thirty, give or take a year or two. He was tall, much taller than she was, with a lean build and long arms and legs. His rich dark hair was in need of a cut and his clothes were in need of ironing, but even with him being slightly disheveled, she still found him a handsome man who was shy and unsuspecting.

Why was he a dentist? Teeth and mouths were far from exciting. In her case, the work was a necessity, and being a woman, her options were limited, but he could have been anything.

A commanding lawyer or a dashing doctor. She pushed the thought aside, realizing it was a tad early to judge his motives.

"Is there anything else I should know?" Hazel asked, breaking the silence.

"Most of it I'll teach you as we go. But, well, I do want you to know that my patients—ours, now—matter a great deal to me. I want them to have the best care."

She stepped a little closer to him and with genuine conviction said, "Then that is what I will give them."

He held her gaze and nodded. "I believe you will. We discussed the particulars when you first arrived. I'll show you tomorrow where we clean the instruments and how to keep notes. If you have no questions, then I think it is settled. I appreciate your help."

Glancing once more around the room, she admired other paintings that hung throughout the simple but comfortable building. Working with him did not seem daunting, and neither did filling her days attending to the patients' needs. She could do this. There had been a time in her life when it would have been an ill fit, but now, she felt immense gratitude. The patients did not scare her, and the teeth, well, she'd manage. Perhaps Providence had led her down Front Street on the very day Gilbert Watts was interviewing for a reason. A pleasant warmth filled her heart, and for a moment she felt less alone and less afraid.

Grinning, she said, "I'm very thankful. I'll be here tomorrow."

Gilbert Watts watched Hazel leave. She'd said she was twenty-five, and he'd believed it when she walked in. She'd been so prim and proper, not a bit silly like the younger female interviewees had been. But now, seeing her skip away, he didn't think she seemed all that different.

No matter her demeanor, he'd given her his word, so there'd be no changing his mind—at least not until after he gave her a chance. Ladies in attendance, once a novel idea, were on course to become the norm. And he saw the benefits. With a lady in the office, his young female patients could come more freely rather than having to find a chaperone. With good help, he knew he could work faster. And with the demand for his services so high, he'd be able to help additional patients.

Despite the obvious rewards of having help, he worried. He'd mulled the decision over in his mind for many weeks before putting up the "Help Wanted" sign. Somehow he'd become a creature of habit, comfortable in his bachelor-dentist ways. Hazel may wish to prattle aimlessly about everything and nothing all at the same time. Or worse, she may cry at the sight of someone in pain or be too delicate to handle the bloodier side of dentistry, and he had no experience with tears or with prattle.

Looking out the front window again, he caught one more glimpse of Hazel before she turned the corner. He'd thought her hair was brown, but now with the sun shining on it, the color looked nearly red.

In dental school, the other men called redheads *spitfires,* and they swore they had tempers that matched the hue of their hair. The thought of a hot-tempered woman working for him made his palms sweat. He wiped his hands on his pants, turned away from the window, and retreated to the art room, where he threw his nervous energy into Rebecca Weidel's bridgework. He'd been working extra hard on this one and wanted it to be perfect. Poor Rebecca had lost both of her front teeth as a youth, and now she was about to marry her sweetheart. The teeth, the wedding. He knew it was all expensive and important. These teeth would be a work of art that Rebecca and her future husband would never regret spending their savings on.

CHAPTER
TWO

"Ina!" Hazel shouted as she burst through the front door of the women's boardinghouse. "Ina!"

Her new friend emerged from around the corner with a pile of papers in her hand and concern written across her face. "What is it?"

"I have a job!" Hazel danced around the room, unable to control her excitement. "A real job. And it's not stitching or cleaning like I'd feared."

Ina set down her load and grabbed her friend's hands, pulling her into an embrace. "Oh, I'm so glad. This day was going so horribly wrong, and now you've brightened it. Tell me everything."

The two had met only a week ago when Hazel first arrived at the boardinghouse, but already they shared a sisterly bond. Hazel's years in prison, with its ever-changing social dynamic, had taught her to make friends quickly and to never take a kind heart for granted. On Hazel's first night at the boardinghouse, Ina asked Hazel to go for a walk with her and they talked without ceasing, proving that the bonds of friendship did not require excessive time to cure.

"Why was your day so horrible?" Hazel stopped prancing about and studied her schoolteacher friend, only to find her sunny disposition darkened. "What happened?"

"Tell me about your job first."

"I can't. Not until you tell me what happened. Otherwise I'll worry more than I already am."

Ina ran her hand along the raised red birthmark that covered the majority of her chin. Hazel had inquired about the mark shortly after their first meeting, and Ina had returned her question with a bucket of tears as she told Hazel how it was her curse in life.

"Tell me about your day," Hazel pleaded. "I want to hear."

"Very well. Dolores, another teacher, had her brother, who she's been telling me about for years, meet me for our noon meal. I'd dreamed of this encounter. I imagined he would see past my ugly mark and find me charming." Ina continued to touch her face, her fingers sliding back and forth along her jawbone. "He stared at my chin but didn't ask about it. His eyes weren't kind—they were disapproving. Worse than that, they made me want to lock myself away where no one could see me." Her shoulders slouched. "If only I could stop myself from dreaming, maybe I could be content with what I have."

"I'm sorry." Hazel set a sympathetic hand on her friend's arm. She understood wishing for things to be different, but poor Ina's remorse was not of her own doing. And unlike Hazel's,

26

perhaps it could be overcome. "Someday someone will see you for you. There must be a man out there—someone smart enough to know what a treasure you are. Whoever he is, that is who you truly want to be with."

"You're sweet to say it." Ina's gaze wandered around the poorly lit parlor they shared with the other boarders. Dark wallpaper and heavy curtains only added to the gloom. "I'm twenty-three, and even though I'd like to escape this place and move into a home of my own, I think I need to accept that this is my life." She raised her shoulders and laughed. "It's just a bad day. I'm sure tomorrow I'll cling to my romantic notions again. Now, tell me about your job. I've no doubt your good news will lift my spirits."

"It's for Doctor Watts, the dentist. Do you know of him?"

"I've taken girls with toothaches to see him. He's handsome in a quiet sort of way."

Hazel hadn't expected to see stars in her friend's eyes again so quickly. Although she should have. In the short week they'd spent together, Hazel had found Ina's sunny disposition and affectionate yearnings endearing. "What do you know of him?"

"Not a great deal. I know he grew up here and leads a quiet life. There doesn't seem to be much else to tell. He's not married. He's just a dentist."

"He can't be *just* a dentist," Hazel said,

picturing the man she'd met. He'd been quiet, but she'd sensed that there was more to him than he'd shown her. And when he'd looked toward his art room, she'd seen a spark in his eye. "No one is *just* a dentist."

"I don't know much about him. When I've been there, I've just sat and admired him while he treated the girls. I don't think there's a rule against staring at a dentist, is there?" She giggled. "I envy you—spending all day with a handsome man."

"I suppose to some he is attractive, and with a little cleaning up, he'd be ever so much more. But it makes no difference. He made himself clear that he has no interest in anything beyond a working relationship. Oh, Ina, it was so funny. I nearly burst out laughing." She mimicked Gilbert's nervous stance. "He shifted around, telling me he needed to make sure I understood. 'I have every intention of remaining *unattached*.' He said it just like that."

Ina laughed, but Hazel sensed a hint of sadness behind the jovial sound. "I suppose you and I will never make a match." She frowned, then rallied and straightened her shoulders. "At least we know how to make our own joy. You have your flute and I have my books, and we can find comfort in our ability to care for ourselves."

"You're right. Work is a blessing. Although I'm not sure I'll enjoy looking in people's mouths." Hazel scrunched up her face and groaned.

"I wouldn't like that either. But I wouldn't mind looking at Doctor Watts all day. Even if he isn't the marrying sort."

"I'm not sure I'm the marrying sort either," Hazel said, cringing at the irony of her words. "But I've never been against staring at one of God's finer creations. I shouldn't jest. He seems a good enough man. I'd better go and press my dress for tomorrow."

On her first day as a lady in attendance, Hazel asked many questions and twice had to fight the bile that rose in her throat at the sights and smells she saw in people's mouths. But she never let on, and she worked hard, grateful for the tireless work she'd performed at the reformatory and the work ethic she'd left with. Gilbert spoke little, but more than once she saw him nod or smile as she worked. And once, he said, "You have a way with people."

Her second day, she asked the same questions again just to be certain she knew the answers. And she only wanted to run for a bucket once when a Mr. Loffer came in with a bulging cheek that nearly exploded when Gilbert drained it.

Later, when Davey Smith came in with a toothache, she held the boy's hand. He squeezed back tightly as Gilbert pulled his tooth. When he was about to leave, Davey threw his arms around her and she wondered why it'd taken her so many years to truly care about others.

By her third day, she was moving about the office with ease. Between patients she tackled the floors, scrubbing years of dirt off the wide wooden planks. Gilbert nodded when she caught his eye, and then to her surprise, he got his own rag and joined her.

"I can do the floors," Hazel said when he knelt beside her. "I'm not sure it's proper for a dentist to scrub the floors."

Gilbert dipped his rag into the bucket. "I've never cared much for how others saw me." He knelt beside her. "You've not stopped working for a single minute. I think I ought to take a lesson from you."

A week in, and she could hand him the tools he wanted without being asked. In that same amount of time, she'd grown accustomed to Gilbert's near-silent ways and made herself at home in the small office.

On her eighth day of attending, she was beginning to believe she knew what to expect at the office, until little Bianca Carluccio, with her round cheeks and black curls, arrived. The poor child shook with fear, whimpering her nervousness in Italian. Hazel grabbed the dental file Gilbert was holding and balanced it on the tip of her finger. Bianca's eyes followed her as she walked on her tiptoes, then pretended to dance like a vaudeville star. Bianca clapped her hands, and then she laughed. And then Gilbert laughed.

Hazel stopped what she was doing, and the metal instrument fell to the floor. Dumbstruck, she gaped at him, mesmerized by the sound of his deep, warm laugh. How sweet the sound. Tears crept into her eyes, threatening to spill over. Five somber years spent locked away from laughter and now here she was surrounded by its stirring melody.

"Let me try." He picked up the file and placed it on the tip of his finger. Up on his toes he went, but before he could frolic across the floor like she had done, he dropped it. With a clang, it hit the freshly washed planks. Again, he laughed, and Hazel knew working for Gilbert, no matter how professional their relationship was to be, would also be fun.

"Mr. Murdock, the doctor needs you to hold still and stop acting like a baby," Hazel said, imitating the authoritative voices the matrons at the reformatory had used so often.

"I'm trying," the large man said as he squirmed, rocking his head back and forth. Beads of sweat ran off his face, dripping onto the floor. "I'm just awful scared."

Hazel bent over him and looked him straight in the eye. "You are going to have to try harder. You hold still or I'll spread word all over town that you were a worse patient than Willard Pierson, and he's six years old."

Mr. Murdock nodded twice and then held his body perfectly still like a giant statue, mouth ajar. Gilbert slid the goat's foot elevator under Mr. Murdock's bad tooth. Blood seeped from the gums, but he didn't flinch. The stubborn tooth now wiggled slightly. Gilbert's forearms flexed, and his face grew tense as he gripped the tooth with the forceps and worked it in a figure-eight pattern. With the steady movement, the tooth worked itself looser and looser until it finally came free. Hazel released the breath she'd been holding and patted Mr. Murdock's shoulder.

"It's out." Gilbert held out the tooth in front of the man so he could see it. Hazel handed Gilbert fresh bandages, and he busied himself stopping the bleeding. "The pain may take time to go away completely, but it'll subside now that the source of the pain is gone."

Mr. Murdock turned toward Hazel with somber, bashful eyes. Gilbert pumped the chair and returned the man to sitting. She smiled at their patient. "I'm sorry I had to be so stern with you."

Mr. Murdock's cheeks, and even his multiple chins, turned pink. Then his lips spread into a sheepish grin. With cloth dangling from his mouth, he said, "I'd planned to be much braver. I'm right sorry about the way I acted. I hope I can trust you to keep my behavior between the three of us."

Hazel gave him another reassuring pat. "Of

course. Having a tooth pulled is no small matter. Besides, Doctor Watts isn't too much of a talker, so no need to worry about him, and I can keep a secret when I need to."

"I wasn't sure about having a woman here, but you're something else. You're something special."

"That's a lovely compliment." Hazel breathed easier knowing Mr. Murdock would not hold a grudge against her for her firm words. "When you're ready, I'll take you to the other room to rest. We'd like to know your mouth is done bleeding before you go home."

After settling Mr. Murdock in the recovery room, she went back to the chair to clean it before the next patient. Gilbert watched her, amazed at the efficient way she went about her tasks as though she'd spent years, not days, at the dental office.

"You think I was too blunt?" she asked Gilbert after wiping the head of the chair dry.

He stopped writing in Mr. Murdock's chart and rubbed the scruff on his chin. "Naw, he seemed rather taken with you. I don't think he minded." He chuckled softly. "I've wanted to say things like that for years."

"You should try it. I can't imagine how you would ever get that tooth out otherwise."

"You admitted to him yourself that I'm not much of a talker." Gilbert smiled at her.

Unbeknownst to her, even this conversation was out of character for him. "I've been quiet so long, I hardly remember how to say what must be said."

She gathered up the dirty instruments and put them into a pot. "With a little effort, you could be a regular conversationalist."

"I doubt I could ever be as firm as you were."

She elbowed him as she walked by. He startled, then relaxed when he saw the twinkle in her eyes. "There was a time when I was known for speaking my mind. I guess it's good you found me."

"I guess it is." He raised an elbow, surprised by his urge to respond with matched playfulness, but he held back, unsure what to make of this budding friendship. "I have a few patients who will make up tooth pain just to spend a little more time with you. We will be busier than ever."

"I'm glad I'm not scaring the patients away." She wiped the puddle of sweat from the floor.

"Wait until you see Murdock in the dead of summer. He's like Niagara Falls, never stopping."

Would she still be there in the dead of summer? It was early fall now. Summer was a long time coming. He swallowed the lump that rose in his throat when he thought of having the office to himself again.

"I'll be sure to have extra rags on hand."

"Maybe by next summer I'll remember how

to carry on a conversation and the office won't be so quiet for you." He lifted the chart he held higher and lowered his gaze, embarrassed by his bold words.

"I wouldn't stop you from conversing a bit more, but rest assured that you are an easy man to work for." Hazel dipped her dirty rag into the bucket and stood up. Her voice took on a different tone, one he couldn't quite decipher. Pensive, heavy—he couldn't decide. "I've enjoyed it more than anything in such a long time."

If his tongue hadn't been so slow to speak, he'd have inquired after her meaning, but she backed from the room muttering something about checking on Murdock before he could spit the query from his mouth.

Women had always made him nervous. His own mother died when he was young, leaving him with only a few scattered memories of her— hardly enough to help him navigate the world of women. His father had been a soft-spoken man and his brother, Eddie, well, he was louder, but he'd left without teaching Gilbert how to be at ease in the presence of the opposite sex, and he hadn't heard from him in years. His school years were spent at an all-boys school, and then dental school was all men. His friends had talked him into escorting ladies out from time to time, but it was never with enough frequency to feel comfortable, and that'd been years ago. Of course, he'd had women patients over the years. There'd been no way around that. But he'd said only what was necessary and busied himself with fixing their teeth.

And now here he was spending every day with an intriguing woman. She was pretty too. He'd been surprised the first time he'd thought her pretty, but he was not blind. Any man could tell she was well put together and full of life. Though there were times when he caught her out of the corner of his eye, and he thought he saw something sad in her countenance. The heaviness was fleeting, but it was there, and he wondered what part of her story caused the lingering sadness.

Normally, though, her brown eyes, with their green flecks, sparkled when she entered the room. Watching her boss Mr. Murdock around today was a thing of beauty. Gilbert was now entirely convinced Hazel's hair was red rather than brown. He'd never dreamed there was a way to get that man to hold still, but she'd done it. Perhaps redheads weren't the worst thing to have around a dental office.

How was it that someone so agreeable and hardworking had no husband or beau? Sure, she could be loud. He'd been able to hear her laughter through the entire office when Cicily Saxton was in, and when Naomi Koster, an opera singer, was waiting, Hazel had insisted on trying to sing a song with her. She could also be presumptuous and overly bold. When Anthony Pewter was in, she'd told him if he'd been dating Ramona for so many months already, he ought to either marry her or let her find someone who would.

Yes, she was bold and lively, but nothing she'd done all week had led him to believe she was unkind. It made no sense, her being unmarried.

Gilbert shook his head. Women were a mystery, that was for certain. And Hazel was no exception.

CHAPTER
THREE

"Why dentistry?" Hazel asked one day while writing notes in a chart.

"Haven't you heard the drill?"

Hazel raised a brow. "The drill? The one that sounds like a sick animal as it spins?"

"The way it squeals is soothing." Gilbert's face remained stoic, giving her no reason to think he was anything but serious.

"I guess one could find it soothing, though I don't think it's generally thought to be," she replied, masking her surprise. The dreadful squeal of the drill was piercing to her ears, leaving her wincing. "I would not have guessed that was the reason."

She looked closer at him and saw his shoulders shake ever so slightly—a suppressed laugh. Who would have thought the man had wit!

"Oh!" She laughed, utterly delighted by his humor. "You're awful. What is the real reason?"

He met her laugh with his own.

"Everyone hates the sound of the drill, but I don't mind it." He paused a moment, leaving her hungry for more and eager to understand the puzzle of a man she now worked for. "I knew someone would need to take over my father's practice. He loved his patients, so I thought he'd want to know they were in capable hands. Dentistry didn't excite me much at first, but soon I realized I would get to be an artist."

"An artist?" Hazel tilted her head, perplexed by his words. Mouths were filled with saliva, abhorrent smells, and rotten teeth, not with art.

"Every day I get to build dentures and bridges. Tiny sculptures that may never be appreciated, but I know they make life better and easier for the receiver. I know I could do careless work or I could slow down and ensure they fit properly and look the way the patient wants them to. I consider myself quite blessed to use my hands to make such important art. I see great value in it, even if others do not. To give someone a smile and teeth to eat with . . . it's rewarding."

"I'm glad it's not the sound of the drill that keeps you coming in day after day." She looked between the art room door and Gilbert and then down at her own hands. They'd produced so little to be proud of. She let her hands fall to her sides and forced a smile. "You are a fine artist."

He picked up a hand drill and fiddled with it. "Thank you. I could . . . I could show you how I make bridges. If you wanted to see."

Hazel looked toward the clock and groaned. Bridges and dentures had never intrigued her before, but now she wished she could stay and pepper him with questions. "I can't."

"Of course. I shouldn't have asked it. Your hours are done." His cheeks filled with color. "It was wrong of—"

"Some other time, please. I would like to see."

Oh, how she wanted to linger. A deep yearning to sit beside him and coax him into telling her about his ambitions and marvel over his artistic skill bubbled inside her. Instead, she bid him goodbye, offering no explanation for her rushed departure.

The night before, she'd slept restlessly, waking again and again in a cold sweat. In her dreams she was a girl living at her parents' home again, sleeping in the same four-poster bed with the lush, thick blankets she'd taken for granted. Her sisters came into her room and sat beside her, begging her to play with them. It was all so familiar and real, yet out of reach.

And then the room went dark, and her dream filled with storm clouds and thunder. She saw the flash of a knife and heard a piercing shriek. Gone were the loving feelings, having been replaced by a tight grip of fear that seized her so firmly, she woke beaded in sweat and gasping for air.

It was merely a dream, she knew that, yet the feelings were tangible. Darkness, loneliness, regret. Once fully awake, she'd resolved to try again to reconcile her past. Her sentence might always mar her record, but was there a way to escape the fear, to live free and honestly?

• • •

"I'll let Mr. Beck know you're here. I'm not sure if he'll see you or not," a stout woman with a threatening look said after Hazel knocked and stated her reason for coming. The biting winds of autumn blew her skirts about and sent a chill racing through her. She'd chosen to solicit Mr. Beck's help after asking another boarder if she knew any trustworthy judges. After work, she had hired a ride to Cheektowaga, hoping it would prove worth her time. "Wait here."

It was already midevening now, which was far from ideal, but there'd been no way around it. If she were to ask for time off, Gilbert might question why, and she didn't want to lie to him again. Guilt already riddled her conscience every time she heard him use her alias, Miss McDowell.

The intimidating woman returned and led her to an office on the far side of the house. In the center of the immaculate room was a giant desk covered in papers, and sitting behind it was a well-dressed man who didn't bother to rise when she entered. A cigar dangling between his fingers held his attention.

"Sir," she said when he didn't look up.

"What do you want?" he asked, his mustache arched downward with an exaggerated frown. "Do you know the hour?"

"Sir."

"I don't take visitors." He tapped his cigar on

the silver tray on his desk. "You should have made an appointment during the day, not come begging at my doorstep like some stray dog."

"I'm sorry for the inconvenience. I've recently taken a job and could not ask for time off." Fidgeting, she looked at the empty chair, then back at him. Did she dare sit without an invitation? "It's of the utmost importance. I assure you."

"Five minutes." He took a long draw from his cigar and watched the smoke puff from his mouth and rise like a cloud.

Hazel sat despite his never asking her to. The chair was lower than she'd expected. She sat as straight as she could, hoping to convey confidence. "I need a closed case opened, and I need to have the evidence reexamined. I was wrongly accused of a burglary. I stole nothing, and I've already paid dearly for it."

"A case from here? I know them all. I've been a judge here for twenty years." The man's brow formed a deep ridge down the center.

"It's from Buffalo. I can't go back right now, and I'm not sure I even trust the law there. I need someone from outside to help. That's why I came to you."

The man leaned back in his seat and drummed his fingers against the desk. "It's not my jurisdiction, so I can't help you. Besides, I'm not going to go stirring up trouble."

"I thought . . . I had hoped you would help me." Emotion laced her voice despite her efforts to remain calm and unaffected. "My life was stolen from me. I spent five years in a reformatory and now I carry the mark of an ex-convict." She paused, swallowing the lump that had risen when she said the words aloud. "I can't go back to my family, not until this is set right. I need someone—"

"If they closed the case, if the time's been served, they had reasons for it. Without valid cause, I can't go investigating whatever I want. Let it go or hire someone. Perhaps a private solicitor would help you."

"I don't have money to hire someone." She kept her spine tense, refusing to cower. "I'm asking you to hear the details. Let me show you my innocence."

"You're telling me you're a perfectly pious girl who happened to be accused of burglary?" He snorted. "I imagine there is more to this story, but I don't have time to sit and listen to your one-sided account of injustice."

Hazel frowned, reminded once again of her mistakes, like wounds that lasted much longer than the initial sting, forever leaving their scars. "I'm many things, but you're right, I'm far from perfect. I've made mistakes, I own that, but I never stole. I had no reason to and—"

"Best move on." He puffed on his cigar.

"No! Their reasons for closing my case were wrong and their conclusions unjust. It's hurt so many people . . ." She stopped before she named names. He didn't deserve to hear them, not if he wouldn't stop smoking that cigar and start treating her like more than worthless chattel— disposable, unimportant. She wrapped her fingers around the arms of the chair and clenched tightly.

"Don't take it personally. The courts are overflowing. We're overworked as it is." He tapped his cigar on the tray. "Best cool your temper and accept that what is done is done. Go west and start over. The law's different out there. No one would know your past if you didn't tell them."

Even if her five minutes weren't up, she knew her verdict was decided. He wasn't budging—the set of his jaw told her that much.

She forced one last plea. "My family is here, not out West. Please reconsider."

He rolled his eyes, confirming his lack of interest in her and her cause. Why should he care? Nothing was in it for him other than the pleasure of knowing he'd done the right thing. And she knew that didn't matter much to a vast majority of the population. A majority whose ranks she'd once been included in. She stood. "I'll find my way out."

"A word of advice," he said without moving from his leather chair.

She waited.

"Bury the past and cling to whatever future you have. Some things are best forgotten, left closed."

She pursed her lips together, knowing she shouldn't say anything. Her words would do no good, but she snapped back at him anyway. "Some things are best set right. I believe that is the purpose of the law."

CHAPTER
FOUR

The sun was low in the sky and the streets nearly empty as Hazel stepped away from the judge's house. Her heart raced, and she feared she wouldn't be able to find a ride back to Amherst. With her skirts in hand and her feet moving briskly, she approached three different people and asked if she could pay for a ride and was rejected every time. She could waste no more time asking for aid that would not be given, as the sun would not wait and neither could she. She would simply walk the seven miles back. With her shoulders straight and her head forward, she set off, feigning composure. Beneath her façade, she shuddered from the cold, the growing dark, and the memories of other shameful solitary walks.

An owl silent as the setting sun soared above her, a coyote yipped, and men argued in the distance. Hazel's feet throbbed, but she didn't slow. The reformatory had taught her to persevere, to keep going when she wanted to quit, and above all else, to find solace in prayer. The solace hadn't come all at once, and she knew she still had far to go, but little by little she'd learned to give her burdens to the Lord. In the dark of night, with fear and heartache surrounding her, she whispered softly, believing her words were heard despite her solitude.

When she finally arrived at Mrs. Northly's boardinghouse, the moon was the only source of light in the sky. She banged on the door, rapping until her fist throbbed, desperate to be within the boardinghouse walls and away from nature's eerie shadows. At last the matronly woman opened the door, slowly peeking out through the narrow gap, her face uneasy.

"Who is it?" she whispered in a hoarse voice.

"It's Hazel. I'm sorry it's so late. I lost track of the hour." She looked over her shoulder at the long shadows created by the low-hanging moon and shuddered. "Please, may I come in?"

"I don't put up with such behavior. There will be no staying out until the wee hours and thinking there will be no consequence. You girls nowadays have no respect for propriety."

"Please, Mrs. Northly. I was doing nothing improper." Hazel shifted her weight from foot to foot, trying to ease the pain shooting through them from the newly sprouted blisters, but it did little good. "The weather's turning cold, and I'm ever so tired. Let me in?"

"Do you have any idea the number of girls who have stayed here over the years? They always say they are virtuous, but I've seen enough to tell you nothing good ever happens when the sun goes down." Mrs. Northly folded her arms across her chest and glowered at her. "You can't pull the cloak over my head."

Forcing a penitent look, Hazel spoke through gritted teeth. "I am sorry I'm late. I realize I've interrupted your sleep and given you reason to question my character, but believe me when I say that I would never willfully submit your establishment to anything undignified. I promise you, I never meant to tarnish the boardinghouse's fine name. I've too much respect for you to ever do such a thing." She had several more sentences of apology on the tip of her tongue but was spared from delivering them.

"Don't get all mawkish on me." Mrs. Northly softened. "I'll give you another chance. But it can't happen again. Be in before the door locks or you will need to find a new residence. I have plenty of interest in my rooms. I can replace you easily."

Mrs. Northly issued the threat softly, but it still stung. There was a time when Hazel had felt irreplaceable and important. But now, she was merely a rent payment. A wayward soul with no real place, and the reminder was humbling.

"Thank you."

Hazel stepped past Mrs. Northly and made her way up the narrow stairs toward her rented room at the end of the hall.

"Hazel. Is that you?"

48

"Yes," Hazel whispered through Ina's door. "I'm sorry if I woke you."

"Come in and tell me where you've been."

Hazel pushed the door open as quietly as she could. "I had to run an errand in Cheektowaga. I hired a ride after work, but when I was done I couldn't find a ride home, so I walked. It was so far, and now my feet are sore and blistered." She groaned. Would life ever get easier? Perhaps it was her tired state that made life's injustices seem extra daunting. "Mrs. Northly has threatened to throw me out."

Ina sat near the head of her bed with her legs bent and tucked up near her chest. "You are always so mysterious. An errand, in Cheektowaga? Whatever would make you go all the way there? We have shops here for anything you need."

"I don't mean to be mysterious."

"Then tell me where you were. What errand had you traipsing about so late at night? I can't imagine what would possibly be so important that you would brave the dark for it."

Hazel crossed the floor and sat on the end of her friend's bed. A sliver of moonlight shone through the solitary window, giving her enough light to see her friend's face. "Well, I was—"

"Were you with Gilbert?" Ina whispered. "Mrs. Northly fumed all evening. She was certain you were with him. She thinks it's improper, the two of you spending so much time together."

Despite her melancholy, Hazel muted a laugh. "She thinks evil is lurking at every corner. But no, I wasn't with him. I only ever see him at work. I was doing nothing improper, and I certainly don't have a suitor." She let her body fall back across the bed. "I don't think I'll ever have a suitor again."

"Does that mean you have had suitors before?" Ina's eyebrows rose. "I envy you. Even if I never married, it only seems fair I should get a taste of romance. Something to dream about through the long winter nights. Don't you think?"

"I don't know. What if your suitor broke your heart? Then you'd be left with tragedy for company."

Ina's white nightgown shone in the moonlight as she left her bed and went to her window. "At least then I would never wonder. I could hold on to the ache and tell myself being alone was not so bad."

"I'll pray hard that some dashing man comes along and sweeps you off your feet." Hazel stood then, wincing not only because of her feet but because of the cruel realities of life and romance. "But I will pray even harder that you never feel the pain of a broken heart."

"Hazel, when you had a suitor, did you feel like the world had more meaning? Every story of love seems to testify to that truth." Ina turned from the window. "What was romance really like?"

"It's not all moonlit walks and gentle caresses." She shivered and wrapped her arms around herself. "Remember when we played chess?"

"Yes."

"My experience with courtship is much like chess. You spend half the game trying to figure out how you can win and the other half afraid you won't. Romance is more of a battle than anything." Hazel rubbed her tired eyes. This talk of love and possibilities only added to her weariness. The last thing she wanted to do on a night like this was relive her own heartaches. "Maybe there is a way to play where everyone wins. But I've never played it that way. It's late. I'm probably not thinking straight."

Ina remained at the window, gazing into the darkness. "Get some rest, but someday I hope you'll tell me all your secrets. I know I can seem simpleminded, but I'm not. I could handle whatever it is you are hiding."

"I believe you are idealistic and sweet, but I've never thought you a simpleton." Hazel smiled softly. "We'll talk soon. Not tonight though—it's too late."

Once safely in the confines of her own small room, Hazel paused, letting her eyes roam over the space she called home. A simple room with simple furnishings. If Mrs. Northly kicked her out, what then? Other girls like her had done their time at Mrs. Northly's. Where were they now? Had they married or taken new positions, or had they simply moved on because they did not want to admit there was nothing else for them besides life in a boardinghouse? Or had she sent them away?

She reached beneath her bed, pulled out her hatbox, and lifted the lid. The envelope on the top was the last note she'd received from her parents. They'd sent it to the reformatory, along with her trunks of clothes, her flute, and her other belongings. Her heart had broken reading their words, which had not been a complete surprise.

To our beloved Hazel,

We're overjoyed knowing you're about to leave the walls of the reformatory that have kept you from us for so long. That joy is dimmed by the reality of life here in Buffalo. Your sisters, as you know, are no longer little girls. It is our wish that they will find respectable matches. Your charges and past indiscretions have left a mark on the family, and we fear if you return, that stain will mar your sisters' chances. Whereas if society believes we've parted ways, they will have ample opportunities to secure their well-deserved futures.

As parents, our duty is to think of all our children and ask what is best for the whole. You have strength and spirit, and with the skills you've acquired while serving your time, you have a way to make it on your own, and so we ask that you not come home. Not now, but perhaps with time.

We've sent money and some of your belongings to the matron on your behalf so you'll be able to care for yourself. Be careful, dear girl, and know that even though you do not sit beside our hearth, you are in our hearts and prayers. Someday when the shame has faded further and the other children have secured their places in this world, we hope to be reunited with you.

Until that time, you must not come to the house or contact your siblings. As hard and painful as this will be, we feel it is for the best.

Your loving Father and Mother

Hazel wanted to wad up the letter and throw it in a blazing fire, but they were the last words from her parents. And no matter how much she hated the feelings and the pain they brought, she loved the authors. For five years she'd dreamed of being reunited with her family, and now she was uncertain if she ever would.

If only she'd been more like her obedient and

proper siblings. Tears burned her eyes whenever she let herself walk the dismal road of what might have been.

Curling onto her side, she held the letter tight to her heart and allowed herself to feel the loneliness she had tried so hard to ignore. But tonight, she felt it all. The hurt of being rejected by the world she had known. The loss of her family. The lies, the mistakes, the darkness. One tear at a time crept from the vault around her injured heart, then faster and harder the tears streamed from her like a river overflowing in a rainstorm.

No matter how sorry or dire her circumstances, no matter how she ached with homesickness and longed for the touch of her mother, she would not return home—not until she could return with her honor reinstated. She'd disregarded her parents' wishes often as a youth, but now as a woman she'd honor them and obey. Until the past was settled or they bid her return, she would eke out an existence for herself. And if the good Lord allowed, she would find some joy along the way.

Crinkling the paper in her hands, she thought of her parents. One moment she felt deep sorrow and the next anger. Why send money? Why not hire a lawyer and fight to reinstate her into their world? Why hadn't they done that right away, when she was first sentenced? But she knew the answer, and perhaps that's what hurt most of all.

They were not convinced she was innocent.

"Be cautious," her mother had warned the youthful Hazel before her real troubles had begun. "Things that seem so insignificant now can have far-reaching effects."

"Stop worrying," Hazel snapped back. "I think you would keep me from ever having any fun if you could. You want me to grow into a dull spinster or you want to marry me off to a fool. I don't want that for myself. I want to enjoy my life."

"You're wrong. I would not keep you from having a good time. I love few things more than the look on your face when you are truly happy. But, Hazel, your eyes sparkle when they are full of joy. These past few years, your eyes have turned dark. You are more than headstrong. You are reckless, and the cost of your thoughtlessness will catch up to you. Your father will not tolerate the behavior you've displayed forever. You will tarnish not only your name but ours as well. Besides, what good am I as a mother if I don't try to keep you from harm? If I don't call out your indiscretion and steer you back to safety?"

Hazel brushed her mother's concerns away, insisting that she fretted too much.

"I can take care of myself," she'd said, her free

spirit adamant that nothing horrible could ever befall her.

More tears came with the memories and the realization that her mother had been right. The years of hardship and pain as she served her sentence and now the months of severed ties all felt like a heavy cost for a bit of foolhardy recklessness. An ounce of wisdom and a measure of discretion, and she could have avoided it all.

When she had first left the reformatory, she had headed back toward Buffalo and the world she'd known, stopping mere miles from the family she could not claim. A small rented room and days filled with nothing followed as she struggled to make sense of her future and regain her confidence in a world with no walls. One afternoon, weeks after her arrival, she dared to venture up into the nearby hills in search of anything that might enliven her spirits. It had been a beautiful day, with a light breeze and flowers in full bloom. For the first time in a long while, she felt hope. Hope that was swiftly shattered. She returned to find that the money from her parents that she had so carefully rationed had been stolen. Only the meager amount in her reticule remained.

She yearned to run home to her parents and beg them to rescue her from this path of endless trouble. What she wouldn't have given at that moment to be held and coddled and taken care of like she'd been as a child. Instead, she packed her bags and began searching for a job and more affordable living quarters.

There would be no going home. Not now and probably not ever. She put the note back in her box and shoved it forcefully under her bed.

CHAPTER
FIVE

Gilbert looked at the clock. It was three minutes past nine, and Hazel hadn't arrived for work. She usually pranced in ten minutes before her scheduled time with a smile on her face and her red hair bouncing behind her.

When he finally heard the familiar squeak of the front door, a strange flutter raced through his chest, followed by relief. But when his eyes left the schedule in his hands and wandered to the door, they did not see Hazel. There was no red hair, no good-morning smile. Instead, there was Alberta Robertham, with her mouse-brown hair in a tight bun and her all-too-familiar frown plastered across her face. No other patient made Gilbert's innards clench like Alberta did. She was never satisfied. She constantly told him how she hated being there, and she was convinced she knew all there was to know about teeth, despite the fact that she rarely cleaned her own.

"Good day, Miss Robertham," he said as he rose from his seat.

"How can you call this a good day? Do you not see where I am?"

"I suppose we will just have to make the best of it." It did suddenly feel like a miserable place.

58

If only Hazel were there, she might add some bit of light to the darkness. He glanced past Alberta to the door.

"What are you looking at? Is there something back there?"

"No, not a thing." He kept his voice level. "Come along."

"If you're looking to see if the door is closed, of course it is. I wasn't raised in a barn," she snapped at him. "I have a tooth that's ailing me, and I expect you to do something about it." Red splotches appeared across her face as she fumed. The effect made her look like someone who'd had an encounter with a patch of poison ivy. "I'll need it fixed quickly, and I need there to be no pain. I plan to attend a social this afternoon." Alberta hoisted her wiry body into the chair, not waiting for an invitation. "Go on, get to work."

Gilbert fought the urge to groan aloud. Instead, he busied his mind by thinking up terribly rude things he could say to Alberta if he were only a little bolder.

For an entire hour he endured the rigors of working on Alberta's ailing tooth. Even with his instruments in her mouth, she still managed to complain with her wicked birdlike eyes and deep scowl.

As the moments ticked by, he missed Hazel more fervently. A few weeks together and already he knew she'd be able to appease the unpleasant

Alberta. Come to think of it, he knew a lot about Hazel. He knew as the day heated up and the little office grew warmer, she'd use the back of her arm to wipe the sweat from her brow. At noon she would take a brief walk outside and her hair would look a brilliant red. When she came back in, her cheeks would be rosy and she'd be smiling. She would ask him questions he would have to think about and might even struggle to answer, but once he did find the answers, he'd be glad she'd asked. Somehow she had created a spot for herself in his little office. Even the sound of her going from room to room was unique, and he missed it now.

"Just about done," he said to Alberta as he removed the dam he'd used to protect her gums and make it harder for her to talk. With its removal, he braced himself for the flood of words he knew she had been holding back.

"That took long enough. I remember your father. He moved with a great deal more speed."

"I'm sure he did." Gilbert leaned away. "He was an excellent dentist. I believe he would be pleased with the work I've just done."

"Adequate, I suppose, but it's not worth telling folks about."

"No praise needed. I'm content knowing you are out of pain."

A few more words shot from her mouth as she paid, then she left the office. Gilbert closed the door behind her, then sank into one of the waiting room chairs, tipped back his head, and closed his eyes. He had survived Alberta Robertham, and that was no small feat.

Hazel burst through the door. "I'm so sorry I'm late!" She paused when she saw him. "Oh, Gilbert, are you all right?" She dashed to him, a look of genuine concern written across her soft face.

"No, I'm not all right. I had to endure Alberta Robertham without you. Where were you?"

"Alberta?"

"You haven't met her, but you will. She always comes back. Then you'll know why I am near death now." He moaned dramatically until his antics turned into a laugh. "I don't know why I'm laughing." His shoulders continued to shake. "She really is a horrible woman."

The worry left Hazel's eyes and was replaced by their usual sparkle. "I look forward to meeting your Alberta. She has you acting practically giddy. I do believe she brings out a new side of you."

"She is not *my* Alberta." Eh, the very thought of it. Nothing would entice him to attach himself to someone who drained the life out of him like Alberta did. "This"—he pointed toward himself—"is not what giddy looks like."

"Come now. She must be quite a woman to have you so beside yourself." Hazel muted a laugh. Even with her hand covering her mouth, he could tell she was smiling.

"You have misinterpreted the type of woman

Alberta is. She is loud and bossy. She's hard to describe—there is no one like her."

Hazel pursed her lips. "She sounds a bit like me. I've been called loud a time or two, and my nanny always said I was the bossiest child she ever met."

"No. You're wrong," he said with conviction. "You talk a great deal, but it's pleasant and your wit is flawless, and I've yet to see you give orders when it has not been your place. You're not a thing like Alberta."

"I don't deserve such praise." A sad look flashed across her face, and for the briefest moment he knew she was hurting, but he didn't know why. He was not drawn to gossip, but he wished he knew what it was that weighed on her. As quickly as the look of sadness came, she smiled it away. "I am glad you don't find my company appalling or too overbearing."

All joking aside, he held her gaze and in a steady voice said, "I meant what I said. Your presence, it is delightful, a pleasure."

He'd never complimented a woman so openly. He waited, expecting to grow flustered or feel a sense of regret over the words, but he felt none.

"Thank you," she said without looking away. "Now I must apologize again for being late. I hope you can forgive me."

He nodded and waited, hoping for an explanation. In the short time he'd known her, he'd already learned that if he waited and let the silence hang, she'd fidget until she finally said what she was holding back.

"I didn't mean to be late," she said, interrupting the silence. "I was busy last night and didn't get much sleep. It was so late when I finally went to bed . . . I shouldn't even be telling you all this, as it's most improper. But, well, when I closed my eyes, it was for much longer than I had intended. I never would have allowed myself to even sit if I'd thought I would sleep so long. It won't happen again."

Her explanation left him puzzled. What in the world was she doing up so late? Was she with someone? Their first meeting left him with the impression that she had no interest in courtship. Was it a farce? Or had she been trying to tell him she already had someone? Suddenly that first conversation seemed fuzzy in his mind, and he could not remember the words she'd used. A knot rose in his throat. Swallowing was normally an easy task, but now, at this moment, it was presenting a challenge.

Perplexed and somewhat afraid of his own feelings, he walked away from the waiting room. She was a free and independent woman capable of choosing who she spent her time with. "We have three more patients scheduled for the morning. I'm going to work on my notes," he said as he put some distance between them.

She hobbled after him. "Wait."

Stopping, he turned back toward her and, breaking character, blurted, "What happened to your feet?"

"You've become so bold." She laughed while limping. "Blisters."

"Your shoes?" He looked at her scuffed boots. "Do you need new ones?"

"I walked too far, that's all. No need to worry." Hazel looked at the day's schedule. "It should be an easy morning. I'm glad. We've been so busy lately, and it'll be a nice change of pace."

"Yes, I thought so too," he said absently, still looking at her feet. "As I am your employer, you will tell me if you are in need, will you not?"

Her face turned a subtle shade of pink, like a soft rose. "That's very kind, but I can assure you that my feet are not your responsibility. You needn't worry."

"I wish to help if you are ever in need, whether it be my responsibility or not. I'm not only a dentist, but I'm also a man." His heart beat faster, but he pressed on. So often he thought of himself as only a dentist. He worked and then went home and did little else, but today he acknowledged that he was more than just his job. "What I mean is, are we not, as humans, meant to look after one another? Not simply when it affects business but at all times. To mourn, to comfort, and to aid?"

"I believe we are," she whispered. "But I've

not met many people who do more than talk of their Christian duty." She assembled instruments as she spoke, her eyes refusing to meet his own. "Eloise should arrive soon."

"You'll like her. She never complains," he said, tapping his fingers to the ever-increasing beat of his heart. "I have bandages if it would help your feet."

"I haven't had time to do anything for them. I don't know what will help."

"Between patients, let me take a look?" Heat raced up his face. He'd never looked at a woman's feet, but he did not rescind his offer. A fierce longing to assist and protect her grew with each word he spoke. It burned within him, igniting a flame he hadn't known before. "I wish to help."

"I couldn't." She turned toward the window. "Look, our patient is here."

Their conversation was put on hold as they cared for sweet old Eloise. When she left, she kissed Hazel's cheek and called her a darling girl. Hazel limped beside the older woman as she walked her to the door and closed it behind her.

"Your feet," Gilbert said the moment they were alone again. He retrieved some bandages from a cabinet and handed them to her. "We've a few minutes more before Duncan is scheduled to arrive, but he's often late, so you ought to have at least half an hour."

She looked around but didn't sit. Sensing her unease, he pointed to his private office. "You may go in there if you wish. Then if Duncan arrives early, he won't see you."

She nodded, took the bandages, and smiled weakly at him before escaping to his small office and seating herself in his chair. The door was open, but with her back to him, he couldn't see the extent of her injuries. When he heard her sniffle, he stepped closer to the open door. An ache deep in his chest grew with each painful sound. "Are you all right?"

"Several of the blisters began bleeding again when I took off my boots. There are more than I'd thought."

The office felt warm and sticky, where only moments before it had been comfortable. He wiped his forehead before asking, "May I help you? In my training, we learned more than just teeth. I can handle a wound."

"If you are certain it crosses no line," she said in a voice much weaker than normal.

Two swift steps later he was beside her, where he dared a glance at her small feet. They were half the size of his own and covered in bloody blisters rather than smooth skin. Anger boiled through his veins, but he didn't know who or what to direct it toward. He only knew he wished he had the power to ease her burden and fight off whatever brought this about. He gritted his teeth and reminded himself he did not know enough to judge who was at fault—if anyone at all. What he knew was that her feet would be sore for some time, and proper care would help them heal. "Let me get some water, and I'll wash them before bandaging them."

He left, only to return a moment later with a bowl of clean water.

"I think they hurt worse now than they did last night. But maybe I didn't notice because I was in such a hurry and so tired."

Again, questions were on the tip of his tongue, but rather than ask them, he simply took her small foot and gently washed the blisters. He was not a new dentist, unaccustomed to blood and suffering—so why then was the sight of her pain and the feel of her skin causing his heart to beat so wildly? Her body was rigid, but with each dip of the rag she seemed to relax, trusting his touch. He dared a glance up at her. Their eyes met and held each other. She touched his cheek briefly, sending a wave of energy racing through him.

"Thank you," she said, taking back her hand.

He bobbed his head in acknowledgment and stole his gaze away from her. Inwardly, he chided himself for not having the perfect words to say. Words that would let her know that he would help her if she were ever in need.

He cleared his throat. "I'll wrap them for you. But they will take time to heal. Do you have bandages at your home? Or should I send some with you?"

"I can manage." Hazel reached to help him, and their hands brushed together. He pulled away, startled. She put a hand on his shoulder, and again his throat grew tight. "You were right. You are a man of action and not just words. I had heard that you were *just* a dentist, but that is not true. You are a good man and a friend."

Mindful of the closeness they were sharing, he found that his hands shook. The brush of her fingers, the touch of her skin in his hands, and her affirming words had an unfamiliar effect on him. One thing was certain—he was grateful he was not merely a dentist.

When the last toe had a bandage securely around it, he took the bowl and rag and left her to put her shoes back on. Safely away from the room, he leaned his back against the wall and took several long breaths in a vain attempt to regain his composure.

CHAPTER
SIX

"Come with me to the corn husking," Ina said while readying herself for work several days later.

"Corn husking?" Hazel had grown up going to dances and teas, and even that had been years ago. "I don't know what that is."

"It's a harvest celebration. Everyone is invited." Ina sat before her small mirror, pinning her hair up for work. "You could bring Gilbert."

"I couldn't ask him to come."

"All you've talked about the last few days is how good he was to you when he helped you with your feet. And you always have funny stories from your day. It seems the two of you have become rather close. I don't think he'd object to joining us."

"We have become friends. But I couldn't come even if I wanted to. I have too much to do." Hazel picked up a pin Ina had dropped and handed it to her. "Here."

"You are not too busy to go. Aside from the rare evening where you venture out on your secret escapades, you spend your nights sitting around here just like me. I'm not too old for a good time and neither are you. Let's not be spinsters just yet." Ina looked at her in the mirror, her eyes pleading. "I don't want to walk in alone. Come with me?"

Hazel hesitated, torn between embracing a night of lighthearted entertainment and the nagging regrets. Tucked in the back of her memory were countless nights of mingling, flirting, and associating in crowded, stuffy rooms, making a fool of herself.

"Please come," Ina begged again. "I know you'll have fun, and you'll capture everyone's attention."

"I'll probably be older than everyone there." Hazel kept her voice light despite her apprehensions. "If I went, I'd just spend my time at the refreshment table. Mrs. Northly's cooking could use a bit more variety. We've eaten beans four nights in a row."

"Then come for the food."

"I'll think about it." And she would. And then she would politely decline. It was traitorous to pretend life was fine when she lived beneath a cloud of culpability. "I have to get going. I don't want to be late, but we can talk about this again soon."

Hazel said goodbye, then rushed off to work, where the morning started out exciting enough—two rotten teeth and a perfectly fitted denture—but then slowed to a crawl.

"Some days are like this," Gilbert said. "I don't mind. It'd be hard to never have a lull."

Hazel hardly heard him. A painting on the office wall of a golden wheat field had her thinking about harvests and celebrations. "Have you ever been to a corn husking? Ina told me about it this morning, and I admit I'm intrigued."

"I went when I was younger. My brother was sociable. He loved going and would drag me along."

"You have a brother?"

Gilbert nodded his head slowly. "I had a brother. He left years ago. My father confronted him on something, and they argued." He rubbed his chest as though there were an unseen wound. "I haven't seen him since. I don't even know where he is."

She swallowed, forcing her own homesick heartache away. "I'm sorry. I can only imagine the pain you must feel knowing he is out there somewhere."

"I pray he'll come back someday and we can be reacquainted." Gilbert thumbed through a pile of papers, but his eyes had a far-off look. "He was more of a talker than I am. In many ways, we were opposites. You'd have no trouble getting him to sit and fill the silence with you. He'd have you laughing in no time."

"It's funny how two people from the same family can be so different."

"Is that the case with your family as well?"

"I have a much larger family than yours, but

yes, we are all unique. Though I am the one who sticks out the most." She sighed, wishing once again that she could step through the front door of her childhood home and smell the familiar smell of wood polish and the cook's dinner roasting in the oven. Oh, how she missed her family. "I do hope your brother comes back."

He stopped riffling through the papers and looked at her. "I pray he does. Where are your siblings now? You've never mentioned them. I should think with how much you talk—Uh, I meant . . . I'm surprised you've not spoken of them sooner."

She jerked her head away, fearing he'd see the whole wretched story written across her face if he looked too closely. Somehow she'd gotten too comfortable with him and allowed herself to become vulnerable and exposed. "I don't see my family right now. But it's not because I don't want to. If circumstances were different . . . I love them very much." She swallowed against the knot in her throat. "Tell me about the corn husking."

He stared at her, his eyes gently searching her. "All right, you keep your secrets. I didn't mean to pry." He picked up a peanut from a bowl on the desk and opened it. "Husking corn is a lot of work, so the big farms take turns hosting corn huskings. Everyone is invited, but those who look forward to them the most are the young people. It's a chance to mix work and fun."

"Very clever of them." She'd husked corn while on kitchen duty at the reformatory, and there was nothing thrilling about it. "It does seem there must be something more fun to do than husk corn, even this far from the big city."

He laughed a little under his breath. "Well, it's really a way for the farmers to get their work done quickly. All evening the men have different husking challenges. They will see who can do fifty ears first or who can husk the most in partnerships. One or two ears—or even enough for a meal—doesn't seem too exhausting, but when you work at it over and over, it's tiresome. My muscles were sore for a week after I went the last time." He rubbed at his forearms. "But the competitions are fun."

"And the women? What do they do?"

"They cheer, and the louder they cheer, the faster the corn is husked. They prepare food. Some years there is a table of food to eat, and other times there is a grand feast at the end. But that's not really why the young people go." His statement hung in the air, and a mischievous smile played across his face.

"What's the real reason?" Hazel leaned forward. "Tell me."

"I'm not sure you're old enough to hear such things."

"I'm flattered you think me so innocent, but I can assure you that I can handle the mystery of the corn husking." In her sweetest voice, she pled, "Please."

He hemmed and hawed dramatically.

She turned her smile into an exaggerated pout. "You don't come across as someone who would tease, but you're relentless. I think you're only trying to get me riled up. You're intolerable."

Gilbert met her gaze, then smirked. "I suppose I'll have to find a new attending. It's a shame. I was enjoying your company. But I can't have someone working for me who finds me intolerable. It wouldn't do."

"I take it back. You're not intolerable." She laughed, wishing the playfulness could go on and on. His tease was diverting, muffling all the other noise and worries in her life. "Don't find a new attending. You might end up with one like Alberta."

"Now who is being intolerable? No more talk of leaving, and don't mention Alberta. I felt a chill creep in when you spoke her name. We both know you must stay, so I will answer your question about the corn husking."

Hazel clasped her hands together. "Oh good."

He leaned in like he was telling an impressive secret. "Whenever a man husks a red ear of corn, he gets to kiss the gal of his choosing."

Hazel gasped and straightened. Gilbert's face

flushed pink in the most endearing way that begged her to keep the conversation going. "And have you ever gotten a red ear?"

"I might have."

"You have? Who did you kiss?" Hazel scooted closer to him. "Tell me the story. I know I'm being intolerable again, but I must know. We have to pass the time somehow."

"Has anyone ever told you that you can be quite persuasive?"

"I've been told that before." She shrugged, unsure if he was complimenting her or not. "But I'm not trying to make you tell me if you don't want to. I just think it would be fun to hear a story from your youth."

"Very well. When I was seventeen, I found a red ear. My brother was beside me and tried to snatch it. He was sweet on Lydia Ridge. If he hadn't tried to steal it without asking, I probably would have given it to him. But I was stubborn, so I kept it and held it in the air for everyone to see." He grimaced. "I hadn't thought about the kissing part, only about making sure Eddie, that's my brother, didn't get it."

Hazel was on the edge of her seat, an image of Gilbert holding a red ear of corn in the air vivid in her mind. "Were you sweet on someone too?"

"No. I'd always been Eddie's quiet brother. The girls overlooked me. I don't think they even knew who I was."

"But was there a girl you wished would notice you?" Hazel stared at his handsome, innocent face. One ounce of effort from him, and he could have his choice of devoted companions. If he would only let someone see who he was. Funny, kind, and hardworking. "Did no one catch your eye?"

"Well"—Gilbert shifted in his seat—"I sometimes wished I was brave enough to ask Lillian Everett to dance. She lived two houses down, and we talked occasionally."

"What happened to Lillian?"

"She got married. I think she lives over in Kenmore now. Probably has a houseful of children." Gilbert stared past her as though it were all rushing back to him. "I haven't thought about her in years. It's strange to think everyone's lives go on even if you don't see them."

"They should all still be seventeen," she said, making him smile. "What did you do with your red ear of corn? I'm guessing you didn't use it to kiss the unsuspecting Lillian."

"I stood there with the corn in the air, and then I panicked but tried not to let it show. I looked around and caught Wesley Croft's eye. He was four years older than I was and engaged. I walked over and dropped it in his lap. Everyone cheered when Wesley kissed Emilia, and that was the end of it." Gilbert shrugged. "I bet you were hoping for a more exciting story. But I haven't really had much excitement in my life." He blushed again and lowered his voice. "Especially not with women."

Embarrassment? Regret? She wasn't sure what the distant look on his face meant, only that she wished she'd known him when he was seventeen. She could have coaxed him from his shell, and he could have kept her from trouble. "Perhaps excitement is romanticized and not as fulfilling as we're told. Did you ever find another red ear?"

"I was more careful after that. If I ever saw a hint of red, I'd grab for a different ear. And here I am thirty and still playing by the same rules." Gilbert scratched the back of his neck. "You'd like the corn husking. You ought to go and have yourself some fun."

A night of respite. A night without cares or worries. A night when she could pretend she had no soiled past. The more she thought about it, the more the idea enticed her. Here, away from Buffalo, in this rural area, perhaps she could find some enjoyment.

"Will you go?" she asked Gilbert, desperately hoping he would say yes. With him there, she would not feel so alone. And she'd rather like to watch him husk corn and imagine him as a quiet seventeen-year-old. "Ina wants me to go with her. She says we're still too young to live like spinsters. I don't know if I agree, but it might be my only chance to see what a corn husking is like."

"You don't think you'll be around next year?" His voice quavered when he spoke. "You'll be gone?"

"I don't know where I'll be next year." She sucked in a deep breath, hating how little control she had over her own life. If she were free to go and come as she pleased, where would she be? Where would she go? But she was not free and could not say where the road would lead her. "I'm here now, so I might go. You ought to come too. Join us and rebel against age. You aren't so old that you have to accept a life of permanent bachelorhood, are you?"

It was breaching the boundaries they'd set, but she wanted him to come. The Gilbert who had interviewed her might not enjoy a night out, but she believed the Gilbert who sat across from her now would—if he would only go.

"The future could still hold a surprise or two." He shrugged. "I don't think I have any other commitments. I might just go."

"I've heard women talk about you. No doubt they'll be pleased you're there. If you find a red ear of corn, you could have your choice of willing women to kiss." Hazel laughed at her own comment but instantly wished she could take it back. Something about the image she'd created didn't sit right.

Gilbert recoiled. "I think I'll stay clear of red ears."

CHAPTER
SEVEN

Hazel's emerald dress fit her curves perfectly, then erupted into a full skirt at her hips. Her parents had sent it with her other more practical clothes upon her release from the reformatory. She frowned at her reflection. It was just a dress. And no matter how perfectly it fit, she wanted her family—not a gift and a letter.

"Ina, do you think this dress is too fancy for a corn husking?"

"Are you dressing up for Gilbert?" Ina walked around Hazel, inspecting her. "He will fall all over himself when he sees you."

"I'm not wearing it for anyone," Hazel insisted. But if she were being honest, she would have confessed she liked the idea of seeing his eyes follow her around in her emerald dress. When he sat near her at the office, she would often look at his strong, skilled hands and wonder what it would feel like to have them around her, holding her while they danced. But she could never confess such a desire, not when she wasn't free to court him, assuming he were to ask. "Is it too much? I've never been, and I don't want to look out of place."

"No, you will be the envy of every woman there. You must wear it."

Hazel took a step backward, nearly tripping. "I don't want to be that person. I want to look beautiful but not *more* beautiful than others."

"And you do. I wasn't trying to say anything wrong." Ina fidgeted with the ends of her hair. "Think nothing of my silly prattle. You look picturesque. It doesn't matter how anyone else looks."

"*Picturesque* is overly generous." Hazel tucked a loose strand of hair back into place. "It's nice having a reason to dress up. I rotate through the same boring skirts day after day." She ran her hands along the bodice of the dress, amazed at how well it fit.

Ina smoothed the collar on her nicest dress. It was deep brown and only mildly more attractive than the gray dress she wore to the school each day. It hung loosely where it should be snug and snug where it should flow. Ina, dear Ina, dreamed of romance and marriage. She believed in fairy tales and happily ever afters. Hazel's days of courtship had left a foul taste in her mouth, but perhaps Ina would be blessed with a sweeter bite if given a chance.

"I don't think I will wear this after all. I think I'll wear my blue dress. It's freshly pressed, and I've always liked the cut."

"But this one is so beautiful," Ina said, trying to stop her. "It's so much finer than your blue one."

Hazel shimmied out of the emerald dress, with

its fancy trimmings and perfectly cut bodice, and handed it to Ina. "You wear it. We are nearly the same size. Otherwise it will hang here in my room."

"I couldn't." Ina held the dress in her hands, staring at it. "Besides, no one will ever be able to see past my mark. It's nothing but a waste for me to wear it."

"Maybe tonight you will get your turn at romance, and wouldn't that be more fun in a beautiful lace-trimmed dress? You have not met everyone there is in this world. Don't despair." Hazel was already pulling on her simple blue dress.

"What of your romance?" Ina asked while she stroked the lace cuff of the exquisite dress between her fingers.

"Mr. Murdock at the dental office asked me if I wanted to go for a Sunday afternoon stroll with him. I politely declined. And then just today a Mr. Noriega asked me if I wanted to ride in his new buggy. Had he not been the age of my father, I might have been tempted." She laughed while buttoning the cuff of her sleeve. "I can assure you, I have had my fill of romance for the week."

"That's not romance," Ina said, still staring at the dress in her hands. "That's simply men who are desperate for female companionship. Real romance is thoughtful and kind, and it makes your heart feel like it's alive within you."

"If that's the definition of romance, then I suppose Mr. Murdock and Mr. Noriega were not the romantic suitors I had hoped for. But it's all the romance I can expect."

Hazel looked at her sweet friend. She had one blemish that seemed so unimportant once you got to know her. How unfair that earthly eyes were used to determine such important matters. Others needed to see Ina, to really see her. If Hazel's dress would help somehow, she was willing to share it with her.

"You'll look beautiful in the dress. Won't you wear it?"

"I don't think there is a man out there who will see past the red mark on my face," Ina said. "But if you insist, I'll wear the dress."

Hazel promptly set to work getting Ina ready. She felt only a moment of regret when she looked in the mirror at her plain blue dress. The fabric had faded from what was once a vibrant blue, and it lacked lace and ruffles. Gilbert's eyes would not follow her, of that she was certain. Of that she *should* be thankful.

Turning from her own reflection, she looked to Ina. A powerful feeling of excitement for her friend overshadowed any qualms she had. Loaning Ina the dress was the right decision. A decision her former self would not have made. Perhaps she'd truly been reformed. A tear of happiness, not remorse, trickled down her cheek.

"Oh, Ina," she whispered.

With the dress on and her hair pinned up, Ina looked radiant, the red mark only adding to her loveliness.

Gilbert straightened his jacket as he walked across the field to the Stoddard barn. The large red building, with its nearby rows of fences and huge maples, was a lovely sight. It was the largest barn in all of Amherst's countryside, and this evening it was bustling with more life than normal.

"Gilbert Watts!" A young woman with a large smile pranced toward him like a mare with her eyes on a dangling carrot. "We haven't seen you at a social in years."

He looked closely at her. There was something familiar about her, but he couldn't place who she was.

She tilted her head to one side, the smile still plastered on her face. "Samantha Firth. John's little sister."

"Samantha?" She was barely over waist high when he'd seen her last. "You grew up."

"I did." She batted her eyes at him as though he were a schoolboy. Little did she know the gesture only made him feel infinitely older. Samantha had to be a good ten or twelve years younger than he was.

"How is your brother?" he asked while heading

once again toward the barn, knowing it was polite to make conversation but eager to shake this woman from his side.

"His wife just had their second baby. John's so busy with the store, he hardly notices them." She inched closer. Too close. "Tell me about yourself. It's been so long."

Gilbert took a quick step sideways. "I'm busy running my father's dental practice."

She smiled again as though she'd figured him all out. "Everyone says that all you do is work. Have you come to remedy it and find yourself a wife?"

She'd been a nosy child, and clearly, she hadn't outgrown that trait. He quickened his pace as he tried to think of a way to answer her. "I thought it might be nice to get out for an evening."

"Is it because of the attending lady? I heard she's old but beautiful," Samantha said.

"She's not old. She's simply not as young as she was a few years ago." Gilbert's fists clenched at his sides, his defenses flaring . . .

"Is she beautiful?" Samantha's pace had quickened too. Relentless girl. "Mr. Murdock told me at the store that you had the most beautiful woman working for you. But I don't see how she could be so exquisite and not be married."

"I haven't noticed." He looked ahead rather than at her. "I'd best join the men. I came to husk corn."

"How can you work with a woman every day and not know if she is beautiful or not?" She spit her words at him. "Do you not even see her?"

"Stop scowling at me like that. Some of us from my generation are just a little more private with our compliments. But if the only way to keep you from making that face at me all night is to tell you the truth, then I will." He mustered his courage and said, "Miss McDowell is an attractive woman. Indeed, she is the loveliest I've seen. But she is more than a pretty face, she is lively and fun and good and kind. She brightens a room with her presence. And one of her finest qualities is her ability to converse without being overbearing. A trait I'm afraid your generation seems to lack."

With each word he spoke, Samantha's face changed from contempt to adoration. With her hand on her heart, she said, "Oh, I had no idea you were so eloquent. That was compelling. I can only pray a man speaks so highly about me someday."

Gilbert clamped his mouth shut, and his hands shook. Rarely did his thoughts come out so freely and with such force. Uncomfortable with the truth he'd spoken, he rushed away, muttering like a crazed man, "I have to husk corn."

Once inside the barn, he stood alone, feeling awkward in a setting where everyone was laughing and socializing. He walked slowly around the mound of corn in the center of the barn, pretending to be interested in its size.

A woman in an elegant emerald dress came walking in, and his eyes and those of all others went to her. He recognized her as someone he'd seen at the dental office, but he could not recall her name. Behind her he saw blue skirts. He held his breath as his eyes traveled up to Hazel's smiling face. His breath caught in his chest next to his rapidly beating heart. Everything he'd said to Samantha had been true, but his words hadn't been complimentary enough. Words alone could not describe the woman he was watching now. Confident, lively, and beautiful.

He took a step toward her, then froze and waited, wondering what to do next. They hadn't come together, but they had both spoken of coming. Did that give him a right to cling to her side? He wanted desperately to be with her, near enough that he could smell the scent of lavender she wore and see the green flecks in her brown eyes.

"Is that her?" Samantha had returned like vermin to its meal. "In the blue?"

"Is that who?" he asked, annoyed that she was back.

"Your exquisite lady." Samantha was watching her now too. "She is pretty. I don't know if I'd be as generous with my praise as you were, but she is tolerable."

Gilbert fought the urge to argue and instead pointed to Mr. Stoddard, who'd overturned a bucket and stood on top of it. "He's about to say something."

The din in the barn died down. "Men and boys, it's time to gather round. The competitions are about to begin. We have a great event planned. There will be games, competition, food, and if this pile of corn is cleared away in time, dancing."

The crowd around Gilbert roared with excitement.

Mr. Stoddard waited for the room to calm down. "I know you didn't all come out here just to help me husk my corn." Laughter sounded in the old barn—some sheepish, some boisterous. "And I haven't let you down. There are red ears in there, folks. Find a red ear and claim your kisses."

The crowd burst with enthusiasm. The eagerness was tangible and contagious. Even Gilbert felt his adrenaline rise. When at last the roar died down, Mr. Stoddard began again. "Ladies, cheer your men along or get those vittles ready to eat. Make yourself at home on the farm, but don't go too far. You never know when a red ear will be found."

This time the din didn't die down as Gilbert joined the throng of competitors. At least no one would know how uncomfortable and out of place he felt if he was busy working.

"Fifty ears husked. Winner gets to lead the opening dance." Mr. Stoddard raised a flag. "Start when the flag waves." The competitors were in the barn's center, and all around them were excited friends and family.

Gilbert stood near the mound of corn, ready to begin, his muscles flexing as he awaited the signal. For no explainable reason, he felt envious of the men with ladies near them, cheering them on. He pushed the nonsense from his mind and focused instead on the unwaved flag.

"Good luck, Gil." No one called him Gil, but he knew the voice. He looked over his shoulder, and there was Hazel beside him, hands clasped together. The corn became more than a distraction—winning mattered.

The flag swished through the air, triggering the men into action. They attacked the pile of corn, tearing into it with enormous speed. Gilbert pushed himself hard. He was no farmer or day laborer, but his forearms were strong from his years of holding instruments and pulling teeth, and his will was solid. Grit, his father had often said, could be learned no matter the profession.

"Come on, Gil!" he heard again from behind him. "Faster!"

And faster he went. One ear after another lost its sheath and was stacked onto his pile. *Forty-one, forty-two.* He was close. His arms burned, but he didn't slow. *Forty-three, forty-four, forty-*

five. He reached for another, only to see the flag waving. He hadn't won.

Hazel stepped closer. "You were so close." She pointed and whispered in his ear, "Those boys over there were so sure of themselves, and I don't think they have over thirty in their piles. Perhaps we aren't too old to fit in, after all."

"Well, I wasn't quite fast enough. I guess that means I don't have to lead the dancing." He brushed the front of his jacket with his hand, and bits of corn husk and silk fell to the ground.

She reached over and ran her hand over his jacket sleeve, loosening even more corn silk remains from his arm. The competition left his heart rate high, and with her touch, it rose further.

"I think you did fine. It's a shame you won't get to lead the dance. You could have had your choice of partners." She reached out again and picked a long strand of corn silk off his shoulder. "Anyone you wanted in the whole barn."

"Doctor Watts, you came." The girl in the shimmering dress joined them. "You may not remember me, but I'm Ina. I've brought girls from the academy to see you. Hazel said she didn't know if you'd make it."

"I wasn't sure myself until today."

"You did well in the competition. I'm sure Hazel will dance with you even if you didn't win," Ina said, earning her raised eyebrows from Hazel.

Gilbert fidgeted, knowing he stood at a

crossroads. If he waited too long, the moment would pass. But did Hazel want to dance? What had those raised brows meant?

"I would love to dance with you," Hazel said before he could work up the courage to ask. "I haven't danced in years, but I believe with the right partner it'll come back to me."

A roar sounded in the crowd. Hazel, Ina, and Gilbert looked around, trying to figure out what the crowd was so ecstatic about. Near the great pile of corn, a boy with ink-black hair stood proudly holding a red ear for all to see.

"I found one! I found one!" he shouted as he wove through the masses, showing off his prize as though he'd struck a vein of gold.

Hazel leaned against Gilbert. "Is that what you looked like when you found your red ear?"

"I like to think I was a little more dignified, or at least more reserved."

The boy ran to a blonde at the edge of the barn. He carelessly grasped her around the waist. The poor girl's arms flailed at her sides. As quickly and awkwardly as it had begun, the kiss ended. The crowd laughed and cheered. The blonde stared, then laughed herself.

Hazel leaned in again. "And is that what you'll do this year if you get a red ear? Wave it around before surprising some girl like that?" She stifled a giggle. "You won't give away your prize again, will you?"

He could feel her breath on his cheek. If kissing was what he was after, all he'd have to do was turn his head and their lips would meet.

"I'm thirty," he said, keeping his eyes straight ahead. "This could be my last chance at a red ear of corn. If I find one, I'll keep it. But I hope I have a more pleasing effect on whomever I kiss."

"And who will you kiss?"

Had she always been so bold? Was she baiting him? Teasing him? He swallowed, stood taller, and vowed to meet her jest.

"I suppose I'd choose to kiss a girl with red hair. It'd match the corn, only seems fitting," he said, then walked away to join in the next competition, his heart racing before the flag ever waved.

"You two looked rather friendly," Ina said when Gilbert was out of earshot. "What were you whispering about?"

"We were only jesting about the red ear of corn." They were being flippant, weren't they? She looked around the barn, searching for women with red hair. Hers hardly counted. It was brown with a mere hint of red, but she saw no one with more red than she had.

Ina raised one eyebrow. "So, you were talking about kissing?"

"No . . . well . . . yes. But not like you're thinking." Hazel's eyes wandered to quiet, kind

Gilbert. She hadn't planned to feel anything for him. Not only was she his attending, but he was nothing like the men she'd chased in the past. Gilbert was supposed to be safe. Her heart wasn't supposed to feel anything when he was near her, yet it did.

"I don't know why you deny an attraction. He's handsome and has a decent job. He seems kind, and that's more important than prestige. What's not to like about him?" Ina asked. "I only wish I had someone half so ideal."

"I saw everyone watching you when you entered." It was true, the girl in the beautiful dress had drawn many eyes. But Hazel had watched, and they'd turned away when they'd looked at Ina's face. "Don't give up," she reassured her friend. Then, grabbing her hand, Hazel pulled Ina toward the center of the barn. "Look, they are about to start the next contest."

"Men, this time you'll be given a basket. Husk the corn, see how many you can fit inside. Man with the most gets first pick of partners for the waltz," Mr. Stoddard shouted to the eager participants. "Anything that topples over or falls out doesn't count."

The flag waved and corn husks flew. Hazel tried not to stare at Gilbert, but her eyes kept finding him. Bent over, tearing into the corn, he moved swiftly. Muscles she'd never noticed in him flexed as he tore the outer sheath from the ears.

Other men could be heard shouting their own accolades, boasting and sneering as they went. But Gilbert worked silently. It wasn't a virtue she'd ever recognized before, but there was something dignified about a man who did not have to drag another man down or puff himself up to prove his own merit.

"Do you stare at him all day like that?" Ina asked.

"Don't be silly. I'm just watching to see if he wins," Hazel said without looking away from Gilbert.

"Of course you are."

The pile of corn in Gilbert's basket grew. A bead of sweat ran down his forehead, but he did not flinch. He was in constant motion—like a clock, all the gears moved in perfect rhythm.

And then all motion ceased. Gilbert was no longer a clock with ticking gears. Instead, he became a perfect statue.

Hazel watched, wondering what had changed. His basket was not so full that it could hold no more. She took two steps closer, trying to discern what had happened. And then she froze.

A red ear of corn rested in Gilbert's strong hand. Without saying a word, he raised it high enough for the crowd to see. The people nearest noticed, their murmuring slowly dying down and causing others to turn their heads. And then Mr. Stoddard saw.

Mr. Stoddard whistled, then shouted again. "Folks, stop where you are. We have another red ear." A hush followed as everyone looked at Gilbert.

Hazel's heart raced, pounding in her chest so loudly she was certain others could hear it. Gilbert pivoted and walked across the barn in slow, calculated steps that brought him closer and closer to her. He did not zigzag or weave through the gathering. He didn't glance at anyone else or put on a show. And then there he was, inches away from her. The rest of the barn may as well have disappeared, because she saw only him.

"It matches your hair," he said, his voice a husky whisper. Holding the ear near her head, he smiled. "Perfect."

Heat crept through her, moving from the tips of her toes all the way to her ears. Her whole body became warm and tense. She'd been kissed before, but never had she felt such fire before even being touched. This meant nothing. She knew it was a silly tradition, but her logic could not calm the flutter in her stomach.

"Kiss her! Kiss her!" the crowd shouted— softly at first, then louder and louder.

Hazel met Gilbert's gaze, only to find a fervor in his eyes. He leaned closer. So close the stubble of his face tickled her skin. Senses she'd not known she possessed came alive as she waited. And then his lips brushed against her cheek, pausing only momentarily as they pressed against her skin. It was the briefest of kisses, a mere touch of his lips.

He pulled away, and there was space between them again. Her face burned where he'd touched her, shouting and pleading for more. It'd been brief, too brief, almost unreal. And yet she could feel it still.

Putting a hand to her cheek, she let her eyes meet his again.

"If I ever see Eddie, I'll tell him I made use of a red ear." He stepped back, putting even more distance between them.

She let a tense chuckle escape her lips. "I'm glad I could help you redeem yourself."

"We do make a good team," he said before walking back to the pile and the competition.

Ina began saying something beside her, but Hazel could make no sense of it. The words were background noise to the flood of emotion awakened by his kiss.

"Hazel! Are you even listening to me?"

"I'm sorry." Hazel forced herself to focus on Ina. Her inner questioning of why was not important. No matter the answer, there was nowhere for her feelings to go. Her heart was closed and must stay that way forever, or at the very least until her slate was clean.

Ina laughed. "I was just saying that now you can say you've been kissed. It was so romantic too. He walked right for you. I always assumed him to be shy, but he seemed so determined. Was it everything you've ever dreamed of in a kiss?"

"I didn't say I'd never been kissed," she whispered to Ina. "I never said that."

"You've been kissed!" Ina's face fell. "I thought you and I were the same."

"I wish we were," she said. How much simpler life would be if the only lips to ever touch her had been Gilbert's. "And we are in many ways." She looped her arm around Ina's. "Tonight let's wander around this barn and see if someone catches your eye."

CHAPTER
EIGHT

Gilbert won the basket fill, came in second for the ten-minute challenge, and lost the hundred-ear challenge to a coin toss. His arms ached, his back ached, even his neck ached, but he didn't care. Spectators, no doubt, believed him lost in his work, but in truth his mind was stuck back in time, still mulling over the red ear, his choice, and the softness of Hazel's cheek.

Time had moved slower during those moments, each step across the barn floor a deliberate decision that took him closer to her and the intoxicating scent of lavender. He'd seen the ear in his hand and decided in that instant to muster his courage and act. He'd chosen to kiss her cheek instead of her lips, believing it'd be safer, but even their brief encounter had been enough to leave him far from unaffected. Even now, the memory touched him.

The pile of unhusked corn grew smaller until only a few stray ears remained. Most of the men had left the corn and gone to socialize. He kept husking, slower now but still as steadily, afraid to step away and face the crowd. Soon the last ear rested in his hands.

"You are the most dedicated man around."

Hazel smiled at him, the corners of her lips pulled high, dimpling the very cheek he'd kissed. "No one else competed in every challenge, and now here you are taking care of the last ear despite there being no prize for it. You've not even visited the refreshment table. I would not have guessed that a dentist would outlast them all."

"I think there are a lot of things people wouldn't expect about dentists."

"I think you are right." She picked bits of corn husk off his shirt. "It's a good thing you are here to set us straight."

"About the red ear . . ." He wiped his sweaty palms on his pants.

"You had to kiss someone. It's tradition." She smiled when she said it, but her eyes lost some of their sparkle. "It meant nothing. I know that, and of course it's better that way."

He scratched the back of his neck and nodded despite his being acutely aware of how much the kiss had meant to him.

"I'm grateful it was you and not that lad from earlier."

They shared an awkward laugh, remembering the boy with the dark hair and his unsuspecting companion.

"There will be dancing soon. I won the partner of my choice for the waltz," Gilbert said quietly, hoping she'd know with her feminine instincts that he wanted her in his arms.

"Will you dance with Ina?" Hazel pressed her lips together and looked toward her friend. "She borrowed my dress and spent so long on her hair. She's beautiful, yet no one sees it. Some of us never get a chance to be the woman everyone is watching. It would mean so much to her to be picked from the crowd."

"Have you been that woman before?" Gilbert asked, wanting to know she'd experienced the thrill she spoke of and at the same time hating the idea of her on the arm of another man.

"Everyone watched when you walked across the floor with that red ear of corn." A far-off look skirted across her face, and he knew there was more to her story. She rallied and offered him a pleading smile. "Ina has never been that woman. Will you ask her to dance?"

He nodded, unwilling to counter Hazel's selfless intentions. It did not matter that he wanted to hold Hazel in his arms or that she'd been the reason he'd worked so hard to win.

"I'll dance with Ina." He reached out, though, and took her hand, pressing it gently in his own before letting it go. "Thank you for cheering me on."

The first dance was a reel led by the winner of the fifty-ear challenge. Gilbert stood near the refreshment table and watched as Hazel danced with a man who appeared to be equal to her in age and seemed to possess a plethora of wit, enough to keep Hazel laughing. He wasn't jealous, of course he wasn't, but he did have to instruct himself not to scowl as he watched. He thought of dancing himself, but the remaining women seemed far too young. And he couldn't work up the nerve to ask, so he sampled the food instead.

Before long, Mr. Stoddard stood on a barrel and whistled for the crowd's attention. "Gilbert Watts has earned himself the pick of partners for the next dance. Ladies, step forward. Gents, step back."

Gilbert set down his plate and went to the center of the floor. He ambled past Samantha and her cluster of giggling friends. He looked at his feet as he passed Hazel and stopped in front of Ina.

With a hand outstretched, he bowed slightly. "May I have this dance?"

She dipped a deep curtsy and took his hand. The music started, and for a moment they were the only ones on the floor while everyone else scrambled to find a partner.

"Thank you," Ina said as they stepped together across the wooden floor. "Hazel is a good woman to give her dance to me."

"She may have planted the idea, but I'm not sorry." He led her around the floor with ease. "I think it's the perfect chance to become better acquainted with you."

"Why have we not seen you at the socials before?"

"I used to come. It's just been a long time. When my father was ill, I stayed with him and never came back." He shrugged. "My friends were married, and I felt old . . ."

"But now something, someone, has given you a desire to return."

"Life has a way of changing when you least expect it."

"It won't for me. I believe I'll continue living at Mrs. Northly's and teaching until I die. All the girls I teach will grow up, and I'll keep doing what I've always done. I'm sorry to complain. My lot is not so bad."

"Those girls are lucky to have someone who cares about them and teaches them," Gilbert said as they floated across the floor. "Did you always want to teach?"

"I don't remember dreaming of teaching, but I do find fulfillment in it."

"I did not dream of dentistry as a boy."

She nodded. "I still *hope* that life has a few unexpected surprises ahead. Do you not?"

He laughed quietly. He'd been so comfortable with his life not long ago, but now the world seemed to be upside down. "I suppose I do."

He looked around at all the young faces, stopping only when he saw the face of an old schoolmate. "Do you know Duncan Franklin? I did not realize he was here."

"I don't think I do."

"He's a patient of mine, and before that we were boys together at the same school. He's only a little younger than I am."

"Show me who he is?"

"Over there near the door. He's the man with the brown vest. If you'd like, I'll introduce you."

"Do you think he'd want to meet me?" Ina's eyes stayed on Duncan. "What is he like?"

"He's lonely." Gilbert let the statement hover in the air.

"Lonely?"

"He confessed to it when he was in the office not long ago. His wife died a few years back, and since then he's not been the same." He told her about Duncan as a boy and how he won every spelling bee and should have been every teacher's favorite pupil, but he also had a fondness for snakes and used to sneak them into the teacher's desk. He told her about Duncan going off to become a lawyer and returning to take over his uncle's office.

"He married Estelle Cline when he returned. She was younger than he was, but they'd known each other their whole lives and naturally took up with one another. She died giving birth to their child."

"Oh, that poor man. What happened to the baby?"

"The last time he was in, he said the little girl was living with his sister. He hopes someday to bring her home. I know he sees her as often as he can. He talks about her like the proudest father."

"I'm sure she eases his grief," Ina said. "I will pray for good things for Duncan."

Gilbert offered his arm when the music ended. "I too hope he finds happiness. Perhaps you can brighten his day."

"Me?" Ina's hand shook as they neared him.

"Duncan." Gilbert greeted his friend by shaking his hand. "I'd like you to meet Ina. She's a friend of my attending lady, Miss McDowell. I believe you met her when you were in last."

"Only briefly. She was helping someone else most of the time," Duncan said.

"Ina teaches at the young ladies' academy." Gilbert took a half step back so they could have a proper hello.

Duncan's balding head and expanding middle might not have caused many women to swoon, but his presence brought a flush of color to Ina's face. He reached out a hand to Ina. "It's an honor to meet you."

Ina grinned. "Gilbert was telling me you like snakes."

"I do." He looked at her intently. "I'll tell you about them if you'll dance with me?"

"Yes," she whispered, taking Duncan's arm. "I'd like that."

Gilbert couldn't keep the smile from his face.

Pleased with himself, he watched the pair set off into the crowd. Then he made his way to the table of food that had caused his mouth to water with the scent of apples, cinnamon, and sweet potatoes.

"Does the man who never desires a match do matchmaking work?" Hazel asked, startling him and keeping him from loading a plate with vittles.

"When I saw Duncan—you remember him, don't you?—it just made sense."

"I met him briefly when he was in the office but hadn't thought to pair them up. I'm delighted. She's told me many times that she longs for romance."

Gilbert nodded. "I've heard everyone wishes for romance."

"No. Not everyone. I'm told that some people intend to remain unattached, always," Hazel said with only a hint of mischief in her voice.

"I've been told that those are the famous last words of many a married man." Gilbert's voice matched hers despite the fact that his palms were sweating. "Even the most stalwart fall to the right foe."

"And that is what marriage is, is it not? A battle of two foes." Hazel's retort was surprisingly terse. She scooped out a slice of pie and flopped it onto a plate with far more force than necessary. "Mrs. Northly never makes pie."

He stayed by her side despite her shift in manner. "I don't make pies either."

"Maybe if you had a wife, she'd make you a pie from time to time. Or maybe you should learn to make your own. It would save you from having to fraternize with the enemy."

"What's wrong, Red?" Gilbert asked. "You don't have to like romance to see that your friend does. Look at her smiling. And he's laughing. They hardly look like foes."

Hazel studied her friend, relaxing as she did so. "She does look happy."

"So does he." He searched for safe words. "How is your pie?"

"Whoever baked this did a fine job." Hazel froze with a bite in midair. "Do you cook all your own meals?"

"No. Clara Ervin was a friend of my mother and father. She decided long ago that I am a poor orphan boy and brings me meals a couple times a week. I pay her for the food, and we both win."

"You eat alone?"

"I have a dining room with a table covered in dust. I tend to eat near the fire or by the stove. Eating at the table without my parents or my brother has never felt right. Besides, a quiet man is well suited for a quiet meal."

She put a hand on his arm. "Keep saying things like that and I might just join Clara and take pity on you. Meals around a table are a treasure far too few cherish." She took another bite and ate it slowly. "You do look a bit like a poor orphan boy who has no one to care for him."

"I do?"

"You could use a haircut." She looked him over. "A little trim would help. I thought dentists were barbers too."

"They were in the old days. Have you forgotten we are almost to a new century?"

She nodded. "Time is propelling forward so quickly. Nights like this, I wish it could slow down. Why is it that the pleasant moments go so much faster than the disagreeable ones?"

"I'll have to ponder that. You have me talking more than before, but I'm still not a philosopher."

A girl's laughter interrupted their conversation, drawing their attention to the corner of the barn where a young woman stood surrounded by a cluster of men.

"That's Florence Calbert. I don't get out much, and even I've heard of her," Gilbert whispered. "People talk to me at the office, saying all sorts of things when they are nervous. I've heard stories about Florence."

"Is she always like that? With everyone all around her?"

Gilbert shrugged. The idle gossip he'd heard meant little to him. "I hear she breaks hearts."

"I feel sorry for her," Hazel said in a soft voice. "Someone ought to tell her that having one good man's eyes on her is better than having a crowd of gawkers."

"It'd be better to feel sorry for the men she is ruthlessly leading along."

"I feel for them too. But I wonder if she really knows what she wants, or if she'll wake up one morning and wish she'd done it all differently."

"Florence is young yet." He wasn't looking at the cluster of men around Florence any longer. "A new song is starting. Care to dance with this poor orphan boy?"

"I've recently discovered I have a soft heart for orphans." She took his hand, and they danced to the lively country music together, laughing as they tried to keep up with the fiddle.

CHAPTER
NINE

"It was perfect," Ina said as she pulled pins from her hair, allowing her fine yellow locks to fall loose at her shoulders. "Did you see the way Duncan looked at me? It's like he could see the real me. He danced with me three times. Can you believe it? And we never ran out of things to say. We talked about books we like and our favorite foods, and we talked about being lonely." She sighed before pulling another pin from her hair. "When we talked, he looked at me in the kindest way."

"He couldn't keep his eyes off you," Hazel said. "Even when you were dancing with Gilbert, or with that boy who looked to be fourteen, Duncan's eyes were always on you."

"I always dreamed, but never thought it would happen." Ina smiled at her reflection. "I truly felt like a princess on the arm of a prince."

"He seems like a perfect gentleman. And you were the fairest princess there." Hazel used the back of her hand to cover a yawn. "It was a good night."

"Do you think he could grow to care for me? I know it's unlikely, but do you think it could be possible?"

"Maybe no one has cared before because you are meant to be with Duncan. Perhaps it's all part of some grand design." She said it and she wanted to believe it for Ina, but she wasn't so sure there was any sort of design for her. "If there were only some way to look ahead and see what will come of it all. But then you'd have to forfeit the magic of the mystery."

"For now, I'll have to be content with this one evening. I want to remember it all. The way it felt being led onto the dance floor. I wish I could live it again and again. I would never tire of it." She fell back on the bed with a squeal of delight. "I'll relive it in my mind whenever I feel discouraged."

"I should go so you can dream." Hazel grinned, loving the atmosphere of hope that permeated the room.

"I've been rambling about Duncan. What about you and Gilbert?"

"I don't know what to think about Gilbert. He seemed to enjoy my company tonight, and of course there was the kiss, but I don't know if any of it meant anything. I don't know if I want it to, or that he does either. I don't even know if I could want it to." Hazel wished the night could have gone on and on. When she was in his arms, dancing with him, she was able to simply feel and not think. "It's all so complicated."

"Again, you are a mystery." Ina frowned. "I've

met no one else who answers questions without ever really answering questions."

Hazel sat beside Ina on the bed just like her sisters had sat beside her so many years ago.

"Tell me what you can tell me," Ina begged. "We've been friends now for well over a month. There must be something you can share."

"I can tell you this. I've never attended a social I have enjoyed as much as the one tonight."

"What sort of parties did you used to go to?"

"When I was young, I went to fancy parties. I attracted plenty of attention in my younger years, but I was too naive. No, that's not true. I wasn't naive. I stubbornly believed that the more men I could flirt with, the more important I was. Men thought I was beautiful, but I wasn't, not like you. Any charms I possessed went no deeper than my skin. You wouldn't have liked who I was. Those careless days of flirting were only the start of my troubles. If I told you more, you'd lose that happy glow, and I'd hate to do that to you when you've had such a perfect night." Hazel stood up and moved to the door. "You were truly beautiful tonight."

"You think I'm beautiful?" Ina wiped a tear from her face.

"Perfectly beautiful. You should never question that." If Hazel could go back in time, if she could undo her wrongs and erase her past, she'd change her course and seek innocence and beauty like Ina's. But the past was locked, sealed, unchangeable, and tirelessly heavy to drag around. It was always there sneering at her and taunting her when she was tempted to be truly happy. Even now it dampened what would be a perfect night. "Go to sleep and dream of floating across the dance floor with Duncan."

When Hazel was alone, she wrote several letters, hoping to solicit help from a different judge or a lawyer. Thus far her efforts had been in vain, leaving her with little hope of ever escaping the chains of her past.

She finally crawled under her patched blanket, closed her eyes, and tried to think of anything but Gilbert. It was much harder than she had anticipated. At first when she drifted off, she dreamed his hands were around her waist, leading her as they danced in the old barn. He stopped, smiled, reached into his pocket, and pulled out a red ear of corn. Her heart beat faster as she tilted her head back and wet her lips. He inched closer, his lips so close to her, but then the barn disappeared and they were in the courthouse. A judge was pounding his gavel and shouting, "Guilty!" in a ferocious voice. She tried to lean against Gilbert for support, but he backed away. Tears glistened in his eyes, but he didn't come to her for comfort. Instead, he turned and walked away, leaving her alone and heartbroken.

She woke in tears, sobbing about the future

she could almost reach out and touch yet could never have. Gilbert, with his quiet ways and simple goodness, appealed to her more than any man she'd ever met. She buried her head in her pillow, then pounded it with her fist. *Be grateful you have a friend in him,* she reminded herself when the tears slowed. The reminder helped a little but not enough to remove the ache.

Gilbert strolled home from the corn husking in no hurry for the night to be over. Despite his slow tread, he arrived at his Amherst home long before he was ready to enter the empty abode. Aside from his years away at school, it was the only home he'd ever known. When his father grew ill, Gilbert was beside him, consoling and caring for him until he left this life and went on to the next.

If he could have his father there again, he'd pull up a chair next to him and plead with him for advice. He would dig deep, looking for wisdom and guidance. Begging for answers about life and what matters.

If he were there, his father, always so wise, would set his book or his newspaper aside and listen to Gilbert's uttered pleas and read in his eyes the ones unsaid.

"Tell me how you knew you loved Mother," Gilbert wished he could ask, knowing his father would tell him something profound that would help him understand the storm of feelings he was experiencing. "I'd planned to spend my days quietly working," he'd say to his father if he could. "I thought that was enough. I thought there'd never be a woman I felt at ease around. But now my world is changing. There's a woman who loosens my tongue. She awakens something in me I've never felt before."

Gilbert imagined his father patting him on the knee. "When you've found someone to fill the quiet, you never feel so peaceful alone again. But that new noise you've found is a tune you'll be forever grateful for. There's nothing like the music of companionship."

Is that what his father would say?

His childhood house was much the same as it had always been, with its old wallpaper, furniture, and even the same lamps. But the home was quiet now, when before it had been filled with the sounds of family. The floorboards groaned beneath his weight, and he realized their din had become his most frequent companion. He was thirty, and even though he told everyone he never planned to marry, he hadn't pictured himself being thirty and alone. It had just happened. One year after another he lived out his life, and now here he was a homeowner, a successful dentist, and alone.

Since hiring Hazel, he found he was eager to get up in the morning to go to work and a little sorry when the day was over and he was back on his own. Tonight, walking away from the social, he'd felt like something was missing. He would have liked to have had someone on his arm. Someone to go home with. Someone to talk to.

Hazel had changed him.

A void he'd been oblivious to had grown over time, first with his brother leaving and then with the loss of his father. Each year since, it'd grown wider and deeper. Tonight he felt the barren emptiness that until now he hadn't realized was meant to be filled by another soul. Holding Hazel while they danced. Laughing with her over nothing. Brushing his lips to her cheek. For a few brief, fleeting moments he'd experienced what it would feel like to have someone.

He tipped his head back, closed his eyes, and for the first time prayed that this home would someday be filled with family again.

CHAPTER
TEN

"Good morning," Hazel said two days later when she walked through the office door with a basket swinging on her arm. "I go by an apple tree every day on my way here. I finally asked the owner if I could pick a few." She held up a bright red apple. "Isn't it lovely? If I had my own kitchen, I'd make you a pie. But Mrs. Northly doesn't permit us in hers, so we will just have to slice them and eat them plain." She set down the basket and pulled off her coat.

He instinctually walked up to her and reached for it. "Let me hang this for you."

"Thank you."

"If you are set on a pie, you could use my kitchen," he said over his shoulder as he hung her coat beside his own.

"Are you sure that doesn't cross one of your lines?" She bit her fingernail while scrutinizing him. "I'd love to, but—"

"As I see it, a happy employee works harder. And I can tell by the look on your face that pie would keep you smiling." He picked up three apples and attempted to juggle them, only to have one fall to the floor. "I'm only thinking of my work and how to make the office run as smoothly as it can."

She reached out and snatched an apple from the air. "All this time I thought you were a kind and generous man, but alas, I find you are just another man who thinks only of—"

"I know what you are about to say. No more of your wittiness. I want you to come over and make an apple pie, and not because I believe it will improve the office one bit. I lied." He put his hand on his heart. "Want the truth?"

"Yes, of course."

"I love apple pie. You come over and make pie, and I'll make dinner."

She narrowed her eyes.

"Say yes."

"I'm not sure." She fidgeted with the stem of an apple, twisting it until it popped off.

When she didn't readily agree to his plan, he amended it. "I hadn't meant a meal for just the two of us." He hoped his red face did not give him away. "It'll be the perfect chance for us to have Duncan and Ina together again. It'd be a house party."

"Yes! That's perfect. Ina has been longing to see Duncan again." Hazel squealed, the apprehension from moments before gone from her face. "Let's do it."

"I'll make the arrangements. Perhaps this Friday evening. You bring the apples."

"You never cease to surprise me." Hazel used the knife she'd brought to cut him a slice of apple. "Surprise me again. We still have a few minutes."

"Surprise you?" He took the apple from her. Slowly, he bit into the crisp fruit and let the sweetness fill his mouth while he stalled. "I don't know what you want to hear."

With the tiniest twitch of her shoulders, she shrugged. "Anything. I just thought it'd be fun to hear something else about you. There's so much I don't know."

He chewed his slice of the apple a moment before saying, "I once solved a crime. Does that surprise you?"

"Indeed! First a matchmaker and now a lawman. I would never have guessed. Tell me the story." Hazel pulled over a chair and settled in beside him.

"I was working when a pair of officers showed up in their formal uniforms. I wondered when they walked through the door what they could possibly want with me."

"Were you suddenly afraid they would discover your life of crime?" Hazel giggled at her own bit of humor. "Did your conscience eat at you?"

"Of course not. I've nothing to hide. Perhaps you suggest it because you are hiding a guilty past." He pursed his lips, attempting to match her wittiness, despite having no true fears about Hazel. No one as kind as she was could harbor secrets that would scare him off, but jesting was entertaining. "Have you some dark secrets you aren't ready to divulge? Some secret life of pillage and deceit?"

"And if I did?"

"Well, as a law-abiding citizen, I'd have to turn you in. I can't have a criminal in my house of employment."

Hazel stuck the knife deep into the apple and pushed it aside. Something shifted in her countenance. "I suppose I must find a new job where my list of offenses can remain hidden. Now finish your story. I need to know what the officers wanted with the least suspicious man in town."

"I'm going to take that as a compliment."

"Take it however you'd like. But Alberta will be here soon, and I want to hear your story."

"Alberta?"

"She wasn't happy with whatever it was you did last week, and so she's coming back. There was a note under the door."

At least he wouldn't be on his own with Alberta this time. But even with Hazel nearby, he still dreaded Alberta's presence. He found only a small measure of solace in the fact that he'd survived all his encounters with her in the past, and odds were in his favor that he would again.

"Finish your story before she comes."

He forced Alberta from his mind, refusing to

let the sour woman rob him of this moment with Hazel. "The officers had a denture with them. They'd found it on a body that had been burned to an unrecognizable state. They were going from dentist to dentist, hoping whoever made it could identify the teeth and therefore the body."

He stood and puffed out his chest a little. "Turns out you are looking at the man who solved the case. Don't tell me that dentists aren't exciting."

"You pull teeth for a living. Who would ever argue that it is not an exciting profession?" She laughed. "Who was the dead man?"

He feigned offense. "You sound like you think my crime story is more exciting than my ordinary days of pulling teeth."

"Come now, you know I find mouths and saliva to be very . . . um, interesting. Who was the dead person?"

"It was an older man I'd known for years. He was a drunk who the police believed may have been the cause of the fire that destroyed the Henley building." He walked up beside her and put a hand on her shoulder. Looking as heroic as he could, he said, "If you ever need someone to solve a case for you, you know where to turn."

"I may have you honor that promise someday. One never knows when they will be in need of a crime-fighting dentist. Now tell me more about dear Alberta."

"The clock moves slower when she is here," he warned. "But time will pass, and eventually she will go."

His warning hung in the air for only a moment before the door swung open and in walked Alberta with her bony frame poised for attack.

"You told me to enjoy the social," she said. "How was I supposed to enjoy a social when a good half of my head was throbbing? The pain has never gone away."

She walked right up to Gilbert until she was only inches from his face and opened her mouth. "Look here."

He winced as foul breath drifted toward him, alarming his senses. His gag reflex was well trained, but this caught him off guard, threatening to overturn his stomach. He took a moment to force the bile that had risen in his throat back down.

"Half my mouth is red. See there." She moved even closer, once again assaulting him with her words and air. "See how red it is?"

Hazel interrupted her. "You must be Alberta Robertham. I've heard a great deal about you. We're so pleased to have you today."

She scowled at Hazel with beady eyes. "Who are you?"

"I'm Doctor Watts's lady in attendance. My name is Hazel McDowell."

Alberta continued scowling as she finished her

appraisal. "You look too young and prim to be of much help."

"I'm flattered you think so. However, I'm twenty-five. And quite unconventional, as you can tell, since I just told you how terribly old I am." Hazel linked arms with Alberta. "Let me walk you back to the chair. I've no doubts the good doctor will have you out of pain in no time."

"Twenty-five? You married?" Impatient for a response, Alberta snorted. "Are you? Or aren't you?"

"I am indeed twenty-five," Hazel said. Her features showed no obvious signs of annoyance, but Gilbert felt the strongest impression that she was battling to keep her temper under control. "And I do *not* have a husband. In fact, I do not even have a suitor. Seems all the men I know have no plans to marry. Odd, isn't it? That men would choose to be unattached when there are so many eligible females around?"

Alberta patted her arm. "Be wary of bachelor men. Especially those who have remained bachelors into their thirties." She darted a look back at Gilbert. "There's always a reason they don't settle down."

Gilbert's and Hazel's eyes met for a brief moment, and with no words spoken, they communicated how utterly shocked they were by her manners and ghastly remarks.

"Be cautious," Alberta warned again. "I often have men trying to woo me and persuade me to follow them to dark and dismal places. I have never given in to the sly workings of men, no matter the persistence of their attempts."

Gilbert covered his smirk and turned away. Surely these enticing men had malicious plans, but he doubted they were the plans Alberta envisioned.

"You must be strong too," Alberta said to Hazel. She leaned in closer and whispered, but not soft enough to leave him out of the conversation. "Even with your fading looks, I'm sure a few men would still take advantage of your vulnerability. Some men are not the least bit particular. Be especially wary of the doctor. I heard he kissed a girl at the corn husking."

Hazel coughed and then coughed again. "Excuse me," she said between fits. "I think I need a drink of water." She slipped from the room without another word.

Drat. It was just him and Alberta again. She walked up to him and shook her finger in his face. "You leave that girl alone. I don't approve of this men and women working together nonsense. Trouble will come of it."

"She has no need to fear."

The finger poked him in the shoulder. "Keep it that way. I won't keep patronizing your establishment if I catch wind of you being anything less than a respectable man."

So there was a way to scare Alberta off. Nothing had ever tempted him to lower his moral standard so much. Hazel returned, a stifled smile on her face, and the two of them teamed up to keep Alberta under control.

"Tell me, Alberta, was there popcorn at the social?" Gilbert asked, a mock smile on his face.

"There was," she mumbled while Gilbert worked.

"A kernel of corn." He held it up a few moments later for her to see. "This is the culprit. We've found the source of the inflammation."

"I'm sure the pain wasn't from that. It was from whatever you did to my mouth." Alberta pulled herself from the chair and folded her arms across her chest.

"Your mouth should start feeling better right away," he said, remaining outwardly calm.

"Unlikely," she said.

"Nonetheless, I do believe you'll be feeling like yourself before long." He moved toward the door, herding her out as he went. "I suggest you buy a toothbrush. They're becoming more common and easier to come by. There are tooth powders you can buy as well. I believe you'll find them quite effective."

Alberta scowled at Gilbert, turned on her heel, and stormed from the building.

"It was lovely meeting you," Hazel called to the woman's back.

When the door swung shut behind her, both Gilbert and Hazel plopped down in the waiting room chairs and sighed.

"She is every bit as audacious as you said." Hazel shook her head. "Someone ought to turn that woman over their knee and give her a swat."

"I don't think a swat would change anything. She's been like this for as long as I can remember."

"I'm glad you said I wasn't like her. I'm not sure I could live with myself if you'd seen one bit of resemblance."

Gilbert shook his head as he looked at Hazel. There was no resemblance—not a thing about her was like Alberta. Hazel was easy on the eyes, with her soft curves and dimpled cheeks, all framed by her gorgeous red mane. Alberta was wiry, with a face that scowled and intimidated.

"Your looks aren't fading," he mumbled.

She brought a hand to her face. "You heard her say that?"

"I did. And I about boxed her ears in when she said it. It's not true." He thought of saying more, of pouring out all the compliments he'd inwardly composed, but that would surely cross the line. He straightened in his chair. If he drew the line, he could move it, could he not? They were his rules. Didn't that mean he could change them? If she were willing, could they be more than doctor and attending?

"You're beautiful," he said so softly he wondered if he'd said it aloud. "Very beautiful."

Hazel shifted in her seat until she faced him and their eyes held one another, his look as gentle as a caress. "Thank you. I do wonder sometimes. Now that I'm older, I see all the young girls about town and wonder how it is that I am twenty-five. I'm so out of fashion, and I've found a gray hair among the brown. Time can be cruel." She smiled her easy smile again. "Alberta offered me some good advice."

"The bit about avoiding me at all costs. I heard that too. That was right before you ran from the room *coughing*."

Hazel smirked. "If I'd stayed one moment longer and heard one more word, I would have been on the floor laughing. Or I'd be behind bars for having walloped the woman."

"She took advantage of our time alone and told me to keep my distance from you." Gilbert scooted his chair a few inches away from Hazel. "Does that make you more comfortable?"

"It does." She scooted her chair in the opposite direction, putting even more space between them. "That's about right. I think at this distance I'm safe from your conniving ways. Thirty and unmarried." She shook her head and clicked her tongue disapprovingly.

He gave her a look of artificial hurt, which only made her laugh. She moved her chair so close, her leg touched his. "I don't have to be far from you to feel safe. You are the man I feel the safest around. I wish I could say the same for all men."

He cleared his throat. "Have . . . have there been men who have made you feel threatened?"

"Some men have made me feel uncomfortable. Your sex can be rather presumptuous, bold, and even forceful at times."

"It's my hope to never be lumped in with those sorts of men."

"I shouldn't be so hard on all men. My father is a good man. And my brothers are honorable. Most men aren't so bad, I suppose." Hazel fidgeted with her cream-colored cuff. "Not all women are pious and innocent. We have plenty who shame the group, at least at times."

"The men who are bad, they kept you from ever marrying?" He stood and walked across the room, unable to sit still. "I shouldn't have asked that. I'm as bad as Alberta."

"I'm sure we both have our reasons for having lived our lives the way we have," she said before rising and stepping beside him. They stood in silence, reflective and thoughtful. "This is a lovely painting. They all are. I adore the one behind your desk."

"You do?"

"Yes, the rolling hills with their autumn colors. The little house at the edge of it all. I feel like I've left the hustle and bustle of town when I look at it. Besides, autumn is my favorite time of year." She brushed a stray hair from her face. In this lighting, her hair looked like the color of autumn. Like a leaf about to change from red to brown. "What's your favorite?" she asked.

"Painting?"

"No, season."

"I've never thought about having a favorite season. I guess spring. It's not as dramatic as autumn, but I love walking home past all the drifts of snow and seeing the grass breaking through. My father loved spring." Gilbert was grateful to be digging up a happy memory of his father rather than thoughts of him on his deathbed. "Now that he's gone, it reminds me of him."

Hazel's shoulder brushed against his as she walked back across the room. "I remember the freedom I sensed when winter ended. We could finally run about outside without having to wear layers of clothes. It was liberating. I'd like to experience that free feeling again."

"Do you feel trapped now?" Gilbert scratched at the back of his neck while he watched her. He'd never been an employer before. Perhaps he was doing something wrong, and he was the reason she felt restrained.

"In a way, I do believe I'm limited. I don't think I can make you understand, but I'm both trapped and free right now." Hazel shrugged like she always did when she couldn't put into words what she felt. "I've made life much too complicated, and I can't find a way to untangle it." She looked down at her hands. "I meant to ask you. Do you think I could leave early one day this week?"

"Yes, if you must." His voice had become a hoarse whisper. He looked about his little dental office, noting how small and old it was. "Do you not like working here?"

Hazel put a hand on his arm and left it there. "I love working here. It's not that at all. I have something I must do."

"Go whenever you need to. Friday is going to be a slow day."

The door jingled open, and the two of them stepped apart. He became the doctor again, and she became his lady in attendance.

CHAPTER
ELEVEN

Tuesday became Wednesday, then Thursday, and soon it was Friday, the day of the dinner party. Hazel and Gilbert grew closer each day, their friendship proving to be more than a passing fancy. Their constant conversations filled the office and pulled them closer still. His deep laugh and her much lighter one were a perfect harmony of happiness.

"I have to finish a bridge," Gilbert said, walking toward the art room.

"Will you show me?" she asked. "All I ever see is the masterpiece at the end."

The art room was where he'd sat beside his father as a boy and started his early dental training. It was now his personal refuge—a sanctuary when he needed to lose himself in his work.

"You can come." Welcoming her confirmed that, despite it being her idea, he wanted her to share his oasis. "My father used this room," he said after opening the door. "Many of his old tools are still here. Relics now, but I can't part with them."

"You loved him. I can tell." She stated the truth while peering at the walls. Wax, molds, and tools were stacked neatly on shelves. Projects half-finished rested in clamps, waiting for his attention. His eyes followed hers, seeing it anew. "It's so clean."

"My father always said a clean workspace was a happy workspace. I've never been able to leave it askew." He watched her run her finger over an old dental pelican, a set of dental keys, and a finished denture.

"I see why you call it an art room. You're gifted."

"Thank you." He picked up a file and flipped it back and forth in his hand. "Do you want to try making something? I'll let you make a mold."

"Could I?"

"Sit here." The counter was high enough that a project could be worked standing or sitting atop a tall stool. He pulled a stool out for her and, once she was seated, handed her a block of wax and several small carvers. "Etch whatever you'd like, then I'll help you pour it."

She picked up the tools, studied them, then shaved a bit of wax from the block. Several long moments passed as she carved more and more away.

"Help me," she said without turning away from her project. "When I try to take a little piece off, I take too much."

He stepped nearer and observed. When the carver slid out of control, he put his hand on hers. She turned when he touched her and stared up into his eyes, waiting. His mouth went dry.

"Cut straight down where you want to stop. The back cut will help you control the amount you remove." He guided her hand, and together they made a cut and carved slivers of wax away from the mold. "You'll get better."

"If you keep helping." She looked over her shoulder, their faces inches apart. "You're a fine teacher."

Her breath was a gentle breeze against his skin and sent his heart beating faster. He released her hand and staggered back a step. "You've nearly mastered it already."

"Hardly." She smiled. "Where are you going? I thought you had a bridge to work on?"

He cleared his throat. "I do . . . you're right."

"I'll wash the instruments from the last patient. I don't want to be in the way." She stood, leaving the wax on the table. "Thank you for the lesson."

"Stay. I'll get another stool and you can keep me company. I'll boil the last batch of instruments later."

"You want me to stay?"

"I do."

Hazel glanced at the clock. "I want to, but—"

He opened the art room door. "You have somewhere to go. I forgot."

"I'll hurry and help clean up first." Hazel appeared flustered.

"Just go. I've cleaned this office many times on my own." She seemed reluctant, but she washed her hands, grabbed her lunch tin, and left. Gilbert closed the door and turned back toward his office. Somehow it seemed darker without Hazel—and far too quiet. A different job, marriage—someday something could pull her away for good. He was acutely aware that if that day came, he would have trouble ever going back to the way things were before. She had changed the office, and she had changed him.

Hazel headed first to the post office in hopes one of the queries she'd sent requesting help with her case had been answered, but as usual there was no reply. Discouraged but still determined, she went to the small police station at the edge of town.

Mustering as much courage as she could, she knocked loudly on the station door. It was the first time she had dared to go right to the police. She'd always quietly gone to a judge or a lawyer, hoping they would take on her case.

"What do you want?" an older man with thin lips and bushy eyebrows asked. "You need something, miss?"

"I need to speak with someone about a crime."

"Come in, and I'll get Tom." The man motioned for her to follow him into the dim building and down a narrow hall to a small, sparsely furnished room.

"Wait here. Sorry it's not more comfortable. We don't get many ladies in."

Hazel tapped her fingers on the table and fretted over the reception she'd get. Was this the right choice? Or could it somehow put those she loved in danger? What if someone evil was behind what happened before? Could he still be out there? If he heard she was stirring up trouble, could he come after her or her family? Maybe Mr. Beck had been right, and she should accept the past and move on.

She thought about her sisters, Bernice and Mathilda, and wondered what they thought of society. Had they been warmly welcomed? And her brothers, what had they been doing? She wanted answers, resolution, and justice— all things she could not have without the help of those in authority. If there was a way to set things right, shouldn't she take it? But fear was a beast that arrived uninvited, unannounced, and with force. It came now, sweeping over her and stealing her breath.

She looked down the hall in time to see a man with a severe face approaching. Without waiting to see if his disposition matched his expression, she fled. Too much a coward to face rejection at this man's hands.

"Miss, did you need something?" she heard a voice call to her back.

"No, thank you," she said, quickening her pace and keeping her face straight ahead.

Like a fool, she ran outside. If only she could

so easily run from it all. Months of bottled-up tears chose that moment to spill from her, racing down her face. She trudged back toward the boardinghouse, making no attempt to contain the grief and turmoil that raged within. One moment she was shedding tears, knowing she'd played a part in her own misery and that of others, and the next she was sobbing over the cruelty of her seemingly lifelong sentence for what she'd never done.

"Hazel?"

Through her tears, she saw Gilbert walking toward her. Running away and pretending she hadn't heard him was not an option. He'd seen her—tears and all.

"Are you all right?" he asked, lengthening his stride.

"Don't worry on my account." She tried to smile through her tears.

Gilbert shook his head. He opened his mouth but didn't speak and instead put an arm around her as though he wished to shield her from the weight of her worries. At the touch of his arm, she turned toward him and buried her head in his chest. He wrapped his other arm around her too, and his arms were strong and comforting, and for a moment she allowed herself to be weak in his embrace.

He gripped her tighter and let her cry. Whispering into her ear, he said, "Come with me."

Blinded by tears and sorrow, she let him lead her away, past the school and the church, up a little hill at the edge of the village.

He laid his jacket across a fallen log. "Sit down." Always a gentleman. She did as he asked, and he sat beside her. "I'm not the best with words, especially with you beside me and with your tears. I can talk about teeth and the weather—those things don't scare me."

She pressed a finger to his rambling lips. "Shhh, you're just fine with words. Don't belittle yourself."

"I could use more practice."

"Practice on me." She sniffled.

With a tender thumb, he wiped away a fresh tear. "What's wrong? Your eyes aren't sparkling like they should be."

"You are perfect with words." She leaned her head against his shoulder and let more tears roll down her cheeks as she mourned the past, knowing it would forever keep her from what she now wanted so badly.

"Did something happen while you were away?" His voice cracked. "Is it something I can help you with? If it is, I will."

"I don't know how you could. It's all a big tangled knot, and I don't know how to unravel it. I worry that if I try, I will only make it worse. But if I don't, my life can't go anywhere."

Gilbert stopped her rambling by pressing a

kiss to the top of her head. She froze beneath his touch, closed her eyes, and savored his compassion.

His voice was gentle. "I wish I knew how to ease all your worries. I know that ever since you walked through the door of my office, I've been grateful for the noise and fire you brought in with you. I want to help you."

She pulled her head off his shoulder and looked up at him. His benevolent deep-brown eyes held hers. "I have never had anyone tell me they liked my noise."

"Forgive my choice of words," he whispered.

"Don't apologize. They're not the polished words of the snakes Alberta warned me about." She laughed a little through her tears. "You're always so good, it scares me. I feel inferior beside you. Where I am weak, you are endlessly strong."

He shifted, and she worried she'd scared him off. Men like Gilbert did not always take praise well, preferring instead to quietly offer charity and kindness, needing no fanfare. To her great relief, he did not leave.

"Look over there." He pointed toward autumn's greens, reds, and yellows in the leaves. "See that cluster of trees?"

She straightened, recognizing the setting as one of the paintings at the office that had so often swept her away. "You are the painter?"

"When I was a little boy, I had a terrible time speaking. I'd try to talk, but my words wouldn't come out how I wanted them to. I avoided people whenever I could so I wouldn't have to talk. One day my father bought me a paint set. I think he knew I needed something I could be good at." Gilbert wiped another one of her tears. "Only my father knew I painted. Well, and Eddie."

Hazel put a hand on his forearm. "Your art should be somewhere public."

"I used to dream of being a world-famous painter. But then I started painting my heart into my pictures. The places I loved, and that brought me peace." He hesitated. "I didn't want my heart to be on display." He picked up a red leaf from the ground. "It matches your hair."

"My hair is what this leaf will look like in a few days when it turns brown." She ran a hand through her unruly tresses.

"I thought your hair was brown when I first saw you. But when the sun hits it, it is decidedly red." With a cautious hand, he took a strand of her soft hair and ran it between his fingers. "It's a beautiful color."

If the past were not looming all around her, she would have crept deeper into his touch and relished the feel of his hand in her hair. With new tears threatening to spill over, she stood and walked a few steps away.

He followed.

"I'm sorry," he said. "I'll be more careful what I say and do."

"I've wanted a shoulder to lean on." Running her hands along the pleats of her dress, she attempted to brush aside all the emotion that swirled within her. With renewed composure, she said, "We should forget all these tears and talk about our dinner with Ina and Duncan."

"If that's what you want. Duncan stopped by the other night to tell me he bought a new suit for the occasion." Gilbert looked out at the horizon. "The two of them together is a good thing. I hope they find happiness."

"What do you think he sees in Ina?"

Gilbert's brow furrowed as he thought. "I can't speak for his heart, and he may not even know yet. But when I saw him, he said he felt at ease in her presence. And perhaps that comfortable feeling can blossom into something more."

"You and I will just have to help them realize they are meant to be with each other."

"I think if anyone can nudge them together, it is us." He stooped and picked up a leaf only to send it into the gentle breeze. They watched it sail and then land. "Tomorrow I plan to paint."

"You do? What are you going to paint?"

He shrugged. "I don't know. I only know I feel the desire to create."

"Paint this tree. Put it up in the office, and when

I see it, I will think of the time you let me cry on your shoulder."

He offered his arm to her. "My shoulder is yours to cry on whenever you need it. Let me walk you home so you and Ina can get ready for our dinner. And tomorrow I'll paint this tree. It'll be for you."

"Can I come?" she asked, reaching for his arm. "Can I watch you paint?"

"I never let anyone watch me paint."

"I don't have to," she said, realizing she'd been presumptuous. "I didn't mean to assume—"

"But since it's your painting, you may come." He squeezed the hand that was wrapped around his arm. "No more tears?"

"No more tears," she said, grateful to have even a moment of contentment.

There were two meals Gilbert could make. The first was eggs, and the second was vegetable soup. Neither seemed appropriate for such an important evening. Ever since the date for their pie making had been set, he'd agonized over the meal. In the end, he'd asked sweet old Clara for help.

"I've been praying you'd find yourself a nice girl," she'd said when he'd asked for her help. "Maybe after you get married, this house will be filled with laughter and children. Just think of it. Children in this home again."

He hadn't had the heart to tell her that he and Hazel were not courting, and so all week he'd let Clara think what she liked. Her excitement had overpowered her practical side. The result was a feast—roast, potatoes with gravy, and fresh rolls.

"She'll be here soon," Gilbert said to the matronly woman. "She wants to use the kitchen to make a pie."

"You've told me twice. I'm hurrying. I'll clean up and then scurry away. I brought a whole stack of mending to do. I'll go in the back room and stitch away while you have your party." Clara grabbed a rag and wiped the table where she had cut vegetables.

"I told you, you don't have to stay. We've spent plenty of time together."

She waved a hand in the air. "Nonsense. Your mother would like knowing I was keeping things proper."

He fought the urge to roll his eyes. "Stay if you must."

Clara set down the rag and walked over to him. Patting his cheek, she said, "I haven't seen you this happy in years."

A rapping sounded at the door. She was here! Hazel was here at his home.

"Go get the door, dear," Clara said when he didn't move toward the sound. "Don't leave her waiting. I'll finish up."

Glancing into the hall mirror, he made sure

his hair was smooth, then looked once more at his home. It was dated, all of it, but there was nothing he could do about that now. His house had not had a woman's touch in a long time, not since before his mother's death. Aside from Clara, a female had not set foot inside in years. Now Hazel was here. Perhaps this moment was not monumental, but it felt pivotal to him.

She knocked again. He stopped dallying and reached for the doorknob.

"Let me help you," he said when he opened the door. She was standing on his porch with a basket of apples in one arm and a little box in the other.

"Take the apples. The box is for you for later." Hazel grinned as she stepped over the threshold. He watched her eyes roam across the front room.

"The box is for me?"

"It's a present of sorts."

"Hello there." Clara stepped into the front room, brushing her hands on her apron. "I'm about done in the kitchen, and then it's all yours for your pie. I took the liberty of starting your piecrust." She turned her attention to Gilbert. "The food will just have to be taken out and served."

"I think I can manage," Gilbert said. "Thank you for helping."

Clara sucked in her bottom lip. "I've been wanting to see you with a lovely girl for so long, and she's just beautiful. Your father and your dear mother, bless their souls, must be smiling down on you."

Hazel shot Gilbert a questioning look. He shrugged, well aware that he'd have to explain it to her later.

When Clara finally snuck off to the back of the house, Gilbert had Hazel all to himself—at least until Ina and Duncan arrived.

He set the dining room table as he spoke. "Clara has all sorts of ideas in her head, but not because I said anything."

"And what does she think?" Hazel asked, already setting to work on the apples.

He stopped setting the table and looked at her. She was in his kitchen with an apron around her waist. It took very little imagination for him to pretend that this was her kitchen and that they shared this home. If only the image could linger and she did not have to go. "Clara often tells me she worries I'll live a life of loneliness. She believes you are my remedy. And I suppose in a way you are. This table has not had anyone sitting at it for far too long."

"It's a lovely table." She smiled. "It's kind of her to worry over you. And good of her to cook for us. I had worried I would not have time to cut the apples *and* make the dough. She's thought of everything."

He grinned sheepishly, remembering his promise to cook the meal. "I'd planned to cook myself, but I decided my cooking skills were not suited for the occasion. I wanted Ina and Duncan to have a special night."

"It smells like you made a wise decision." She set the apples aside and rolled the piecrust out. "I only learned to cook a couple years ago and that wasn't by choice, though I do love it now. This dough looks better than anything I've made."

"I am guessing you won't tell me why you were forced into the kitchen, but I'm hoping you will tell me what's in the box."

She pressed the piecrust into the tin. "Open the lid if you'd like."

Gilbert didn't have to be told twice. He picked up the wooden box, unsure what he'd find inside. The box was wooden with three latches along the front holding it tightly closed. He opened each, only to discover a velvet-lined box with an instrument resting on the soft fabric. A flute? He looked at Hazel, hoping to understand.

"Don't worry. I don't expect *you* to play it. I brought it because you shared your painting secret with me. You paint your heart in your brushstrokes, and I play my heart into my music. Or, rather, I did. I haven't played in a very long time." She set the crust aside and went back to the apples. "I thought I'd play it tonight."

"Will you play it now?" Gilbert asked, holding the delicate instrument in his hand. "Let me hear what your heart sounds like."

"I will once this pie is in the oven." She tossed him an apple. "Come slice with me. If I don't hurry, I won't have it in before the others arrive."

He had wondered what it would be like to have her in his home. And now here he stood beside her. He felt perfectly at ease, comfortable. More than that, he sensed a growing desire to always have her near. They made quick work of the apples, and not much later the pie was in the oven.

Brushing her hands on her apron, she sighed. "Thank you for letting me use your stove. I've missed baking."

"I believe my mother would be pleased. She loved it when this house was filled with the scent of good food." He rinsed his hands and stepped away. "Now we only have to wait, and then we can eat it. I can hardly wait."

"I will play for you. Otherwise, I think you will just sit there with a watering mouth as you wait for your slice of pie." She took the flute from the box and pieced it together before bringing it to her perfect pink lips.

Closing his eyes, he listened as the soft music filled the room. His own heart responded to the sound, hurting as she played. It was a sad song, a melody that sounded like weeping. On she played, and he knew she was giving him a precious glimpse into her soul.

When at last her lips moved away from the flute, the room was silent except for the beating of their two hearts.

He took a cautious step toward her, and then another, unsure what he would do when he got to her but unable to remain so far away. She took a small step toward him. Was she uncertain too? How they closed the gap, he did not know, but somehow she made her way into his arms. No sensation had ever felt more right than the feel of this tender woman leaning against him. If only he could hold her always. Could they not remain as one, leaning on and supporting each other? He yearned to hold her so long and so gently that never again would she play a sad song.

The room filled with the fresh scent of warm apple pie as they stood embracing. He dared to lean his cheek against the top of her head, her red hair brushing against his face, tickling his skin, and sending heat racing through his body. Everything about having her near felt good.

A knock on the door pulled them apart. Reluctantly, they separated to greet the other half of their party.

Before opening the door, Gilbert took her hand in his own and pressed his lips to her fingertips. "Thank you," he said, hoping she knew it was for more than the pie. "All of it was a gift like none I've ever received. Your music, your heart"—he cleared his throat—"it was beautiful."

· · ·

The hour was late when the party finally ended.

It had been a night of both laughter and joy, and above all else it had been an escape from the weight of their worries. Hazel had nearly been beside herself with happiness when she saw Ina and Duncan holding hands while she played her flute after dinner. Gilbert complimented her pie and ate nearly a quarter of it himself. When she insisted he'd helped, he gave her all the credit.

All too soon the evening ended. The group stood and moved toward the door. Oh, how she wished the night could go on forever. That time would stand still and she could sit beside Gilbert and relish the companionship and comfort she felt with him nearby. Duncan offered Ina his arm as they readied to depart.

"Walk with us?" Ina said to Hazel. "I hate to think of you walking alone in the night."

"I've already asked if I could escort her home," Gilbert said before Hazel could speak. When their eyes met, he winked at her, sending a flurry of excitement through her. The night was not over. Soon she'd be on his arm, which was exactly where she wanted to be.

"We won't be far behind you. I insisted I help clean up, and then we'll set out," she said, willingly joining the conspiracy.

"Very well. Thank you for a lovely evening," Ina said from beside Duncan. They stepped over the threshold and onto the street, leaving Gilbert and Hazel.

"I thought they could use some more time together," Gilbert offered as an explanation once they closed the door. He went to the table and gathered an armful of dishes. "I think we did well tonight. It wouldn't surprise me if they get their happily ever after before long."

"I wasn't sure I believed in fairy tales, but I think you may be right." While Hazel helped clear the table, they talked amiably about the night. She started washing, but he came up behind her and put his hand over hers. "I insist you leave these. Let me walk you home before it gets any later."

"I hate leaving them for you."

"I don't mind." He kept his hand over hers. "I promised Clara I'd let her know when we were done. I'm sure she's asleep in her favorite rocker. Let me wake her, and then we'll be on our way."

Moments later they were arm in arm, walking the streets toward the boardinghouse and talking about everything and nothing as they went. She wondered if her prattling bothered him, but he seemed engrossed in their meandering conversation. The warm night allowed them to go slowly and enjoy the end of a perfect evening.

"What is your favorite book? The one you love more than any other?" she asked.

"I've never ranked things in order like you do. Let me think."

"You don't have one you just know you love?"

"Do you?" he asked.

"Of course. Whenever I'm feeling any pity for myself, I read *Jane Eyre*. Her life is full of trials, yet she's persistently moral and relentlessly determined. She may be an odd hero, but I long to be like her. Now tell me yours."

"When I was small, my mother read to us every night. I remember sitting beside her as she read, wishing I could step into the images. That is my favorite."

"I like your memory," she said. "I think Clara was right."

"About what?"

"That your father and mother are proud of you." She stopped and pointed. "That's the tree the apples are from. Do you have a favorite type of pie?"

He laughed aloud. "Another favorite. After this evening, I'd have to say that apple is my favorite. Let me ask you one."

"Very well." She waited.

"What is your favorite time of day?"

"That's easy. I love the morning when the sun is just coming up, but I do also love the afternoon when the sun is warm. But I think I'll still pick morning. You?"

"Strolling in the evening with you." His voice was soft, almost lost in the night air. This talk of moonlit walks crossed a line, and she knew it. She should run from it all, but she could not. "And the mornings when you come through the office door with a smile on your face," he whispered as they rounded the corner near the boardinghouse. "And the afternoons when you come in from your walk."

"I see." She swallowed and fought to keep her voice steady. "You love the morning, the afternoon, and the evening."

"It's hard to choose a favorite."

"This evening was one of the finest ones I've ever spent." What a beautiful reprieve it had been. The boardinghouse loomed, reminding her that it was coming to an end. "Thank you for it, and for walking me home."

He pressed his lips together and nodded. "It was a night I will always remember."

"I'm glad I got to make my apple pie," Hazel said, trying to keep the conversation from ending. If only she could slow down this night, stretch it out, and make it big enough that she could climb inside it and never leave. For one magical night, the world made sense. When she stepped away from Gilbert, she feared it would all become chaos and worries again.

He looked at the luminous moon in the sky and said, "I suppose I better get you home."

Mrs. Northly was at the door when the pair stepped onto the porch.

"Say goodbye to her at the door. We don't allow callers inside, except in the parlor if they've made arrangements ahead of time and there is a proper chaperone."

Hazel released Gilbert's arm. "Mrs. Northly, I'd like you to meet Doctor Gilbert Watts. Gilbert, this is Mrs. Northly. She owns the boardinghouse."

"You the man who kept Hazel out all night a while back?" Mrs. Northly interrogated.

"No, I wasn't out with her," Gilbert answered, giving Hazel a sideways glance.

Heat ran up her neck and into her cheeks. With Mrs. Northly watching, she turned to Gilbert and said, "Thank you for seeing me safely home."

"I'll be by in the morning for you so we can paint." Gilbert's voice had lost its easy tone and once again seemed slow to come.

"Two outings in a row," Mrs. Northly said, interjecting herself into the conversation. "And you work together. Remember what I said about only housing wholesome women."

Hazel let out a gasp. Through gritted teeth, she said, "Mrs. Northly, I am a grown woman who is well aware of the ways of men. Doctor Watts is honorable. You needn't worry."

"Perhaps it's not the doctor I'm worried about." Mrs. Northly's voice was terse. "Go inside."

Hazel obeyed. At first, anger was the only sentiment she felt, but then guilt joined it, reminding her that there was truth, at least some, in Mrs. Northly's appraisal of her character. Soon her heart ached and her head throbbed. All this was a lie, and an innocent man was involved—a good man who deserved to live a life free of lies. How did one escape the bonds of dishonesty? She wrestled for an answer, searching for one that would not put a wedge between her and the man she was coming to care so deeply for. In the end, the only way to counter lies was with the truth. For Gilbert, she would confess it all.

CHAPTER
TWELVE

Tired eyes greeted Hazel when she looked in the mirror the next morning. Sighing, she pulled her hair up and neatly pinned it in place.

"Why the long face?" Ina asked from the doorway.

"I didn't sleep well."

"I didn't either. I was dreaming of Duncan. When we walked home last night, he held my hand and told me about his daughter. Her name is Amy. Don't you think it's a perfectly charming name?"

Hazel pressed her palm to her pounding head, attempting to find relief but getting none. "I do think it's a charming name. Are you going to see him again?"

"He asked to take me to church on Sunday and invited me to meet his daughter afterward. I'm going to go out today and find a gift to take her. I'd ask you to join me, but I know you will be with Gilbert."

During her sleepless night, Hazel had resolved to confess her past to Gilbert, knowing it was only fair to let the man judge her character for himself. Since she'd reached her conclusion, a nauseous feeling had settled in the pit of her stomach. It was right to tell, she knew it was, yet she wished it were not so.

"I don't know how long I'll be gone. I might be back before you've found the perfect gift." Hazel stood to leave, only to stop and put a hand on Ina's arm. "Be glad you have no past, that there was no one before. All the lonely years will be worth it. You can have your Duncan."

"He is not *my* Duncan."

"I saw the way he looked at you. I am no predictor of the future, but I believe you will get more than a small taste of romance." She squeezed her friend's hand. "Gil says Duncan is the best sort of man."

"I believe he is," Ina said. "And it's all so much sweeter knowing you have someone too."

"I have no one. Not really. I'll be back later."

Hazel and Gilbert walked up the small hill in relative silence. He whistled in a carefree way, and she grew increasingly more ill at ease with each note of his cheery song. On the crest of the hill, he pulled out his painting supplies and set up his easel, then he laid a blanket on the ground. "Sit by me?"

She settled herself beside him despite her restlessness. Stalling, she asked, "Was this your mother's quilt?"

"I don't know. My mother died before I ever thought to ask." He turned toward her and reached for her hand. His hand, large and strong, felt warm and comforting. She should pull away, refuse his touch, but she bit her lip instead and allowed one more moment of closeness. "I can't say for certain, but I believe it was the loss of my mother and later my father that caused me to fear getting close to people." He ran his thumb along the ridge of her knuckles, a gesture that, on a different day, would have had her heart swooning. But on this day, it made a lump of sadness swell inside her. "I grew accustomed to the quiet and then you came, and suddenly everything changed. You've given me reason to hope for something more for my future."

"Oh, Gil." She pulled her hand away. "Don't say those things to me."

"Have I read you wrong?" he asked, but she would not look at him. He straightened his back and reverted to his businesslike manner. "I'm sorry. I thought you felt something."

In a small voice, she said, "It's not that. If I had a different past, I'd tell you my heart was warming to the idea of a future with you, but as it is . . ."

Her voice failed her. Instead, she focused on breathing, in and out, in and out.

"Tell me what it is that holds you back. Help me understand, please." He scooted closer, urgency written across his face. "And after today, I'll never speak of it again. If that's what you want."

He put a hand on her shoulder, such a gentle touch—one that begged her to melt into it.

"Please."

She raised her head and watched as a brilliant red leaf dropped from the nearest tree and sailed slowly through the air to the ground. Its path was not its own. It soared at the mercy of the wind until it settled on the ground to wait for the rain and hail to beat upon it.

"I was . . . I *am* going to tell you, but it is so much harder than I had expected. I want so badly for it all to go away. Then we could sit on this hill and savor this beautiful day." She took a deep breath and forced herself to look at him. There he sat, his forehead creased with worry, dark-brown eyes searching her, pleading for understanding. "If I'd only had the foresight to see all of this. To see you. I would have lived so differently."

"Tell me." He brushed a strand of hair from her face. "You can trust me."

"I know," she whispered. "It hurts, knowing that you'll never look at me the same way again. I love how you look at me."

"I'll still look at you just as I am right now." His innocent face, so naive, so full of kindness and hope. "Whatever it is, tell me."

"My mother," she began, "says I was notorious for getting into scrapes even when I was small. I have a few scars to prove it."

"It's a shame you didn't have your nursing

experience when you were young," he said, the tips of his mouth pulled into a slight smile. "With all those injuries, that would have been helpful."

"It's not as though I would have doctored myself. I was little." She gnawed on her bottom lip. "I may have exaggerated my medical experience when I was so desperate for a job. I do have an uncle who is a doctor, and I did go to his house one summer. I didn't mean to lie to you. I shouldn't have. Can you forgive me?"

"I knew you hadn't spent much time in the medical field from the first day."

"You did?" She was surprised, as he'd never mentioned her inadequacies. "I thought I was convincing."

"Anyone who has spent time in the medical field knows the name of a scalpel. You called it the little knife." He laughed good-naturedly. "I didn't care. You were good with the patients and willing to learn."

"Now you know the truth about my medical experience. I've confessed to one thing today. I think that's enough." Fear took over. She pointed toward his art supplies and asked, "Didn't you come here to paint?"

"Not so fast," he said with enough force that she froze, startled. "I long to sit here with you and smell the crispness in the air and watch the leaves fall from the trees. I want to hold your hand and perhaps be bolder still, but I can't. Not until you tell me what is weighing on you. It's between us. I can feel it, and seeing you wrestle with whatever it is tells me that we must face it or this can't be."

He stood, looked at her, and paused before reaching for his paints.

"What are you doing?"

"I need you to talk to me, but you're not. I think I'll paint another time. I seem to have lost my desire to create."

She grabbed his hand and pulled him back down onto the blanket. "Where has the quiet, pleasant Gil gone? You have your own secrets, don't you?"

"Very few, but I'll tell them to you if you'd like." He ran a hand over his scruffy jaw. "Once when I was a boy, I snuck into the kitchen and ate half a pie without permission. Everyone was shocked, and they sent me to bed without supper."

"That is hardly a damning confession." She threw the leaf she was holding at him. "Is that your worst? Your innocence is further proof that I am not your equal. Don't you see, you are perfect. You're the most moral, kind man there has ever been. I'm sure of it."

"I've never been sorrier that I have so few transgressions. I was late to school a few times, and I'm sure I talked back to my father." He leaned in and spoke with urgency. "And I have unkind thoughts whenever Alberta comes in. I think of all the awful things I wish I could say to her. Surely that's a sin."

She groaned. This budding friendship that she found herself wishing could be something else could never be. Tears stung her eyes, leaving her regretting ever taking a job working for Gilbert, because letting him go was going to be harder than she'd ever imagined. "You are a perfect saint. We both know God will overlook your thoughts about Alberta. He is probably shouting your praises because you have not strangled the woman."

"If it'll make you feel better, I'll go throw a rock through the schoolhouse's window or swipe a loaf of bread from the bakery." He took her hand again, holding it tightly and looking directly at her stinging eyes. "So, our pasts are different. You were a devilish child, and I was an angel. I think we could reconcile that."

She shook her head. "There's so much more."

He sank back on the blanket, propped himself up on an elbow, and waited, so unaware of what she was about to throw at him. "We have all day."

"I *was* a reckless child, and most people just laughed when I was young. Then I grew up, and I don't think anyone knew what to do with me. I lived by my own rules."

"What kinds of rules?" he asked. "Were you a girl who hated skirts?"

"No. I dressed the part of a lady. It was little things when I was small. Once I walked atop the railing of the stairs. It was three stories down to the entryway, and I thought nothing of the consequences of falling. Somehow I grew from railing walking to much more serious offenses without ever putting together the simple fact that actions have consequences."

"Tell me more," he whispered.

"If that's not sufficient evidence of the perfect heathen I was, I'll tell you more. When I was older, I bullied and bossed our maids and nannies into giving me what I wanted. I ran through my father's pocketbook whenever I could. I owned more dresses than any girl ought to, and I had a closet full of hats I never wore but complained that I didn't have enough. But even that was not as horrible as what I became."

She spoke a little softer when she went on. "My parents threw me a party when I was sixteen to introduce me to society. I remember walking down the stairs after being announced, and everyone turned and stared at me. I liked the way the men's eyes lingered on me and how the women's eyes burned with envy. I became like Florence at the corn husking." She shook her head. "No, I wasn't like Florence. I was worse."

He sat up stiffly, forsaking his casual pose for a tense one, like a man braced for a blow. Gil's soft eyes turned away from her. "So my walk across the barn was not your only moment as the belle of the ball. You've been that girl before."

"I wish I could tell you it was the first time," she whispered. "I wish it had been."

"And these men, you . . ." The words he wanted to say, the questions he harbored, he couldn't voice. It was too ugly, too painful.

"I'd pick a man from the crowd, toy with his emotions, and never think of the damage I was causing." She put her hands over her face. He went to reach for her but held back. "I don't know that I'll ever forgive myself for the person I was. I tore couples apart. I treated sacred things as though they were trite."

"I don't understand." And he didn't. What she was saying did not match up with the woman he thought he knew.

"I don't either. I was so wrong. I came and went as I pleased, I danced with whom I wanted, and . . . and . . ." She looked off into the distance. "I kissed them when I wanted to. I told myself it was romantic to sneak off with a man, skirting every rule I'd ever been taught. I was foolish."

The tender kiss in the barn had awakened something deep within Gilbert. He'd believed, or at least hoped, that what he felt, she felt as well. But now, hearing her talk of flippant kisses and careless flirting, he doubted. A heavy sadness overpowered him.

"Do you still play those games? Was I—"

"No!" She wiped the tears that were streaming down her face. "You don't have to believe me, but I am not the girl I once was. If I could do it all again, you would be the only one."

"What happened? What ended the charade?"

"Rumors were often flying about me. My father heard more than one story of my recklessness. He said he'd put a stop to it."

"How?" He didn't want to know, but at the same time he knew he had to. "What did he do?"

"A new boy, Charles, arrived in town, and I of course tried for his attention. He would have nothing to do with me, so I tried harder." Hazel paused. "I'm sorry I have to tell you all this."

"I asked you to," he said, but he too wished it were not real.

Hazel took a deep breath. She let the air out slowly. "One day Charles's friend Edward sent word letting me know that Charles wanted to meet me in the park at night. When I got this invitation, I felt victorious, like I'd won. I can still remember climbing out my window, smiling as I went. There was one moment, though, when I paused and wondered if what I was doing was wise. I didn't stop, but I wish I had.

"When I got to the park, a man I knew only a little named Nathaniel was there. We argued as we tried to figure out what happened. The whole thing was malicious from the start, and I should have expected it."

"I don't understand," Gilbert said. Sneaking out, meeting strangers in the dark—none of it was part of his own youth. He'd been reserved, quiet, and always on a quest to better himself and honor his parents. He tried to picture her tale and to understand, but he couldn't. "Why was he there?"

"Charles, Edward, and some other boys had decided to trap me in the park with a man so they could shame me. They tricked Nathaniel into going as well, and they had the police show up to catch us together. The police said they'd been told we were . . . that we were . . . well, you can imagine what they were told. We tried to tell the police that we'd been set up and that we'd done nothing wrong."

He cleared his throat, willing his words to sound strong despite the weakness that had crept over his limbs. "Did they believe you?"

"No. They escorted us to my house. My father had already threatened me, telling me if I was caught in a situation that would shame the family again that he'd give me a consequence I'd never forget. When he heard what happened in the park, he wouldn't listen to me." She sighed, and he could tell this retelling was painful. "He paced around the house, angry, and I believe he was hurt as well. For once I was innocent of every accusation other than sneaking out, but it did no good. He was determined to follow through, and I believe he thought his consequence would solve some of his troubles."

She paused again. He couldn't bring himself to comfort her or to speak, so he sat, tense and waiting, bracing himself for whatever she was going to say next. It seemed unbelievable, but when he saw the tears glistening in her eyes, he knew she spoke the truth.

"My father is a good man, but he was out of his head that night. He was furious. He ranted about what I'd done. Questioned how he'd raised such a daughter. He reminded me that he'd warned me, and then he sent for Nathaniel's parents and somehow convinced them that it was their son's duty to marry me. We'd done nothing wrong, but there was no convincing my father. I tried to stop it, but I was afraid if I didn't comply, I'd be on my own. And, so, we married quickly—"

"You are married?" Gilbert caught her elbow and turned her toward him. His next words zinged from him like a hand about to slap. "How could you?"

"I *was* married." She grabbed his arm, but he pulled away, too overwhelmed to find comfort in her touch. "I know what you must think of me. First the medical experience and now the name. I know you can never believe me, but I have changed."

"What is your name?" He rubbed his chest. Daggers could not have hurt worse than the stabs of betrayal piercing him. He'd trusted her. "Are you even Hazel?"

"I am Hazel. I was Hazel Bradshaw before I was married, and after I became Hazel Williams. I only told you that lie to protect myself, not to hurt you."

"From your husband? Is that who you're afraid of?" He raked his hands through his hair. How could this be true?

"No," she shouted through her tears. "Not from him. He's dead."

He wanted to shake her and wipe her tears all at the same time. He felt weak, but he also burned with rage. The line between reality and fiction blurred, and he didn't know what to think or what to cling to. This story she told, surely it was not real.

"We were married for six months," she said through her tears. Each teardrop that ran down her face added to the turmoil twisting in his gut.

"Did he hurt you?"

"No. I hurt because of shame and regret, but no, Nathaniel didn't hurt me. He was angry at first, but I can't blame him for that. The whole joke had begun because of me. It was a punishment for my sins, not his. We became friends, but even then, I always wondered if he regretted our marriage. He was a good man though."

He said nothing but handed her a handkerchief.

"Before Nathaniel died, he became secretive, going out at night. I followed him once because I feared he was meeting another woman. But he didn't meet anyone. He went onto one of his father's boats." Hazel shivered. It was not the cold but the memories that affected her, Gilbert could only assume. "It was only a few days later that police brought him home nearly dead. They told me he was caught in a cross fire, someone else's brawl, they said. He woke briefly and said a few words about his parents' boat. I believed his death was not an accident. I went to the police to see if they'd investigate."

"He died then?" Gilbert asked, trying to understand the sequence of events.

"Yes, he died the night they brought him home to me hurt."

"Did you move back to your parents' home?" Gilbert asked.

"No."

He waited.

"I was arrested two days later on charges of burglary. They found jewels in my house that belonged to someone else." Her right hand went to her throat where a necklace, no doubt, had hung whenever she went to a party. "If my parents had not been of good standing, I may have been hung."

"Was there any truth to the charges?"

"I did not steal anything."

"What happened then?"

"I spent five long years at a reformatory for women. The House of Refuge."

"A prison?"

"Yes, in a way. Though we didn't just sit behind bars. We took classes and worked. It was the matron's belief that we could change if disciplined and schooled. She was a modern thinker, and though her methods could be harsh, she truly believed the women were capable of transformation."

"Was she right?" Gilbert's life had never required him to spend time thinking about prisons or transforming convicts. He knew men and women were capable of change, but could criminals be reformed as well? He cringed, not liking the thought of Hazel as a convict.

"Not everyone changed, but some did. At first I was only concerned with learning how to succeed in my new environment and how to avoid punishment, but I watched the women around me and saw what the work and focus were doing for those who truly cared." She looked past him, down the hill to where the small white church was. "I listened to the preachers. They spoke the same words I'd heard my whole life, but they meant so much more to me during those dark days. I believed their words that the Lord could meet me in the lowliest places. I'd started to change who I was while married to Nathaniel, but it was within the reformatory's cold walls that I found the Lord and truly learned to care for others. I'm far from perfect." Hazel faced him again, meeting his eye. "But I'm not the same girl I was before."

He sat silently beside her, struggling to picture the vibrant Hazel as a flippant young girl and then older and playing the part of a criminal, locked away from the rest of the world. How did those sides of her fit with the woman who sat beside him, the woman he knew and cared for? Who was she really? He could walk away right now and never look back. A part of him wanted that. But his old, quiet life before Hazel did not appeal to him like it used to.

When he said nothing, she stood and walked a few steps away. "I should go."

He put a hand out and stopped her, wanting to know more. "What was it like?"

"The reformatory?"

"Yes, all of it. What was it like?" he asked. "Help me understand."

"No one has ever asked me that."

"Tell me?"

"There were rules for everything, even how many letters we could get and if we were allowed visitors." Quickly, she told him of the tears she shed, the women she met, and her movement around the main building and eventually to a cabin on the outskirts. "The women I lived with were mostly poor and uneducated, but we became like family. I taught them to read and write, and they taught me resilience." She sighed, and he knew that whoever these women were and no matter what their crimes had been, Hazel had cared for them. "Some of the wardens were harsh, and there wasn't always adequate food. Many days I felt like those in charge were looking for me to make mistakes so they could issue punishment. But that was not the worst thing."

"What was the worst?"

"Even as we counted down our sentences, we knew we'd return to a world that would never forgive us."

"I've never considered it before, but that doesn't seem fair. Your sentence had already been served."

"I'll be forever grateful for what I gained there, but I'm also keenly aware of all I lost. I lost my future. It's why I gave you a false name. I needed money and couldn't risk losing work on account of my history. Everyone before you turned me away when I told them where I'd come from and who I was. I came to Amherst nearly penniless and did what I had to do. I'm sorry for it."

"What happened next?"

"There isn't much more. My parents sent me money and some of my belongings so I could get by on my own."

He turned his head quickly. "You've not been home?"

"No. I have brothers busy with schooling and younger sisters who are out in society trying to snare wealthy husbands. If I'm there, I'll remind the world that my family has a mark against it." Another wave of sadness swept across her face, darkening her features like a cloud blocking the sun. "My parents have to think of my siblings as well. I can hardly blame them for severing ties. Though I do dream of returning one day."

"You have been on your own since?"

"I used my parents' money to rent a room, and at first I lived quietly on my own. I was lonely but well enough. Then one day all my money but what was in my reticule was stolen. Everything fell apart all over again. I tried to get a job but had little luck until I moved here. My time at your office has been the happiest of my life. Despite my deceitful name, I believe I've been my truest self while with you. I'll cherish the memory always."

"So that's it. You will go?"

She tilted her head, and he nearly came undone. There stood Hazel, his dear friend, with tears racing down her face like rivers of sadness and defeat. "You wish me to stay?"

"I don't know, but I am not ready for you to go. I can't lie to you and say that I'm not bothered by this confession." He scratched his neck while he struggled to decide what to say. "What if you cleared your name? If you are innocent, there must be a way."

"I've tried, but no one will help me." Hazel sighed. "I may go west. Far away where no one has ever heard of Hazel and her notorious history. There are men out West looking for wives. I could have a new life without constant reminders of all I can't have."

"You'd run when you aren't guilty? You'd marry a stranger?" Gilbert clenched his fists so tightly his knuckles turned white. She couldn't run. She shouldn't have to. "And what of Nathaniel's death? Don't you want to put it all right? If you're innocent, shouldn't you refuse to settle for less?"

"We rarely get what we want. I've grieved and beat myself up, wondering how I could somehow make his death right, but I can't. I've tried. Mrs. Northly mentioned a night I was out late, and that's because I was seeking help but was turned away. I've written asking for help, and again and again no one has rallied to my cause."

"It seems only the guilty would run west," Gilbert said with great passion, more passion than he'd anticipated, but he could not swallow the idea of her running to the arms of some unvetted frontiersman. "Fight against all the injustice. Stay and stand your ground."

"And if I know I cannot win?"

"Let me help you. You said you couldn't find help, but here I am and I'm willing." Like a man enlisting for battle, he offered himself. "I might be a fool for it."

"You're a dentist. I appreciate—"

"A dentist in need of a cause and of adventure. Besides, I identified a body once." He squared his shoulders, his presence large and strong. Only moments before he'd wavered, but now a fierce determination grew. Feeling the call to duty, he was ready to rise. "If this can be solved, let's solve it and clear your name. Then you will be free to come and go as you please. You could see your family." His cheeks warmed. "You could marry for love."

"I fall asleep every night wishing for such a future. But why would you want to help when I've confessed my guilty past? I did not steal, but I'm not your equal in innocence."

Gilbert did not speak for a long moment. He'd always imagined they'd lived similarly solitary lives, that she was as naive as he was about courting and romance. And he'd liked believing that the tender rustling of affection he'd felt was new for her also. Did it matter that their pasts were vastly different? He was not sure.

"I'm surprised by it all," he said at last. "More than surprised. I don't know how it will change things, but I do know I have watched you care for our patients. I've witnessed your kindness.

I've seen you light up a room with your smile and pour out your heart playing the flute. Your past is troubling. And it doesn't fit the woman I thought I knew."

She wiped her tear-streaked face.

"But I want to believe you are still the Hazel I know. I told you once that I was a Christian man who believed it my duty to help. I even offered to help you if you were ever in need, and I see no reason to take that offer back. Either I am a man of my word or I am a fraud. I don't believe any verse of Scripture says to help only those who are perfect when none of us are."

She pressed a hand to her chest as though her heart ached. "Duty is a fine reason to help another."

Love, he wanted to say, was a much finer reason, but he held back. He was not certain what he would feel when he had time to mull it all over. For now, duty was motive enough.

THIRTEEN

Hazel ran her hand over the recently painted canvas, enjoying the feel of the ridges and valleys Gilbert had created with the stroke of his brush. She'd sat beside him yesterday as he painted, mostly in silence. When they did speak, it was cautious but cordial.

"He did a fine job," Ina said. "I never would have guessed he had so much hidden talent."

"At first glance he seems ordinary, but he has heart and skill that he keeps to himself." She set the painting on her bed but couldn't take her eyes off it. "I suppose we are all more complex than we seem at first."

"I think you're right. I'm glad Duncan is taking the time to get to know me," Ina said. "His Amy is the perfect little lady. She curtsied when I met her and had the finest manners. I had thought she might comment on my face, but she just smiled."

"Did she like the marbles you got her?"

"She did." Ina told Hazel how Duncan had held her hand and how proud he'd been of his daughter. "And just when I thought the day couldn't get better, Duncan stopped our walk beside the covered bridge and we talked about our dreams." Ina leaned against the wall as though the memory left her weak in the knees. "He said he hoped to find someone to share his life with. Someone who would love his daughter and create a home for her."

"Did you tell him you were that person, and then did he take you in his arms like you've always hoped for and kiss you senseless?"

"Of course not." Ina rolled her eyes. "I told him I loved teaching, but I dreamed of a home of my own and a family."

Hazel nodded. "That was sensible. But I think you should have told him you wanted to be *his* family."

"You're always so clever. You should say those things to Gilbert." Ina laughed. "I can't even imagine myself saying half the things you suggest."

"I'll stop teasing. Tell me what else happened."

"He took my hand and brought it to his lips and kissed my fingertips. I know I blushed, but not because I was embarrassed."

Hazel smiled, pushing her own heaviness aside. "It sounds beautiful."

"It was. I find myself amazed by how naturally we've become friends. I hope your day was wonderful too," Ina said. "Did Gilbert confess his love? Did he kiss you?"

"No, well, he started to tell me something along those lines, but it didn't amount to a confession of love. The truth is, I've done more kissing than I'd ever want to admit. But I have not had the kisses of love you dream of. You and Duncan are like a fairy tale." She swallowed back the sadness that crept in whenever she thought of her wretched past. "You have me convinced that what I thought was romance was something entirely different."

Ina brought her brows together. "I've not pried into your past because it's your past. But don't you think that at some point you ought to forgive yourself for whatever happened and allow yourself to go on with your life?" Ina moved closer and put an arm around Hazel. "You're good and thoughtful, and I know this because I am someone who has learned to fear the judgments of others, and I've never felt fear around you."

Hazel leaned her head on her friend's shoulder. "I'll tell you everything. Then you can help me know what to do, and you'll know why I believe love is not in my future no matter how I ache for it."

An hour later, Hazel wiped the tears that poured down her face and looked at her friend. "It's not a pretty tale, is it?"

"No, it's not. But I still believe there is a way for you to write a new chapter and then another and another and give them a happy ending. Don't you think that's what writers do? If they can't get their characters to end on a happy note, they write more."

"That screams of reason, but I don't know if I can write a new chapter until at least some of the past is sorted out. Otherwise it would be a story that made little sense. I want answers and closure. I wish I could make things right with Nathaniel too. It weighs heavy on me, but I know I can't." Hazel gritted her teeth in frustration. "I want to walk into my family's home with my head held high, knowing no one questions my innocence. There's so much I want to do."

"They're your family. Certainly they trust your word."

"I'm not sure they do."

"Talk to Gilbert. I believe he truly wants to help you. He might come up with some ideas, and I'll think on it. Together we'll find a way." Ina embraced her in a sisterly way. "You aren't alone."

"You don't have to help me."

"I know. But I want to."

Hazel spent the remainder of her weekend deep in thought and prayer as she wrestled with what to do. Torn between what she wanted— love and family—and what reason told her was impossible. Her father had called her stubborn as a child, and the trait had stuck. She determined now was the time to make that weakness her strength. She would see this through to the end, grateful for whatever help she could find and ready to accept whatever consequence followed.

• • •

Monday came, and Hazel arrived at work with jittery nerves. Gilbert had offered to help on Saturday, but would he still want to today? She had fretted and worried about seeing him again, but even with quivering nerves and a plethora of worries, she had not changed her mind about taking his help.

"I've made a decision," Hazel said as soon as she walked into the office.

"You have?" He sprang from his seat and crossed the floor in long strides.

"I'd like your help." She picked up the broom, needing something to keep her hands occupied, and set to work sweeping. "I want to clear my name. I thought we could ask Duncan for ideas. He's a lawyer. I was so caught up in his being Ina's beau, I did not think he might be able to help me too."

Gilbert shoved his hands into his pockets and made a sheepish face. "I don't know why I didn't think of that. I've been racking my brain trying to devise a plan. I should have thought of him."

"I can't pay him until after my name is cleared, and then I know my parents will help me. At least I believe they will." Hazel cringed at the mention of her dire finances. A few dollars in a jar were not enough to leave her feeling financially independent. "Do you think he'd let me pay him after?"

"I do, and if he's unwilling, I'll cover the cost."

"I'd pay you back." Her voice came out as small and weak and desperate as she felt. "I don't want you to do anything you don't want to do."

He could throw so many things in her face if he ever found cause to. Perhaps they had never been on equal ground, but now, with her sins exposed and her lack of funds being discussed, she felt far beneath him. In all their days together, there had never been a more uncomfortable silence. They stood staring at each other, both seemingly unsure what steps to take next. Were they friends? Just a dentist and an attending?

"Ina agrees you are a master painter," Hazel said, breaking the silence.

"You told her my secret." Gilbert scowled, but Hazel saw his telltale signs of humor, and it was enough to give her hope that they still could be friends.

"I did. I showed her what you painted for me, and I told her everything I told you on the hill. I've done an awful lot of confessing the last few days."

"I'm sorry," he said in a sincere tone, and once again she was convinced that he was much better with his words than he believed himself to be. "I'm sorry you're hurting."

"I've brought this, at least in part, upon myself." Patients would be arriving at any moment. Now was not the time for self-pity. "I'll prepare the rooms for you."

"Thank you."

She felt his eyes on her back as she walked to the small exam room and set to work arranging instruments. If the past were put to rest, dare she believe this man could care for her? She believed he had begun to, but that was before her confession. A burst of laughter drew her away from her work. She peered into the waiting room, hoping to know its source. What she saw brought a smile to her lips. Gilbert was grinning at a man whose back she could see. A friend? She stepped closer, eager to know who had brought such good humor from Gilbert.

The men embraced. From behind she couldn't tell much about this stranger other than his height and build, which were similar to Gilbert's.

"Eddie!" Gilbert said. "You came back."

Gilbert's brother was back! Peering around the doorway, she felt like she was observing the prodigal himself returning. Happiness engulfed her heart. Not wanting to interrupt, she leaned against the wall, unseen, and observed.

"We have so much to catch up on. But first, come and meet Hazel," Gilbert said, steering his brother toward where Hazel stood. She saw the stranger's face . . . but it wasn't a stranger at all. She knew this man.

Her past and her present collided in one catastrophic thud, leaving her breathless and ready to run.

Standing before her was Edward. It couldn't be, but it was. She'd not seen him since the night at the park . . . the night when so much had changed. When he'd sneered at her from the trees.

His parted dark hair, his dimpled chin—the memories rushed back. Memories from before, when she'd been a different person—a heartless person and then a married-against-her-will person.

She couldn't be here. Not with him. All hope of reconciling her past immediately vanished.

She ran through the back door. No goodbye, no looking back. Her lungs burned by the time she reached Mrs. Northly's, but she refused to stop and catch her breath. She grabbed her carpetbag and shoved her few belongings in, not worrying about careful packing or future wrinkles. Leaving was all she cared about.

CHAPTER
FOURTEEN

"I don't know where she went," Gilbert said as he rushed through the office, checking each room for a second time. "Something must be wrong."

"If she was just here, she must be fine. It's a dental office. Nothing dangerous happens here." Eddie looked out the window. "Perhaps she had some sort of womanly emergency."

"Possible, I suppose." Gilbert knew little of women and their struggles. "I want to hear all about your travels and what has brought you back, but first I need to find Hazel, er, Miss McDowell."

"I've never known you to chase after a woman." Eddie's brow furrowed. "Is she more than an employee?"

"That's unimportant." He paused near the door and turned his open sign to closed. "I don't know how long I'll be. No need to sit and wait."

"Even better. I'll kick off my boots back at the house."

"Do what you wish," Gilbert said as he stepped out onto the street and headed toward Mrs. Northly's. He ran to the front of the house and pounded on the door. When no one answered, he ran to the back of the house and pounded again.

No answer. A sickening panic took over, stealing his ability to think rationally. Desperate to find her, he twisted the handle and found the door was unlocked.

Reservations shouted at him to stop, but he couldn't. In an uncharacteristic act, he pushed open the wooden door and stepped inside. His eyes took a moment to adjust to the dark interior. The home was simply furnished—practical straight-backed chairs around a fireplace, stitched verses in frames mounted on the walls. Reminders, no doubt, of how a proper lady should behave.

He called out for Hazel, and when he still did not hear her or anyone else, he went up the stairs. It was wrong to enter the sleeping quarters of a woman, and until this moment he'd never done so. His heart raced and his palms grew sweaty, but he didn't stop. He knocked and peered into the first room, but large boots near the door told him it was not her room. The next room exploded with color, décor, and belongings. Again, he moved on, knowing it was not Hazel's room since she had few possessions. The next room was simple, and he believed it could be Hazel's room until he saw Ina's name on a letter. Guilt gnawed at him, assaulting his conscience, but he had to know if Hazel had fled and he had to know quickly.

At the end of the hall was one more room. The

door was open. He stepped over the threshold and the instant he did, he knew. Hazel was gone. The armoire hung open and had nothing hanging in it, not a single dress. Frantically, he searched for some evidence that his instincts were wrong. Under the bed he found a faded and worn hatbox. He lifted the lid, and his heart sank when he saw Hazel's name on a stack of letters.

Hazel had left and not even said goodbye. Like a physical wound, a stabbing pain twisted deep in his insides. Never had a woman affected him the way she had—her laughter, her sparkling eyes, her friendship. It had all come to mean so much to him, and now it was all gone. Taken without his consent or even a farewell.

Everything in him wanted the world to stand still so he could make sense of what had happened. But that was out of his reach. He had to go. Taking the steps two at a time, he rushed through the house and out the back door.

"What are you doing here?" Mrs. Northly's voice nearly knocked him over.

Hoping his voice did not give his guilt away, he said, "Looking for Hazel. Have you seen her?"

"Not since this morning when she left for work. Did she not come?" Mrs. Northly, for all her overbearing ways, looked genuinely concerned.

"She was there and then she left. I'm not sure where she's gone."

Lines of worry folded across the woman's

normally stoic face. "I do hope she is all right. You've not had a tiff, have you?"

He took a deep breath, telling himself not to panic. Knots could be undone, and so could this. "Nothing of that sort. If you see her, will you tell her I'm looking for her and would very much like to talk?"

The woman nodded. "I will. Keep that girl out of trouble. I sense an unruly streak in her."

"I have to go," he said to Mrs. Northly, but with no leads to follow, he didn't know where to look. He stopped at the tree just beyond the boardinghouse and leaned his back against it. This couldn't be real. Time passed in strange fashion, the sun rising higher and higher in the sky as he stood motionless, unsure what to do.

"I have to leave."

Gilbert's head shot around the tree at the sound of Hazel's voice. There she was on the doorstep, talking to Mrs. Northly. A miracle.

"You don't have to go," the matron said. "Come back in and unpack. I saw that dentist of yours frantically looking for you. Talk to him."

"I thought he might come." Hazel's shoulders slouched. "I'll mail him a letter."

"The other night you shouted about what a good man he was. If you were speaking the truth, then you know you're going to hurt him by running away. Good men feel things. They hurt just like us women do, even if they don't show it." Mrs.

Northly handed Hazel a handkerchief. "Stop your crying. Likely you've brought this on yourself. Now, if you've had a dispute, talk to him and set it right, or tell him off if you must. But there's no need to flee."

"I have brought this on myself." Hazel wiped her face. "He is a good man. I was telling you the truth, and I have no reason to quarrel with him."

"Then why run?"

"I'm not running. I . . . well, it doesn't matter why I'm going, only that I must go. Thank you for your hospitality while I stayed here."

Mrs. Northly patted Hazel on the arm. "Well, if you must go, then go. But why spend your life running from one set of problems only to get another? Troubles are lurking around every corner. Face them. With God's help, you can move mountains."

"It's a sentiment I easily believe for others, but . . . I fear I am not strong enough to face the demons I saw today." She picked up her bag. "Goodbye, Mrs. Northly."

Hazel moved away from the boardinghouse that had been her home. She carried her carpetbag on one arm and the hatbox dangled from the other.

She walked toward him, but with her eyes down she didn't see him. Gilbert stood frozen in the moment, watching her. Her once-bright eyes were dark, the lightness of her step replaced by a heavy, determined gait. There was no time to stand and watch or to think of an eloquent way to confront her. Giving it no further thought, he hurried out of the shadows and stepped up to her side.

"Don't go," he begged. "Don't leave."

"Gil." She looked at him, softening for a moment before she set her jaw and said, "I have to go. I only came back for my hatbox."

"You don't have to go. You have a job, you have friends, and we will make a plan together. Why run from all that?" Without asking, Gilbert took her heavy bag from her.

"Because here in Amherst I'm still close to everything from before. I have to go away. Somewhere far."

"So, you will go west and start a new life? You'll just forget us?" He swallowed hard, knowing for him it would not be so easy. Forgetting her would be impossible. She consumed too much of him.

"I know your brother." She stopped and faced him. "I know him from a long time ago. Everyone called him Edward, and I didn't realize he was your brother. But now, this morning when I saw him at the office, it was like the present and the past were colliding, and I knew it could never work between us. I remembered how it felt to be heartless. I remembered every wretched thing I've done and . . . and that others have done. You don't want to spend your time with me. It sounded nice and I almost believed it could work, but it can't."

Hazel reached for her bag, but Gilbert held it tight. "Let me decide who I want to spend my time with. I might be quiet, but that doesn't make me inept. I have a heart and feelings, same as you, and a mind of my own."

"I don't understand you," she said, raising her voice. "You should be grateful I am saving you from all the shame." She reached again for her bag, and again he pulled it back. "Just let me go. With me gone, you can have whatever life you want. You could find a sweet, innocent woman. Someone your equal."

"Fine!" He held the bag out for her to take. "Go if you must. But I'd like a chance to tell you what I want before you do. At the very least, can you grant me the chance to say goodbye?"

For a long and agonizing moment, he stood waiting. Hoping she would agree. His eyes held hers as he waited, silently pleading with her. Knowing whatever she said next would affect the course of their futures. Knowing if she chose to leave, he'd be left with a hole forever in his life.

In a voice no more than a whisper, she said, "You're right. I should have let you say goodbye."

They walked side by side in awkward silence to the dental office. Like strangers, they averted their eyes and kept a good amount of space between them.

"I'll put a sign up letting our patients know I'm not available. I'll leave it up so we can talk," Gilbert said as he closed the door behind them, the tension palpable in the air as they shuffled to the back of the office. "Sit down if you'd like."

She didn't sit. Instead, she stood in front of the serene painting closest to her. "I was thinking while we walked, trying to figure out what to do next, but I can't decide."

"You stay, and we face it together like we discussed." Gilbert had been thinking as well. He wondered how close Eddie and Hazel had been. Had she toyed with him? Kissed him? And then he asked himself if it mattered, and he wasn't certain if it did or not, but he wanted time to find out. "You've changed. Surely Eddie has too. Whatever happened between the two of you, it's history."

"History has a way of haunting me." She cleared her throat. "You and I have been skirting all the lines we once talked about. I feel strongly that if I'm to stay and we're to work together, it has to be different now."

He nodded, knowing from her fidgeting that she would not negotiate. "It feels different already."

"I'm sorry for it." She rubbed her temples and sighed. "I do still wish to be your friend, if it is possible. I'd cheer on your happiness no matter what."

"My friendship is not so easily lost."

"Will you help a friend, knowing there is no future beyond that?"

"I heard you tell Mrs. Northly that you would write me. If you had, what would you have said?"

"I would have said"—Hazel's voice trembled—" 'dear Gil, I hate to leave you, but I must.' I would have pled for your forgiveness and your understanding, and I would have confessed to wishing it could all be different—"

"It can be different."

"No! It can't." She looked away. "I would have finished by telling you that I hoped you would fill the void you confessed to having with family. I would have wished a wife and children for you. You'd be such a good father." She stared down at her hands. "And then I would have said goodbye."

"There may still be a way for us." Tears burned in his own eyes. The dream he'd never known he wanted stood before him but out of reach. "Once we sort this all out. Tell me there is a chance then."

"I can't. It has to be this way."

"Because you won't forgive yourself or because you're afraid I think you are guilty of stealing?" he asked. "Or is it because you've committed some indiscretion with my brother? Tell me what your relationship was like with him. Put it out in the open and let me judge it for myself."

"Edward, he hates me because I'm the reason

his friend did not marry the woman he loved. He hates me so much that, well . . . ." She moved a few feet away from him. "I won't tell you the rest unless you promise you will not speak of it with him. I will not come between you and him. I will not break up your brotherhood, your family. I've already ruined too many things."

"I promise," he said, afraid of what he'd committed to. "I won't speak of it."

"He was there the night I was cornered with Nathaniel in the park. I saw him in the trees. He could have stopped it all from happening, but he didn't. He watched. He hated me and rightfully so. I did horrible things."

"He was there?" Gilbert leaned against the wall. "And do you hate him? Your father forced you to marry Nathaniel because of what Eddie did."

"I did hate him and the others. I hated him when I was first married and again when I was first at the reformatory, but I let that go. And I want you to do the same. Don't be angry with him. Promise me you won't speak of it and you'll go back to being thrilled he is here."

Gilbert nodded.

"I know the loss of family, and I don't want that for you." She wiped tears from her cheeks. "The past may never be sorted out, and your brother may forever hate me." She stood and put her hand out. "Do you accept my friendship?"

He took her shaking hand in his and wished he could bring it to his lips, but he knew better. Instead, he held it gingerly, all the while wondering if he would ever hold it again.

"I accept," he said when he let go. "And I will not cross your lines unless you give me permission to."

To Hazel's great relief, Mrs. Northly had not rented her room as quickly as she was always telling the girls she could. The older woman, in her own way, had even seemed pleased to see Hazel standing on her doorstep with her bag in hand.

Ina's reaction that evening was far more volatile. "You almost left! You didn't say goodbye!"

"I left my dress for you."

"That's no substitute for your presence." Ina threw her arms around Hazel. "Never leave again."

"I'm sorry, Ina." Weariness set in as Ina released her embrace. "When I saw Gilbert's brother, I realized I'd never fully be able to set the past right even if I did show the world I was not a thief."

"None of us can change everything, but look at the life you are leading now. That must count for something. We all know how remorseful you are, and I've seen you praying often enough." Ina touched the painting Gilbert had done. "It's not right the way you berate yourself all the time. You smile and enjoy life, but only so much— never fully. Why not see what God has in store for you? Trust that he is willing to give you a future even if you feel you don't deserve it."

"Let's clear my name. That will help rid my family of the shame I've brought to them. And then I'll think about the rest."

"Will you be happy until then?"

She thought of the terrible first days at the reformatory and how she'd learned to find good despite her circumstances. Those were hard-earned skills, perfect for a time such as this. "I will be the happiest that I can be."

Ina hugged her again. "In that case, I will tell you what Duncan and I talked about today."

"I do want to hear that!" A real smile spread across her face. She moved to the bed and sat with her legs crossed, ready to listen to her friend's good fortune.

"Well, at first we talked about my teaching and about his daughter. And then he told me about his wife who died. It was all very sad."

Hazel had expected a happy story, not a tragedy. "He must trust you."

"I felt honored that he would share something so dear to him. Then he told me that since meeting me, he feels like he can smile again. He said when we danced that first time and I looked up at him, he felt something." Ina blushed. "Maybe it wasn't as fine a compliment as you've been paid before, but to me it was perfect."

Hazel picked at a loose thread on an old blanket. "I've never received so fine a compliment. What else did he say?"

"He told me that although he is grateful for his sister and all she's done to help with Amy, he is hoping to have his daughter live with him again soon." Ina squealed, and Hazel's heart soared. "He wants her home, and I tried not to assume. Oh, but I hope he meant what I think he did."

"I'm glad I didn't leave. If I had, I would have missed watching your happiness unfold."

Ina put her arms around Hazel. "Someday you will realize that you are part of that happiness."

"Tell me where you've been," Gilbert said to his long-lost brother after arriving home for the night. He'd done his best to abide by his promise and simply be happy for his brother's return. Surely, with time, Hazel would see that Eddie was not the lad he'd been before. "Did you go to sea?"

As a boy Eddie had always talked of leaving home and becoming a cabin boy and then first mate and finally the captain of a large and well-known ship. Exotic places, adventures at sea, and even battling pirates had been parts of his youthful ambitions.

Eddie sat at the table eating cold meat and bread left from one of Clara's meals. "I never went to sea. It's not a bad idea though. Maybe I'll do that next."

"Still a dreamer?"

He took another bite. "We've all got dreams. Even you must."

Gilbert sat in a seat across from his brother. In many ways it felt like they were boys again living under the same roof, yet they were not. They were men, with lives and passions that had changed since they'd last occupied this home together. "Lately I've been dreaming of a family."

"You never even talked to the girls when we were boys. Has someone broken you from your shell?"

"I've met someone now who has loosened my tongue. I can talk to her and even laugh. You would be surprised by my unhinged tongue."

Eddie set down his bread and stared at his brother. "The girl from the office? The one you were so worried over when she left?"

"Hazel."

"Does she care for you in return?" Eddie asked between bites.

Three or four days ago Gilbert would have told his brother he believed she did, but now he was unsure. And according to his agreement with her, they could never be more than mere friends.

"It's only a dream. Like going to sea, perhaps someday. But that's not important right now. I want to hear where you've been. You left and you never came back, or even sent word."

"You should hate me."

"What purpose would that serve? Tell me where you've been. I've often wondered."

"When I left eight years ago, I went to stay with Carl Kaine. Do you remember him?"

Gilbert nodded. "He was your friend from school. His family was from Buffalo. That's only miles from here. Have you been close this whole time?"

"No, but I did stay with him when I first left. I thought about coming back and trying to set things right with Father, but I always pushed it off for another day and then another. I was there a couple of years." Eddie's face, always confident, showed signs of regret. "I was stubborn. Then Carl had a bit of wretched luck. It wasn't really luck. A silly, thoughtless girl came between Carl and his fiancée. Anyway, we headed west. Tried our hand at prospecting." Eddie ate another large bite, leaned back, and rubbed his stomach.

Gilbert waited, hoping for more details of his brother's adventures. "And now you've returned? What brought you back?"

With his mouth still half full, Eddie said, "It didn't go well. The big vein we were always looking for didn't show up. Besides, Carl married, and the cabin felt too crowded for three, so I decided it was time for a new adventure. I'm not sure what that will be, but I'm here to find out. For now, I'm content eating your food and putting my feet up for a while." He brushed the crumbs from his hands, letting them fall on the floor. "Tell me about Father. I heard about his death through Carl's family. They sent a clipping from the paper."

"He was sick a long time—"

"After I left, I wondered about him and worried some, but I always knew you'd be there to take care of him."

"I think he would have liked having you back. When he was dying, he often spoke of you. He even called your name when he was delirious or sometimes in his sleep." For a long time, Gilbert had been angry with Eddie. Angry that he'd left, that he wasn't there when their father died. Angry that he was alone when he had family. But with time he'd come to realize the anger did no good. It would not bring his father back. "We were all hurt by your leaving."

"I should have come back, but I was too proud and then so much time had passed."

"Why did you leave?" Gilbert at last voiced the question that had plagued him for so long.

Eddie pushed back from the table. "You never asked him?"

"No, it was your quarrel."

Eddie walked over to the mantel, where a portrait of their father sat in an oval frame. "Suffice it to say that I was wrong. I made a mistake, and when he confronted me, I ran. And when I considered coming back, I was too stubborn."

His brother picked up the old frame and studied the picture. Eddie sighed, but even the exhale did not seem to release the burden of remorse.

"You're here now, and he's glad of it," Gilbert said. "He knows you're here. I know he does. He always believed you'd come back."

Eddie didn't speak. He stared at the picture a bit longer before setting it back. His face was pulled tight when he turned around, and Gilbert could see the tears he was fighting.

CHAPTER
FIFTEEN

Two days later, Hazel, nervous and eager, walked the long hill that led to Gilbert's Amherst home. Tonight, Hazel and Gilbert would sit with Ina and Duncan to discuss a plan and begin their joint quest to liberate Hazel from the shackles of injustice. If they failed, what would she do then? She hated the thought.

"Hazel, you're here," Gilbert said as he opened the front door. "Come in and say hello to my brother."

She groaned and thought of fleeing but rejected the notion, reminding herself that she was not the same woman she'd been all those years ago.

"Eddie, come and say hello to Hazel," Gilbert said.

Eddie walked toward the entryway, a grin on his face, his long arms swinging at his sides, and a lightness to his gait. He stopped. He froze. His ease and appearance changed. "Hazel?"

"Hello, Edward."

"What are you doing here?" His once-relaxed features were tight and angry. "I heard you were spending time behind bars."

"Eddie," Gilbert said, "she's my guest."

"You didn't tell him that I worked for you?"

198

Hazel put a hand on her forehead. Could this be real?

"No. I'd hoped we could all move forward peaceably." Gilbert looked from his brother to Hazel and back again. "We're not children. We can handle this."

"Is this the Hazel you were talking about?" Eddie's smug expression was anything but peaceful. "That's one dream that will never come true. Give it up, brother, before you're torn to shreds. Your Hazel is heartless, and she's a thief."

"We have a friend who's a lawyer. He's coming over, and we're going to try to prove her innocence. And as for heartless, her heart seems to be pumping blood through her body same as yours and mine." Gilbert stood firm. "You can stay and help us or you can go."

"I'll stay. I could use some good entertainment. I'll enjoy watching you try to prove the guilty innocent. This woman destroys whatever she touches. She destroyed my friend's engagement and why, you may ask. Was it love? No. I doubt she knows what that is." Eddie walked past her, his shoulder bumping against her as he went. Then he sank into a burgundy wingback and folded his arms across his chest. "This should be amusing."

"I'm sorry about him," Gilbert said to her while glaring at his brother.

"It's all right." Hazel stopped Gilbert from

199

saying more. "He didn't expect to see me. I'm sure it's a shock." To Eddie, she said, "I have never been able to apologize. I'm sorry for the past and for your friend and for so much more."

Eddie ignored her.

"Ina and Duncan are coming. Don't worry about Eddie." Gilbert moved to open the door upon hearing them knock. Moments later, the four sat at the dining room table. Only Eddie remained separate—a quiet, glaring bystander.

"Ina told me what she could of your story. But there is still so much I don't understand. I brought a list of questions I hope will get us started." Duncan had paper ready and a pencil in hand.

"I'll tell you whatever I can."

"Let's start by discussing any enemies you might have had."

Eddie snorted from the other room, earning him scowls from the four people at the table. Hazel did her best to honestly answer Duncan's question, embarrassed by the transparency it required.

When the inquiry ended, they all leaned back and mulled the details. "I'll send messages to a few trusted friends in Buffalo, and then we'll go there together and gather more clues. If I can see the case records, I'll know where the accusations came from, and I can see if the accuser's name is in any other cases. We need to figure out why someone would want Hazel to disappear." Duncan tapped the table. "We'll also see what we can find out about the boat you say Nathaniel mentioned."

"It's been so long," Hazel said. "I don't know if we'll find anything."

"That is an obstacle," Duncan agreed. "But listening to you now gives me reason to hope. Your case was not handled properly. If nothing else, I may be able to prove that."

"Thank you, Duncan, for all of your help."

They stood to leave.

"What are you doing here?" Eddie cornered Hazel as she fetched her coat and hat. "What kind of games are you playing with my brother? There are plenty of other men for you to torment."

In a low whisper, she replied, "I'm not playing any games. I didn't know he was your brother until you came back to town."

"I don't believe you."

"It's the truth."

When he said nothing and only stood scowling at her, she reached out her hand and put it on his arm. "For Gilbert's sake, can we be civil?"

He shook her hand off. "You should go."

"It's a free world." She stood a little taller, trying to convince him and herself that the sight of him was not alarming. "Your brother has agreed to help me. He's my friend."

"Break someone else's heart and leave him be.

He might be thirty, but he's as innocent as a child and doesn't know to be wary of your snares. Haven't you caused enough damage?"

She took a step closer to him. "I stopped playing games long ago, and I've paid my dues. I'm truly sorry for everyone I wronged. If you'd been here these last couple of months, you'd have seen the friendship your brother and I have formed. It's real."

Gilbert walked over to them. "Are you ready to go, Hazel?"

"Yes." She looked once more at Eddie and in a slow, piercing voice said, "I never stole anything."

Eddie turned his back on her and walked away.

"What was my brother talking to you about?" Gilbert asked once they were alone and heading toward the boardinghouse.

She kicked at a stone in front of her, sending it rolling down the street. "He doesn't think I should be here with you. He's just being a big brother and worrying." She shivered in the cold, or was it from the memories? "Do you think our plan will work?"

"I agree with Duncan. If someone was hiding something, then we need evidence before we can make an accusation. I guess we will know a lot more this weekend when we all go to Buffalo."

"What if it's not safe? Everyone said Nathaniel's death was an accident, but I never believed it. Something more was going on, and it still may be. I don't want anyone to get hurt." She stopped and looked at him. "Promise me you'll be cautious. I have no desire to move forward with our plans if they'll put you or anyone else in jeopardy. I'd rather go west and leave all this behind than have harm come to anyone."

"I've made it past thirty with no major harm befalling me."

"But that was before you met me. I have a trail of damage behind me." She looked over her shoulder. "I'm surprised anything I touch still stands."

"We've worked together for months, and I have never once felt threatened."

Hazel laughed despite the tension of the night. "You work in a dental office. Of course you've been safe."

"I stuck myself with a carver once. It was a nasty cut. Accidents can happen anywhere." He held up his thumb. "See that little scar?"

"You are brave. You've survived a duel with a dental instrument."

He puffed up his chest. "And I'll survive this too."

"You better. And the jewels. Do you think Duncan will find out something about the owner so we can try to figure out who put them in my home?" She'd lost countless hours of sleep mulling over possible scenarios but could never think of an adequate motive—unless Nathaniel's death was no accident and somehow linked to the jewels. Many people did not care for her back then, but she couldn't think of anyone who would have stooped so low.

"I believe it'll all come together."

"I find myself wondering again how it is you are not married. Look at you, helping me like this."

"None of that flattery."

"Mrs. Northly and the girls at the boardinghouse are always rattling on and on about how unmarried men over thirty have some secret to hide. She must be right or else you'd be married."

"I've heard that myself. Alberta loves telling me I'm a wolf in sheep's clothing."

"Why didn't you ever marry?"

A dimple in his cheek was the only evidence of humor. "Let society think me a menace if they want to, but it's really the fault of a very peculiar lady friend of mine who has drawn lines and made rules that I've promised to abide by. I blame her for my unrelenting bachelorhood. If she would only rescind her rules, I'd beg for her hand."

She elbowed him. "What have I done to you? You were a man of so few words before and now you have me always wondering what you'll say next. I'm certain this lady friend of yours had good reasons for her request."

He scrunched his face up and shook his head. "I doubt that. But I keep my word when I give it."

"That's honorable of you."

"Or foolish, but aren't we all fools when our hearts are at stake?" Gilbert slowed again. They were near Mrs. Northly's. "Hazel, I can only imagine how difficult all of this is for you." His voice was serious now. "We'll look out for one another, and I trust Duncan that we can get to the bottom of it. You've spoken to me of your faith, and I believe too. We'll be in good hands."

"I only worry for you and the others."

He touched her cheek. "You, my dear friend, are worth worrying over too. Don't ever think otherwise."

Wind rustled the bare branches, sending eerie shadows dancing in the moonlight. Hazel's hair blew across her face. She closed her eyes and leaned against a tree. Being worried over was not easy to accept, but it felt good to be cared about.

"What time is the door locked?" Gilbert asked.

"Ten o'clock. I should go, but I don't want to. I have so many worries, and for some reason out here in the moonlight, I feel less afraid."

"I wish we could linger." He looked between the house and her. "Best hurry inside. I'm not sure how many more chances Mrs. Northly will give you. Don't worry though. The week will go quickly, and soon we'll put together the pieces of this puzzle."

"I do hope so." She picked at the tree bark. "Thank you."

"Good night, my redheaded friend."

Swallowing the emotion that wanted to rise without her permission, she stared back, wondering what her eyes gave away about her. "Good night, Gil."

"What is he doing here?" Hazel whispered to Ina two days later when she spotted Eddie waiting on the front porch of the boardinghouse with Gilbert and Duncan. The rest of them were to set off for Buffalo as planned, but Eddie, what was he doing?

"I don't know. He doesn't look happy."

"He's certainly not happy if I'm present," Hazel grumbled. She could feel the excitement that had been building all week drain from her. "This is bad. I can't spend a weekend with him."

"It doesn't look like we'll have much say in that. But you won't be alone." Ina waved at Duncan. "I better go say hello."

She stepped away just as Gilbert walked over and took Hazel's bag. "You pack light."

"It's only for a couple days. What is Eddie doing?"

"He insisted on coming. He says he wants to help." Gilbert shrugged. The man was innocent to a fault and likely believed Eddie's altruistic lies. "I didn't see how it could hurt. The more people on our team, the better."

"I'm sure he will be most helpful." She couldn't keep the sarcasm from her tone.

"Isn't this weekend about setting things right? You could start by reconciling with Eddie."

"I think he wants to be the one to watch me walk the plank."

He put a hand on the small of her back and led her away from the boardinghouse. "Only guilty people walk the plank."

"Not in the real world."

On heavy legs, she made her way toward Eddie but couldn't bring herself to look him in the eye. Instead, she stared at the collar of his shirt. The dread she felt about the impending adventure multiplied exponentially at the thought of him being there.

"Next to me or across from me?" Eddie asked when she climbed inside the carriage.

Nowhere near you, she thought. But aloud she said, "Next to you." At least she wouldn't have to look at him. It was crowded inside with Eddie, Hazel, and Gilbert on one side and Ina and Duncan on the other.

"Your brother tells us you tried your hand at prospecting. What is the frontier like?" Duncan asked, filling the uneasy silence.

"Dirty." Eddie put his hands on his knees and leaned forward. "It was dirty and picturesque all at the same time. There was so much open space and everyone was hopeful, at least at first. Some men lost their wits when they didn't find piles of gold, but the rest of us still saw it as beautiful until the end."

"Were there Indians?" Ina asked.

"A few, but not how you imagine them. They weren't fierce. They either got along or they stayed away. It was the miners who could be a fierce and rough sort. It takes a hardy man to make it out there."

Hazel dared a glance at Eddie and was surprised to see a smile on his face. His eyes were not boring holes into Duncan or Ina, but rather the opposite. He seemed content sharing his adventures.

"When I first worked my claim with the men I'd hired, we were certain we'd strike it rich. Every day felt like a treasure hunt from the books we'd read as boys, except it wasn't someone else's story—it was ours." He rubbed his shoulder absently. "The novelty wore off, but we kept going."

"What changed?" Gilbert asked.

"One by one, they gave up, and Carl married. As the men left me, I realized that friends and even working men were temporary. I started thinking that this was the right chance to come home. At least for a while. Someday I might go back."

There was passion in Eddie's words, so much so that it baffled Hazel. Not the flippant passions from younger years, but the steady and focused passions of a man willing to work to bring his goals to fruition.

"I don't know you." She uttered her thought without meaning to voice it aloud. "I'm sorry. It's only that you are very changed from when I knew you before."

When he turned to face her, his expression changed from a man deeply engrossed in thought and reverie to a man filled with contempt. "And you are exactly the same as you were before."

"You have no idea who I am now."

"You don't fool me."

"Then why are you here?" She couldn't understand. He didn't care a thing about clearing her record or reuniting her with her family.

"Gilbert's my brother. And what you've talked him into doing isn't exactly safe."

"I never—"

"Don't." Gilbert stopped her from offering a defense. Then he leaned forward and looked around Hazel at his brother. "You said you'd keep your thoughts to yourself."

"I'd planned to. But you don't know a thing about this woman."

"Do we need to stop and let you out?" Gilbert reached a hand toward the window, ready to get the driver's attention.

"Whoa, there, little brother. You've gone and gotten yourself a backbone. Maybe I don't know you anymore either."

Eddie's comment silenced all the passengers. They froze in their seats, listening to the thudding of their own hearts and the clip-clop of the horses' hooves colliding with the street.

Hazel bit her tongue to keep from speaking out of anger. When her temper cooled, she said, "You never have to think a gracious thought about me. I can live with that. But if you are coming with us, can we agree to work together? Not for me but for your brother?"

"For Gilbert, I will."

CHAPTER
SIXTEEN

"You ladies get settled into your room, and we'll meet you in the morning," Gilbert said after they arrived at the hotel.

"Where are you going?" Hazel asked.

"We've decided to look into a few things tonight." His gaze, which normally held hers, darted away. "Rest. We'll meet you in the morning and catch you up on whatever we learn."

She grabbed his arm, pulling him back. "Tell me where you're going."

"It's better if you stay here and trust us."

"You can't do that." Fear assaulted her. Nathaniel had left one night, only to be injured and then die. What if they went to the docks or somewhere dangerous? She couldn't allow that. "I'll stay up the entire night worrying. Tell me where you're going so I'll know if you are safe."

Duncan looked at his watch. "Don't argue all night. Either tell her or don't."

"We're going to your old house. The one you lived in with Nathaniel. It's been vacant this whole time. Duncan saw the deed, and Nathaniel's parents still own it. We want to see if we can find any clues. Maybe something was left behind." Gilbert immediately looked as though he wished he could take back the words. "But you can't come."

"I'm going with you. You can't stop me."

"It's dangerous. We have to get in and out with no one noticing us."

She pressed her hand to her chest. "I lived there. I know that house. I know which boards squeak and which ones don't." She raised her voice loud enough for Eddie to hear. "Tell him I should go. That I'm the one who should do anything dangerous. Tell him it's smart for me to come. Besides, if they catch us, at least I have a connection to the house. You would be strangers with no reason to be there, but I could claim innocent motives."

Eddie let out a cynical laugh. "I don't want her to come, but I agree with her. She can be our cover if we are caught."

Gilbert looked from Duncan to Eddie and then to Hazel. Through gritted teeth, he said, "Very well. And Ina, will you be joining us? It seems we are *all* going to put ourselves in harm's way together."

"No." Ina shook her head. "I'm afraid this is more of an adventure than an old schoolteacher can handle. I'll stay here, and if you don't return, I'll send the police."

Hazel groaned. "Don't talk like that. We'll be safe."

"Go." Ina picked up Hazel's bag. "I'll be here when you get back."

The group moved away, but they stopped in their tracks when Duncan broke ranks and returned to Ina. Moving on and giving them privacy would have been the appropriate choice, but they all stood together and watched.

Duncan took Ina's hand, then slowly moved it to his chest and held it against his heart. "I'll be back."

"Be safe," she said, looking up into his eyes.

Hazel's breath caught in her chest as she watched her friend living out the tender moments she'd always dreamed of. Duncan, with his balding head and outdated clothes, was Ina's perfect suitor. He pressed a kiss to her cheek before promising again to return.

"It's that one." Hazel pointed to a tall brick home with dark shutters and iron railings around the porch. "I think no one will notice us if we go in through the side gate. The trees are thick over there and block the view. There's a door in the back we might be able to get in through."

Gilbert felt small as he stared up at the large, ornate home where Hazel had lived with her husband. It was twice the size of Mrs. Northly's and had a gold finial on the top. He knew her life was different before, but his imagination never conjured up an image this grand.

"Are there any hidden keys?" Duncan asked.

"I don't know of any," she said, her eyes

sweeping over the home. "Follow me around back."

As stealthily as they could, the four of them stepped through the gate, under the trees, and to the back door. A twig snapped under someone's foot and they froze. But they were alone, and if they could get the door open, they would be inside soon.

"I can get us in." Eddie pulled a piece of wire from his pocket, surprising everyone. "I've picked a few locks before. Brought this just in case."

Had they been somewhere else at some other time, Gilbert would have insisted Eddie tell him where he'd learned such an unusual talent. Tonight, in the eerie darkness, all he felt was grateful that his brother possessed such a skill.

Eddie bent the wire and set to work picking the lock while the others looked out into the darkness. Seconds that felt like minutes passed before Eddie pushed open the door and they entered the abandoned home.

"It's so dark," Duncan whispered. "I don't think we'll be able to see anything."

"If nothing has been changed, then I can find a candle." Hazel stepped past the men and felt her way inside.

"They're still here," he heard her say.

When she returned, candlelight flickered across all their faces. "The drapes are drawn. I think if we are careful, no one will see the light from the candles. I can find more too. We had them stored all over the house and there are lanterns. From what I can tell, everything's just how we left it."

"Why didn't they sell the house?" Duncan asked, taking his candle and holding it up so he could look around the large kitchen. Shelves covered in a thick layer of dust lined the walls.

"I'm not certain. Perhaps because it's a family home. But I never thought they'd leave it neglected."

"I had trouble changing my father's home when he died. Grief can do strange things to us. It's a good thing for us though. We're more likely to find a clue with it all untouched." Gilbert's voice was a low whisper. He straightened and held out his candle in front of him, using the dim light to see what he could of the home. "It's very fancy."

"Nathaniel came from money," Hazel said. "Follow me." They left the kitchen and entered a hallway. "That way is a large bedroom." She pointed. "And that way is the parlor and an office, and upstairs are all guest bedrooms. There's also a library and sitting room. It's all bigger than I remembered. Where do we begin?" Hazel turned to Duncan for direction.

"It's hard to say, but my hope is that we'll find some evidence that Nathaniel had suspicions regarding a crime. Your story seems to point to something involving his parents' boat, but I'm not sure what to look for," Duncan said. "I'll take Eddie, and we will start upstairs. You and Gilbert search this floor. Look for papers, names, whatever might help."

Gilbert nodded, glad someone was taking charge. "We'll meet you back here." Being in the dark house uninvited made him nervous. "Let's all hurry."

Duncan and Eddie headed up the stairs, leaving him with Hazel. Together they went down the back hall and started on the far side of the house. He'd been alone with Hazel many times, but never like this—in the dark, in a bedroom she once shared with another man. A board creaked under his foot and they both jumped.

"I'm sorry," he whispered.

"I used to like that spot. I always knew when Nathaniel was home. I should have warned you."

Raising his candle higher, he tried to decipher the contents of the large bedroom—a four-poster bed, bureaus, chests of drawers, a plush wingback chair, and a washstand. Drapes with golden tassels adorned the windows. Everything was grand—dusty but grand.

"My old dresses are still in here." Hazel's voice was a low whisper. "The dust is all that's changed."

"If we are caught, that will be our defense. We will tell the police you were looking for a dress to wear to a party."

"Do you think they'd question why I had to bring three men with me?" Hazel pulled open a drawer and stared into it with her mouth ajar. "Gil, look. This jewelry was all mine." She rolled a string of pearls between her fingers. "This necklace was my mother's. She gave it to me when I was sixteen. I remember not wanting to wear it because it was so plain. If only I'd valued the simple things."

He stepped near her and looked at the necklace. "You should take it. It's yours. You can care about simple things from this day forward, if you wish." He riffled through the jewels. "Why is this all just sitting here?"

"It's strange, isn't it? They accused me of stealing jewelry, and here sits a whole pile of it that no one cares about. Look, here's a jade necklace, and this one has a diamond in it. Why would I steal jewels? I already had a fortune's worth." She slid the thin string of pearls into her pocket and left the rest. "My verdict was decided before I ever spoke."

"They'll listen this time." Gilbert inched closer to her. The candlelight danced across her face, glistening off the flecks of green in her eyes. The setting was all wrong. It was dark and eerie and they were in the room she'd lived in as a wife, but he couldn't help but admire how beautiful she was. "We'll find a way."

She closed the drawer and moved to the other

side of the room. "Nathaniel's belongings were stored over here. Something may be in them. He often had notes tucked away in his pockets or he left them on the nightstand."

Hazel pulled out a suit, covering a sneeze as she did so. "All this dust gets to me."

"Dust and cobwebs have taken over this place."

"Nathaniel was their only son, and coming here may have been too painful. Elizabeth, his mother, was tenderhearted. I can only speculate, but I wouldn't be surprised if they pay someone to keep this place secure but have never come back themselves, at least not often."

"I've never possessed much excess, certainly not enough to keep a house for spiders to live in." Gilbert searched through the pockets of the finely tailored suits, keenly aware of the fact that he'd never worn anything so fine. He differed from Nathaniel at least in his manner of dress and likely in other ways. Hazel's life with Nathaniel must have been one of ease and glamour—words he'd never pick to describe his own existence.

"Here's a note that lists a boat schedule." She held a scrap of paper near the candlelight. "It's hardly incriminating, but I'll keep it."

"What do you make of this one?" Gilbert held up a faded note to the light. "It says, '*Sally Belle*.'"

"That's one of his parents' ships. The night I followed him to the docks, it was the *Sally Belle* he was sneaking around on. He mentioned it before he died. It's connected somehow, I'm sure of it."

"Is there anywhere else we should check in this bedroom?"

Hazel looked around the room again. "I don't know. It was all so long ago, and I didn't know at the time that I needed to watch him for clues. We didn't talk about his suspicions. We did other things together, ordinary things."

He couldn't bring himself to ask what sorts of things. They were married, after all. "What about under the bed?"

They knelt side by side and peered underneath but found nothing.

"What if he was trying to hide something from you too? Where would he have put it?" Gilbert kicked at the floorboards, trying to find a loose one. He looked under doilies and even moved a side table to look beneath and behind it.

"We can check the library. When he would first come home, he often went in there before he looked for me."

"Let's check there." He moved toward the door, but she lingered in the bedroom. "Hazel."

"I'm sorry. I was remembering . . . I was remembering so many moments. He died in this room." She sneezed again. "I remember when this room wasn't covered in dust. I remember it all."

"Was it a happy home before he died?"

"It was becoming one." She turned her back on the room. "Come on, I don't want to dwell on his passing. I'll show you the library. There's no time for sentiments right now."

They went through the dark house as cautiously as they could. Even moving slowly, he still bumped into a chair, nearly losing his candle as he stumbled.

"Give me your hand," she said. "I seem to still remember my way around."

He took it and let her lead him around the old furniture—her small hand so capable, a perfect guide in the near darkness.

"At night I was often too tired to light a candle. I could navigate the whole house in the dark," she whispered as she walked. "This is the library."

The room was large, with bookcases filled with a fortune's worth of books lining the walls. "Was he a reader?"

"He was. He introduced me to many authors and ideas. In fact, he is the one who bought me my first copy of *Jane Eyre*. Perhaps that is part of why I love it."

A younger Hazel had roamed this library picking up these very books, thumbing through them, and pondering their contents. He rubbed his tight chest, uncomfortable with the jealous feelings that swelled within.

"It's an impressive library," he said while

running his fingers over the spines of the books.

"I've no idea where to begin in here."

"What books would you have never picked up?"

"Latin. I don't read it, but he did, and he had several volumes written in it. They're over here." She pulled a chair over and stood on it. "Shine your light."

He held his candle high while she pulled bulky old volumes off the shelves and fingered through the pages.

"There's nothing here. Just words."

A yellow glow softly floated into the room. Eddie and Duncan followed behind it.

"We found nothing upstairs," Eddie said. "What about you?"

"We found a sailing schedule and the name of a boat. The *Sally Belle*. But that's all." Gilbert reached out a hand and helped Hazel off the chair. "I don't think we are any closer than before."

Hazel pursed her lips. "We haven't finished looking in here, and there's still the parlor and the kitchen. But I don't think he would have kept anything in the kitchen since it wasn't a very private place."

Eddie looked around the library. "Have you checked the desk? Do any of the drawers have a false bottom?"

"I don't know. I never helped with the accounts, so I never opened it."

All four went to the desk that sat by the far wall

of the library. Its drawers creaked as they were pulled open for the first time in years. They held their candles close and riffled through the notes, bills, and letters.

"Look here," Eddie said, holding a leather journal near his candle.

"What is it?" they asked.

"I'll read it." He bent nearer to it and read. " 'I wake every morning and have to remind myself that I am a married man.' "

Hazel reached for the book, but not quickly enough.

" 'I'm trapped, and I will be forever,' " Eddie continued, " 'and all because my father and hers decided it was what we must do.' "

Gilbert ripped the book from Eddie's hands. "Enough."

"Don't you want to see what Nathaniel had to say about his lover?" Eddie filled the room with a wicked laugh. "Are you not curious?"

"Quiet down." Gilbert glared at his brother. "He was her husband. And he's dead. Where is your sense of decency?" He passed the journal to Hazel's waiting hands. "You should have this."

Duncan ignored the commotion and continued looking through the desk. "Let's keep looking. We don't have time to quarrel." He scooped out the papers and handed them to Gilbert to look through, and then he pried at the bottom of the drawer. It stuck a moment before coming open.

They gasped and leaned in closer. Hidden in the bottom compartment was a large folder.

Eddie grabbed it before anyone else could. Duncan moved his candle closer, adding light so everyone could see.

"This is what we're after. It has to be." Eddie waved the now-open folder in the air. "It's a list of names and boat schedules. It even has a list of police officers. I don't know what it all means, but he was hiding—"

"We have to go. We have to go now." Hazel pulled on Gilbert's sleeve. "We have to go."

"Do you hear something?" Gilbert asked, his heart racing at the urgency in her voice. "What is it?"

"No, but this is why he was killed. It has to be." She was breathing rapidly, pulling him with more force than he'd expected. "Someone killed Nathaniel. They killed a good man because of whatever he knew. We have to go."

"All right. We will." He took her hand and squeezed it. "No one is here though. It's safe."

"I saw his body the night he was killed. I know what these people are capable of." She let go of his arm and put her hand on her forehead and paced away from Duncan and Eddie. "They beat him and shot him. Police said he was caught in the cross fire, but someone killed him. They killed him because he knew something, and now we know too."

She was trembling.

Empowered by a protective instinct, he put an arm around her. "It's all right. Nobody knows we're here. We're safe. No one is watching the house." He felt her breathing slow as he soothed her. "No one is coming. It'll be all right."

"We can put the desk back together, but there's no way to hide the fact that we've been here. Let's go. We need to get away and put all these clues together—and quick," Eddie said, breaking the two apart. "Save that for later. You said you were brave enough to come, so act like it."

Hazel glared at Eddie, but she obeyed and led the way out of the house. Only when they were several blocks away did they dare speak.

"I'll go through the papers tonight. See what I can make of them," Duncan said. "But we can't talk to anyone about this until I have a solid case. And even then, if these names are correct and the police are involved, we have to be careful whose help we seek."

"But how will we prove it?" Gilbert asked. This was all bigger than he'd ever imagined, lists of names and boats. Standing in Hazel's old house, where her husband died, made it more real than it'd been when they'd been sitting in his house talking around the table.

"Tomorrow I'll meet with my friend. I've known him for years. He's trustworthy. I'll ask him only about the jewelry case, and hopefully we'll be able to match up a name from this list with one from that case. After that, I'm not sure. We might have to go to the boats and see if we can discover what's going on with them. Assuming that whatever was happening before has not ended." Duncan rubbed his balding head. "I don't know exactly how we will prove anything. But I believe we have stumbled upon something serious. Hazel, you've got to try to remember all you can. Think back."

"I will. I'll think on it all night."

CHAPTER
SEVENTEEN

Hazel raced on bare feet through the house, confused by the pounding at the door. Her nightdress caught on a door handle. She stopped only long enough to pry it loose, then rushed on. The instant she swung the heavy wooden door open, two men rushed past her with a body in their arms.

"He was awake when we found him and insisted we bring him to his wife," one of the men said. "He lost consciousness just after telling us where his home was."

A deafening scream escaped her lips. It was a sound she'd never heard the likes of before. This couldn't be Nathaniel's bloodied face. "Who did this?"

"We heard the commotion and came running. We're told it started as a brawl and then people started shooting. He was caught in the cross fire and left for dead, but there's still life in him. It don't look good. Put pressure on the wound. It might buy him some time."

She forced her shaking hands to rip off the hem of her nightdress and pressed the torn fabric against the wound in her husband's side. "Go, then," she shouted without turning from her husband. "Go for help."

A trickle of blood ran beneath Nathaniel's lip. His right eye was swollen shut and painted in purple. Her breath came rapidly as she scoured his body, searching for other injuries, more marks and bruises, but it was the dark red soaking the compress that brought tears to her eyes.

"What happened?" she pleaded with him in a voice of sheer desperation. "Wake up and tell me what has happened. Tell me you'll be all right."

She put her free hand on his cheek and stroked his face. "Nathaniel, it's Hazel. I'm here."

His eyelids fluttered open, and she felt hope grow. He swallowed like his mouth was dry. With a weak hand, he reached up and touched her face.

"My parents. Their boat." His words came slowly and required great effort.

"Who did this to you?" She grabbed his hand and held it tightly in her own. "What happened?"

"*Sally Belle*," he said. Then a strange choking sound came from his throat. "*Sally Belle*."

When his body calmed, she buried her head in his neck. "I'm sorry. I'm so sorry." She sobbed, knowing somehow she was to blame for his pain. Every bad thing had been her fault, and now a good man, her husband, was lying in a pool of his own blood. "I'm sorry you were stuck with *me*."

"No." He shook his head. "No."

"No?" She lifted her head and looked at him. What was he trying to say?

Once more he lifted his hand to her face, and then it fell to the bed. Anguish followed, tormenting her.

"No!" she shrieked. "No! You can't die."

<hr />

"Hazel." Ina was beside her. "Wake up, you're dreaming."

Dreams and reality blurred together as she struggled to open her eyes. The hotel room came into focus, and Ina was beside her. But her dream, it'd been a replaying of that horrible night. It'd been so real, so vivid.

"I'm sorry." Hazel curled her legs tight against herself. "Going back to the house made me remember. And I have his journal in my bag. I'm afraid to read it. When I do, I might discover how he really felt about me."

"Perhaps he cared more than you knew. There

might even be clues that will help us." Ina covered a yawn.

Hazel rubbed her arms. "I don't expect to find any clues in his journal. He was too smart to leave important information lying around, and his journal was right in the desk drawer." She blinked, hoping her eyes would adjust and she'd be able to see better in the dim room. "I'm sorry I woke you."

"Don't be sorry. I'm glad you weren't alone." Ina moved closer and patted Hazel's arm. "What was it like? Being married. Living in that house."

"It was uncomfortable at first. I hated how we'd ended up together, and so did he. But with time we figured out how to get through the day side by side. He was a good man. I learned that much about him." Hazel's mind kept wandering back to the house, back to before. "I remember how much it hurt when he died. Oh, Ina, it hurt so bad."

Ina put an arm around her. "Shhh . . ."

"I never even got to hear him tell me he loved me. I've always wondered if he did or if he still hated that our fathers had insisted we marry. I tried so hard to be a good wife. Not right away, but when the anger softened, I did. I came to care for him, and then he was gone." She wiped at the tears that ran from her eyes. "It feels like a strange dream. I know I lived it, but it was so long ago. All that's left is the pain and the questions and the guilt."

"He may have died anyway. You had no part in his going to the docks." Ina soothed her in an almost motherly way. "Tell me something good about being married to him. Not just the regrets."

"Well . . . he had a wonderful laugh. I would go to great lengths to hear it. One day he laughed without me coaxing it from him, and I believed that we'd become friends."

"And did you laugh with him?"

Had she laughed with him? "I've never thought about it, but I believe I smiled and laughed along with him."

"A home full of laughter does not sound like a life he would regret. He may not have said it, but don't you believe he was happy?" Ina rubbed her friend's back. "Surely he was not so good an actor that he could pretend such things day in and day out."

Hazel nodded. "I want to believe that, but . . ."

"Your life is good now, and you're doing what you can to sort out the past. With the good Lord's mercy, a bright future can be ahead for you." Ina patted her back. "I hope someday to have a home of laughter. Don't regret that. That part at least is a happy chapter. It's what we all yearn for."

"I've seen Duncan laugh and smile around you. And we all saw the moment of passion you shared before we left." Hazel turned toward her friend. "I did not expect Duncan to be so bold."

"My heart raced for hours after that." Ina clasped

her hand to her heart. "It was the most romantic moment of my life. It was just a little kiss, but I could feel so much from it." Like a schoolgirl, she asked, "What is your most romantic moment?"

Hazel thought of all the stolen kisses, but those kisses no longer equated to romance. She thought of Nathaniel and her months of marriage that ended prematurely. "I believe it was when Gilbert walked across the barn floor with the red ear of corn in his hand. My heart stood still in that moment."

"Go back to sleep and think of Gilbert with his red ear of corn. We don't know what tomorrow will bring." Ina curled back up on her side of the bed. Into the darkness she said, "I think Nathaniel would want you to be happy. I think he'd want you laughing again."

When Hazel settled back down, she closed her eyes and pictured Nathaniel's smiling face as she drifted off to sleep. And for one brief moment, she was convinced she heard his laughter.

"Duncan took the folder we found and went to speak to his friend the lawyer," Gilbert said to Hazel over breakfast in the hotel's dining room the next morning.

"What did he find in it?"

"Lists of officers, cargo lists, notes. Mostly dates and things Nathaniel had observed. The folder won't put anyone behind bars by itself, but it will serve as evidence once we put a few more pieces together." A man brought a plate and set it in front of Gilbert. He waited to eat until Hazel had a plate set in front of her. "Ina went along with him, and he has agreed to escort her while she shops afterward."

"They went shopping together?" Hazel raised a brow. "She didn't mention it when she snuck off this morning. All she said was that it was early and I ought to keep sleeping."

"I saw her before they left. She said you had a rough night."

"I'm not prone to nightmares, but last night I kept seeing Nathaniel's broken body." She picked up her fork and knife and cut into the thick slice of ham on her plate. "I didn't mean to get up so late. I'm sorry."

"You don't have to be so strong." He set down his fork and seemed to let his full attention rest on her. "Death in any form is unpleasant, but you lost someone you cared deeply for and in a terrible way. That's the hardest of all."

"This was the first night I've seen his face so clearly in years. I can't explain it exactly, but I could feel what it felt like to watch him die. It was terrifying, just as it was that night."

"I'm glad Ina was there."

"She's a true friend." Hazel smiled, feeling more comfortable now that the topic had shifted. "I can't believe she's gone shopping with Duncan."

"Would you not want to shop with a man?"

"No, it's not that. I'm just surprised that there are men who would want to go shopping with a woman. I'm glad though. Ina is very frugal but has her heart set on a new dress."

He buttered a biscuit. "I'd shop with a woman if I cared for her. It seems to me that if a man cares for a woman, then what matters to her would also matter to him. Maybe not in the same way it does to her, but he still would care."

"Hmm." She looked skeptically at him. "But what if she loves embroidery or something dull like that? Would you take it up?"

"I don't know if I'd have a knack for it, but I could still find it important. I'd love what she creates, just like I'd hope she'd love my painting and my passion for it." A crumb stuck to the bottom of his lip. He brushed at it with a napkin. "I believe genuine love can create genuine interest."

"I have no doubt many women would be genuinely interested in your painting, among other things." Hazel smiled again. "Where's Eddie?"

"Eddie has gone to visit his old friends."

"His friends?" She raised an eyebrow, but let it go. There were more pressing matters than Eddie and his shenanigans. "What will you do today?"

"This afternoon we will all be meeting to discuss what we've found and decide how to best use the rest of our time here. I thought this morning if you had no plans, we could go down to the docks and see if we can discover anything there. Catch a glimpse of the *Sally Belle*."

"The docks can be dangerous."

"We'll go together, and it's during the day. Duncan told me the *Sally Belle* is there now. She's docked. It seems like the perfect chance." He wiped his face with his napkin. "I know it's been a long time, but some crew members may be the same. Maybe what we are looking for is still there. It's worth a try."

"Very well." She pushed her plate away. "I'm finished."

Gilbert looked at her quizzically, then shoveled the rest of his breakfast into his mouth. Despite her insistence she pay for herself, Gilbert paid for breakfast, then offered his arm.

"Where did you live? Before you were married," he asked once they stepped out onto the street full of couples, working men, and children. Buffalo lacked the quiet serenity of Amherst, but it had its own bustling charm to be found in its constant movement. "Was your home close to here?"

"Yes, it was near here. I've walked all these streets many times before." She slowed and pointed. "See there, that house belonged to a girl just older than me, and the one next to it was owned by a prominent banker." She pressed a hand to her heart. "I was homesick before, but now that I'm back, the desire to run home is so much stronger." She sighed. "And then I recoil and wonder where I fit in this city and if I'll ever be welcomed home again."

"I imagine those are all normal feelings. Wanting something and being afraid at the same time."

"There are good memories too. Every year when it first snowed, we would go outside and fill cups with fresh snow and then we'd stir in cream and sprinkle sugar on top and eat it." She looked up at the sky, remembering the lacy flakes and the excitement they'd evoke. "Memories like that make my heart happy."

He grinned. "And when you have children, will you do the same?"

"If I ever have children, I will. I'd like to take the good from my childhood and pass it on, and leave the bad behind. What about you? What will you do with your children? Do you have plans?"

"I do now. I think I'll help them eat sugar snow. I'll also teach them to paint if they have a desire to learn, and I'll find them a good teacher for the flute. Perhaps you can recommend one." His eyes twinkled with mischief. How many quiet men had she overlooked, thinking they were dull when in truth they were simply more subtle?

"I hear flute lessons are going for an extravagant price," she responded. "It's a shame, but even as a dentist, you'll have a hard time affording them."

"Is that so?"

"Yes." She pulled her mouth into a playful frown. "Though it pains me to say so. The flute is a lovely instrument, and your home would be much happier filled with its sound. But it simply won't be a possibility."

"There must be a way." He put a hand on his chin and thought. "I suppose I must look for a wife who plays and could teach the youngsters. That would solve that problem of the extravagant fees. I think when the children were settled in their beds, I'd plead with her to play for me." He stopped walking and asked in a voice that carried a hint of humor, "Do you know of any flute players who might be interested in a rather quiet dentist?"

"Ha, you are hardly a quiet dentist."

Gilbert sighed. "Very well, do you know of any flute players who may be interested in a not-so-quiet dentist?"

"I think Alberta might play." Hazel struggled to keep a straight face. "Shall I inquire when she is in next?"

"That will never do. I need one with red hair, and Alberta's is not even a distant shade of red."

Hazel laughed out loud, bested by this man she'd once thought lacked a sense of humor. She broke stride and asked, "That seems an odd reason to reject a potential suitor. What difference does her hair make?"

"It makes a great deal of difference." Gilbert put a hand to his heart as he attempted a serious face. "My wife must have red hair. I could never even consider a woman with blonde or black hair. It would never do."

"Why?"

He stepped closer, his body only inches from hers. The closeness unnerved her, excited her, and threatened to break her resolve. Remaining only friends with this man was the proper choice but certainly not the easy one.

"I like the way red hair looks in the sunshine," he said with a wink. "And if we are to go for walks on warm summer days together, then I'll just have to find a wife with red hair."

"Oh." Hazel's voice squeaked from her like the sound of a mouse. She folded her arms across her chest to keep from wrapping them around Gilbert and telling him that her hair was nearly red and she played the flute and if he'd have her for a wife, they'd have a perfect life together. *Foolish girl,* she chided herself before pointing. "Down there. Do you see the large boat? That's the *Sally Belle.*"

He sighed before turning his eyes toward the rows of large ships. "What do Nathaniel's parents use it for?"

"They own that boat and several others.

They run them up and down the Erie Canal and around the lakes. Crops, goods, I think they ship whatever people pay to have hauled."

"Why do you think Nathaniel mentioned it before his death?"

"I'm not sure. But I believe something was being smuggled on the boat. It's the only thing I can think of. Nathaniel was clever, but he was not cautious enough." And she'd not protected him well enough. If they'd been happier, perhaps she could have begged him to stay home at night. But she'd hardly been in a position to make demands. "If only he'd been a little more guarded, things would be different."

"He sounds like a good man," Gilbert said. "I'm sure you often wish it had gone differently."

"For Nathaniel's sake, I wish he'd been more careful. I wish I could have stopped it." She swallowed. This talking of what might have been was confounding. It was unfair to dwell on which path she'd rather walk, the one that led her to this moment or the one that could never be. Long-ago decisions had already dictated the outcome, and they could never be undone. "He should not have died the way he did. Of that I am most certain."

The sound of men yelling on the docks interrupted their conversation, pulling their attention away from each other and focusing it on the water. The *Sally Belle* swayed peacefully beside the commotion—a quiet onlooker. But was she an innocent bystander or did she have a secret?

"Let's get a closer look." Gilbert led them toward the docks. "Maybe we can get onboard."

"No. It's too dangerous."

"We'll be discreet."

They walked near the massive ship, jumping when a man emerged carrying a load of rope. Hazel clung to Gilbert's arm, stealing what strength she could from him. *This was where Nathaniel came the night he died, where everything changed,* she thought.

"Do you work on that large ship?" Gilbert asked the man. "How is it? Traveling up and down the Erie Canal, I mean."

"I been sailing this same boat for years now. I don't think much of it. It's hardly the dangerous life of a sailor out to sea." His long beard made it hard to read his expression, but his eyes seemed kind enough. "You two looking for something? If it's a sailor you're after, you won't find many around here. We unloaded yesterday, so the men are off." He looked at Hazel. "They're just enjoying their time ashore."

"It's not a sailor we're after. We're thinking of having goods shipped and thought coming to the docks was the right place to find a carrier." Gilbert squeezed her hand as he lied. She'd never heard him tell an untruth, and though she knew he had good cause, she hated being the reason for it. "We've heard of the *Sally Belle*."

"What does she normally carry?" Hazel asked.

"Whatever we're told." The man shifted the rope from one shoulder to the other. "If it can fit on the boat, we take it."

"Tell me, do you know the owner well? Is he an agreeable man?" she asked. Then she quickly added, "We'd prefer to work with an honest man."

"Don't know him well myself, but he's a hard worker, always keeping the schedule full. I'm sure he'd meet with you, but I don't think he's here today."

"Since we are here today, would it be much trouble for us to walk through the *Sally Belle*? I've always wanted to see the inside of a boat like her." Hazel plastered a pretty smile on her face and feigned excitement. "If it's not too much trouble, that is."

"Come along, we don't want to bother him." Gilbert tugged on her hand, turning her away from the boats. "He's busy working."

"But I've wanted to for so long." Hazel allowed a little pout to enter her voice. "You know I've wanted so badly to board a ship like this."

"It's no trouble," the man said. "I've got to deliver this load, but you can go aboard. Walk around, and I'll be back shortly to answer your questions."

"That'd be lovely." Hazel clasped her hands together and smiled at the sailor.

Gilbert winked at her as they crossed the gangplank onto the ship. "We do make a good team."

"I never thought you'd be able to pull off a deception so well." The boat was large, but not tall. The deck was covered with large shipping crates secured by lines they had to step around. "What are we looking for?"

"Let's try the captain's quarters first." Gilbert looked at both ends of the ship. "I think it must be that way."

"We can't go in the captain's quarters."

He pressed his fingers tightly around hers. "We have to go there first, and quickly, so we don't get caught. There's no good explanation for us being in there."

"It's reckless," she said but followed him down a narrow stairway.

"Stay here and knock on the door if the man comes back and I'm not done. I want to look around and see if anything seems suspicious."

Hazel's chest rose and fell, her breath coming sharp and quick. She pushed him toward the door. "I'll watch out this window the whole time. Go quickly."

Gilbert ducked under the low doorway, leaving her to watch the docks. Her palms were damp from sweat despite the cold weather. She wiped them on her skirts, but it did little good.

Searching the captain's room didn't make sense, and it was imprudent. She reached behind her and pounded on the door. If the captain were doing something illegal, he wouldn't leave it out to be seen, and what would the man do to them if he caught them in the captain's quarters? The risk was not worth it.

Gilbert's head popped out from the low doorway. "Is he headed back?"

"No. But I think you should come."

"Keep watch. I'll hurry." He ducked back into the dim room before she could plead with him.

The docks were bustling with action, but she couldn't see the sailor they'd met. He'd been wearing a dingy top and had long dark hair.

She craned her neck, looking as far as she could in every direction. The sailor was nowhere to be seen, so she relaxed for a moment. When she looked back toward the gangplank, a man was halfway up it. Not the sailor from before. This man was older and walked like a man in charge. She wasted no time and pounded on the door of the captain's quarters, banging as hard and fast as she could.

"Come now," she hissed in a loud whisper, then left her spot and scurried up the stairs toward the man, ready and willing to do what she must to protect Gilbert.

"Excuse me," she said as she hurried across the deck.

"What in tarnation?" The man swore under his breath as he surveyed her. His mouth dropped open, and Hazel took a step back, afraid he recognized her, but she could not think from where. No matter who he was, she had to keep her composure.

"My husband"—she looked back over her shoulder, relieved to see Gilbert only a few steps away—"and I were hoping to ship some supplies on this boat."

"So you came aboard and decided to have a look around?" Skepticism oozed from his words. "What's your name?"

"Gilbert McDowell," Gilbert said, using her pseudonym. "One of your shipmates told us we could look around. I apologize if that was an inconvenience."

The man's eyes didn't move to Gilbert. They stayed firmly planted on Hazel. "And your name?"

"Mrs. McDowell," she said to the man before turning back to Gilbert. "I believe we'll be late to meet the rest of our party if we don't go."

"I thought you wanted a look around." The man moved closer. "I'm the captain of this vessel. You want to know about her, I'm the man to ask."

"I feel assured that it's watertight and in good condition. I believe any further inquiries can be made later," Gilbert said as he backed slowly toward the gangplank.

The captain spit before saying, "If you're up to some sort of nonsense, I'll find out."

"No need to worry yourself," Gilbert said as they moved away from the captain and the ship. Perfectly in sync, they walked across the wooden docks, leaving the *Sally Belle* behind them.

"We have to go quickly." Hazel tried to catch her breath and calm her shaking hands. "The way he looked at me—"

"He recognized you, but I'm not sure he knows where from," Gilbert said as he pulled her around the corner of a building and wrapped his arms around her. She fell into them, grateful he'd sensed her near-bursting emotions. "You're safe. We'll work fast and get this sorted out before he has a chance to do anything."

"I don't think I've ever met him, but I suppose I could have. I met a lot of people while I was married to Nathaniel. Did you find anything? How can we act fast if we have no clues?"

"Nothing that proves he's guilty, but I found some opium. Not a lot, but the way it was packaged didn't look like a personal supply." He shrugged. "Maybe it was. I don't know how much people typically take at a time, but I think it may be a clue."

"Opium." A sob she'd not anticipated burst from her, and anger followed. It made sense, or it could at least. Opium dens riddled the city. "Nathaniel died for opium. They killed him." She pounded her fists against his chest. "I spent five years—"

"Shhh." He rubbed her back. "This isn't your fault. None of this is."

When the tears slowed, she once again became aware of their need to take action. Later, she could feel it all, but right now she had to think. She wiped her face and quickly apologized for her lapse in control.

"Don't be sorry, but you're right. We need to solve this in a hurry." They stepped out from their alley hiding place and started back toward the heart of the city. "What is Nathaniel's father like? If we told him what we know, what would he do?"

"I haven't seen him since my trial." Hazel shivered. "It was a horrible day. My mother cried, but my father wouldn't even look at me. And all the people I had thought were my friends . . . I could feel them jeering."

"And Nathaniel's father?"

"Hugo Williams." Her heart ached. "He looked so sad and ashamed. I don't think I could ever face him again. He'd agreed with my father and been a part of the marriage, but he hadn't liked it."

"I'm very sorry."

"Hugo's an honorable man. When my father told him my reputation could be ruined because we were caught together at the park so late, he agreed to the marriage and convinced Nathaniel it was his duty. Hugo and I did eventually become friends, but then everything fell apart. I can only imagine what he has thought of me all these years." Hazel shook her head, frustrated and overwhelmed by all she felt at that moment. "If we can find out who put the jewels in my house and link it to Nathaniel's death, then maybe those feelings could be redeemed and Hugo would look at me like family again." Her chin quivered. "Gil, I want my family back."

"Then that is what I will fight to give you." He quickened his step. "We'll set it right."

CHAPTER
EIGHTEEN

"You ever heard of a Patrick Harper?" Duncan asked before taking a bite of bread. The four friends sat around a back table in a little restaurant on the south side of Buffalo.

Hazel shook her head. "I don't think so."

"So no one ever told you whose jewelry it was they found in your home?"

"No, not exactly. The police came to my home saying they suspected I was involved in a burglary. They searched my home without my consent, and when they found the jewels, they arrested me. I was not in my right mind after losing Nathaniel. At the trial, the words and everyone's faces blurred together. They spoke of a woman's jewelry, but they didn't believe me when I said I didn't know her." Hazel set down her fork with a clang. "I believe my guilty verdict was decided before the trial began. I'm partially to blame, as I had no great character witnesses."

"Who is Patrick Harper?" Gilbert asked Duncan.

Duncan cleared his throat. "He's an immensely wealthy man who's made his living off speculating. But my friend believes there may be more going on than just that. We were able to dig up three other cases where he was the accuser. In Hazel's case, he was the one who brought charges against her on behalf of a Charlotte Lowell. We spent the morning asking questions wherever we deemed safe, but looking at all these cases makes us believe Nathaniel was right and there are crooked police involved. The three cases were all absurd—no motives, little evidence, and speedy verdicts. And Patrick Harper's name keeps popping up."

"But why?" Hazel shook her head, still unable to put the pieces together. "I know it connects, but how? Does Patrick have connections to the boat?"

The door of the restaurant opened with a loud squeak. In sauntered Eddie. "Sorry I'm late."

"How are your friends?" Gilbert asked, a hint of annoyance in his voice.

"They're all married." Eddie spat the last word out like he was discussing the plague. He sat and reached for a roll. "It seems that despite *someone's* efforts to keep them from ever settling down, they all have."

Hazel looked at her plate. With her fork, she drew lines in her potatoes. Would the guilt never cease? With Eddie around, she felt as though she were forever doing the dance of shame.

Eddie ripped a piece off a roll and buttered it. "They remember a lot of what happened when Nathaniel died."

"What do they remember?" Hazel asked.

"They remember him talking about smuggling and his parents' boats, but they didn't take him seriously at the time because they figured he was going out at night to get away from his wife, and the boats and smuggling were just an excuse. Married life must have been worse than I'd imagined for him, to find the docks a more enjoyable atmosphere than his home." Eddie leaned back in his chair, a smug look on his face. "They also remember how much they disliked you."

"Is that why no one would plead my case? Their grudge with me was more powerful than their loyalty to Nathaniel?"

He shook his head. "When no one investigated, they accepted the cross fire story and moved on. They all believed you were capable of stealing the jewels, though they couldn't guess why you'd do such a thing."

"But I didn't steal them, and I did nothing to cause his death," she said, only to see Eddie sneering at her. She threw her napkin down. Eddie's company exhausted her. He reminded her of the many times she'd tried to prove how changed she was and how no matter what, there was no changing some people's minds. It was as though they *wanted* to continue seeing her as flawed, unfeeling, and manipulative.

Hazel turned on Eddie and with passion said,

"I was far from perfect. If you would like me to grovel or shout it from the rooftops, I will. But I am innocent in this case. And Nathaniel at least deserved to have people standing up for him."

Gilbert put a hand on hers. "Eddie knows you're innocent. Don't you, Eddie?"

Eddie kept chewing for a few more moments. Just staring at them. "I don't think you had any part in killing Nathaniel, and I don't think you stole any jewels. Still doesn't make you a good person. And you're far from innocent."

"Oh, but she is a good person," Ina said in Hazel's defense.

"Let him think what he likes." Hazel smiled weakly at Ina before turning back to Eddie. "Tell me, what do you think happened to Nathaniel? What's your theory?"

"I think someone found out that he knew about the smuggling."

"The smuggling may still be happening. I found opium in the captain's quarters of the *Sally Belle*," Gilbert said. "It makes sense that it'd be something ongoing like opium to feed the dens and not a onetime thing. Otherwise, I doubt Nathaniel could have compiled much information."

Eddie licked his lips. "Opium dens are hidden all over the city, and if Nathaniel was interfering with the deliveries, whoever is behind them would kill him to keep him quiet. And the jewels.

I think that was to keep you quiet and to humiliate Nathaniel's family. His family is wealthy and could have spent a fortune investigating their son's death. Instead, they mourned privately and hid from society because of the shame brought to their family by their daughter-in-law."

"It fits with everything I've found," said Duncan.

"It makes sense." Gilbert leaned forward, both elbows on the table. "How do we prove it?"

"I don't know," Eddie said. "What difference does it make? She'll never get those years back, and Nathaniel, well, he's not coming back. It's too late for any of this to matter."

Gilbert glared at his brother. "It makes all the difference, and if you weren't stuck in a sour mood, you'd admit it. It means Hazel can walk through Buffalo without the gossips wagging their tongues about her past. It removes the shame from her family and allows her to reconcile with Nathaniel's family. But more than all that, if we can stop what Nathaniel was trying to stop, it means his death amounted to something."

Hazel wanted to applaud Gilbert. Her shy and quiet friend had found not only his voice but also an eloquence of speech.

"You may have your own personal qualms with Hazel," Gilbert continued. "You must sort that out yourself. But if you are half the man I remember you being, then you'll see the injustice of it all."

Eddie chuckled. "Listen to you. You've got no trouble speaking anymore." He stood. "I've promised another old friend I'd meet him this afternoon, but I'll do what I can to help. I have time that needs to be filled."

Eddie grabbed another roll from the table before ambling away as though he had no cares in the world.

"Was he always like that?" Ina asked. "He seems very . . . confident."

"He has always been good at heart, but he can carry a grudge," Gilbert answered. To Hazel he said, "What was he like when you knew him?"

Hazel hated discussing memories she wished to forget. "It's been years. I don't remember too much."

"What are your plans for the afternoon?" Ina asked as though they were on holiday. If only they were and they could explore the city, shop, and relax.

"I think we'll see what we can discover about Charlotte Lowell," Gilbert said. "Do you want to join us?"

"Thank you, but we are going to try to meet with a judge Duncan knows and trusts," Ina replied. "How will you find Charlotte?"

"It won't be too hard," Duncan offered. "Ride with us to the courthouse, and we will see if there are any records in her name. If she's married or if she has any legal records, I think I can find a way to access them. Legal forms should list her address on them. She must be well-known to have jewels worth stealing."

"That's a wonderful plan," Hazel said to Duncan, then turned to Ina. "Before we go, will you show me your dress? I know we have to hurry, but it'd only take a minute."

Ina sprang from her seat. "Yes! We left it at the coat check."

She and Ina bounded away from the table like two schoolgirls despite the looming threats and unanswered questions.

"How was shopping with Duncan?" Hazel asked after they'd gotten the box and stepped down a quiet hallway with it.

"It was so nice. I fear he's ruining all ordinary things for me."

"Ruining them?"

"Now that I've had him with me dress shopping, I'll probably never enjoy it quite so much on my own. Everything is better when he is there." The string came undone and fell away from the box.

The dress was a soft yellow with a few small embellishments, a bit of lace, and a ruffle. Most would call it simple, but compared to her dull gray dresses, it might as well have been a ball gown. "Oh, Ina! It's lovely."

"Duncan plans to take me to a concert. I think I'll wear it then."

"That's exciting."

"Today while we were walking the streets of Buffalo, so many people were around. I don't like crowds of people that I don't know. I never have. He held my arm while we walked, and he introduced me to people during our meetings. I almost felt like he was proud to have me by his side." She fingered her red chin. "It didn't matter much today. He wasn't embarrassed, so I wasn't either."

Hazel put her arms around her friend and kissed her cheek. "Never be embarrassed. You are in a class of your own, and Duncan seems to realize that. We should go back. They are probably wondering what's gotten into us. We need to settle all this so we can fill our days with concerts, yellow dresses, and a little girl named Amy."

"Do you think it's safe to go to her house?" Hazel asked Gilbert as they set out to find Charlotte. They'd talked of renting a ride, but with the weather still moderate, they opted instead to walk. Now, with her legs burning, she questioned the wisdom of that decision. "We don't know a thing about her. I was told she signed a testimony privately. I've never even seen the woman."

"It was all handled poorly. There should have been questioning."

"I can't change that now. But I do worry about you and the others being safe."

"None of this is safe. But we're in this far. Besides, it's been years. There won't be spies hiding in the bushes waiting for you." He put the paper with the address that Duncan had found on a marriage license in his pocket. "Can I ask you a question while we walk?"

"You want to know more about me and Eddie." She'd expected the question, and though she dreaded answering it, she did appreciate his waiting for them to be alone before asking.

"Will you tell me?"

"He was staying with Carl Kaine, the friend he ended up going west with. Carl was engaged to be married to Georgia Upton. They were happy together, and Eddie blames me for coming between Carl and Georgia." She brushed her windblown hair from her face, wishing she could brush the past away as easily. "And he has every right to blame me."

"What happened between you and Carl?"

"Nothing really, or at least it felt like nothing back then. I flirted with him. We went on afternoon strolls, but he didn't realize he was merely a diversion. He called off his engagement, but of course, I didn't want to marry him. Eddie told me I was the reason for his friend's broken heart. I can't remember all the colorful words Eddie used, but I remember how angry he was. The rumor was that Eddie and his friends concocted the plan to catch me in the park with

Nathaniel, but I never knew for certain how that all came about. I do know he was there in the trees the night I was cornered, so he was involved. After that I never saw him again."

"Eddie never courted you?"

"No."

"Why aren't you angry with him for what he did to you?" he asked. "You have every right to be."

"It sounds trite, but I wanted to change. And I began by forgiving others. Besides, I can't imagine he knew how far it would go." Hazel stopped and searched Gilbert's face, hoping to find understanding.

Gilbert stopped too. He tucked the strands of hair that blew relentlessly across her face behind her ears, only to have them blow loose again. "I believe in forgiveness. I always have. Did Eddie ever tell you why he left home?"

"I recall something about a falling out, but I don't think he ever told me the details."

They walked in silence until they rounded a corner. "I think the house is on this street."

"It can't be. Someone with expensive jewels wouldn't live here." She looked at the little houses all lined up in a row, all the same. Boxes with roofs on them and small front yards. "You must have the wrong address."

"It says Southgate Road. Look." He pointed at the paper and then at the road sign. "It's that one over there."

"But this can't be right."

"Let's knock and at least ask after her."

"Very well." They climbed the three steps to the porch and rapped on the door of the tiny Cape Cod house. A baby cried, and then they heard a mother soothing the youngster before they heard the sound of footsteps. When the door opened, a woman at least ten years older than Hazel stood before them. She wore a faded dress with an apron tied around her waist. Stringy blonde hair hung loose over her shoulders, giving her an unkempt look.

"What do you want?" she asked, pulling the baby closer to her.

"We're looking for Charlotte Lowell," Gilbert said. "Do you know her?"

"I'm Charlotte." Her eyes resembled those of a skittish rabbit darting this way and that, afraid. "What you want?"

Hazel looked harder at the woman and decided that at one time she may have been beautiful. Cleaned up and in different clothes, this woman could have owned an extensive collection of jewelry. But looking at her now in this humble setting, it was hard to fathom. This couldn't be the Charlotte Lowell whose words had condemned her to five years behind iron gates. There must be another woman by that name.

"You are Charlotte?" Hazel said, trying not to gawk. "Charlotte Lowell?"

"It's Carmichael now."

Hazel turned to Gilbert, searching him for answers, but found only questions in his expression. He smiled at Charlotte and put out his hand. "We were hoping we could talk to you for a few minutes."

"What about?" A barefoot toddler walked up and grabbed ahold of Charlotte's skirts. "I've got a lot to do."

"Do you know Patrick Harper?"

Charlotte took a step back, her face ashen. "Why?"

"We need your help," Hazel said before bending down and saying hello to the little boy, who smiled shyly back at her.

"I can't help you. I promised I wouldn't." Charlotte backed up farther. "I'm sorry. I'm respectable now. I don't want nothing to do with no one from before."

Gilbert put his hand on the door, preventing her from closing it. In a gentle voice, he said, "We aren't going to get you into trouble, or let anything happen to you. This is about doing what's right."

"Nothing right about that man."

"Patrick?" Hazel inched closer.

"He's bad." Tears welled in Charlotte's eyes. "I don't want to ever see him again."

"Help us, then. And you'll be safe from him." Hazel tried to keep the desperation from her voice, but it was a hard battle. This woman could be the missing piece, the key to her freedom and so much more. "We want justice."

Charlotte looked up and down the street, then motioned them inside. The home was sparse, boasting nothing more than a crooked print pinned to the wall for décor. A stool, two chairs, and a small table were the only furniture in the tiny front room. Charlotte invited them to take a seat, then she sat with the baby and the little boy on her lap. He put his dirty thumb in his mouth and nestled next to his mama.

"How do I know you don't work for him?" She wrapped her arms protectively around her children. Motherly love did not require upholstered sofas or good lighting for it to grow. This woman in this humble abode loved her children and feared for them—it was evident. "I can't do nothing that's not safe."

Charlotte Lowell had been just a name to Hazel up until this moment. Hazel turned to Gilbert for reassurance. Was it right to ask this of her? He reached for her hand and nodded.

"A long time ago, I was accused of stealing jewelry. Now we think that might have been part of an even bigger crime." The toddler waved at Hazel, and she paused her story to wave back at him. "We think Patrick might have had something to do with it. If he's still hurting people, we need to stop him. We know he helped you file the court case. Can you tell us anything?"

Charlotte leaned forward and in a hoarse voice said, "He used to visit the place I worked. I don't do that work no more. He was mean, but sometimes he'd bring the girls presents if we did what he wanted. We took what he brought, but we weren't trying to cause problems. We had so little. He didn't really care about us, and we knew it. He'd hurt us or spoil us—whatever would get him what he wanted."

"I'm sorry, Charlotte." Hazel meant it. She had shared close living quarters with women much like Charlotte at the reformatory, desperation driving their everyday choices. They'd lived miserable lives, selling their bodies in order to eat. It was a wretched life that most were anxious to leave behind. "No one should have treated you like that."

"We was used to being roughed up, but he was worse than most. But then one day he told me he'd give me more money than I'd ever had if I'd get all dressed up and go tell a judge that my jewelry was stolen. He made me practice what to say, and then I did it. I said my words and signed my name. I didn't mean to hurt nobody." She began rocking. "I wanted to get out. I'd see the respectable women, and I wanted what they had."

"I don't blame you." Hazel's heart ached for this woman and her life's journey. She knew what it was like to yearn for an existence that felt out of reach. "Did he say why he needed you to pretend?"

"He said he was trying to lock up someone that was getting in the way of business." Charlotte's eyes kept darting to the door. "He told me I could never tell nobody. He'd kill me if he knew you was here. He said some folks were easier to lock up and others were easier to bury." She stood up and paced the floor with the baby in her arms and the little boy clinging to her leg. "I shouldn't have told you. I shouldn't have told nobody. I wasn't thinking straight." She shook all over, so violently that Hazel feared her baby would fall from her arms. "You come in here dressed up all pretty, being all nice, and I . . . I don't know what I've done."

Hazel went to Charlotte and put her hand on her arm. "We'll do all we can to protect you, and together we can stop him." Her resolve deepened as she spoke. She silently vowed to stand up for justice, to see this through to the end so she could walk free and Nathaniel's death could mean something and this scared mother could have peace. "Tell us everything you can. I know you're scared to trust us, but I promise you that we don't want any harm to come to you. We can stop this together, and you'll never have to be afraid of Patrick again. Can you tell me what business he was in?"

"You'll stop him?"

"We'll do all we can." Gilbert nodded, adding his own resolve to her words.

"Opium. He'd bring some to the girls sometimes. And he was always meeting people selling it. Men would talk at our place and forget we was there, but just 'cause we weren't decent don't mean we wasn't smart. His opium goes all over the city." Charlotte ran her hand over the baby's back. "I'm so nervous. I ain't been this scared in a long time."

"Have you seen him since?" Gilbert pressed on. "Help us and we'll leave."

"I took the money he gave me and left. I got new clothes and a little room and started working a respectable job, and then I met Lewis. He's a good man. Not like the ones that came in with Patrick."

"He sounds like a fine husband," Hazel said.

"I went back to see if I could get one of the other girls out. Patrick was there and he cornered me, slapped my face, and reminded me to keep my mouth shut. That was three years ago, but I saw one of the other girls not long ago and she said he still comes around."

"If we found a judge we trusted and would keep your identity private, would you tell your story again?" Gilbert asked. "It could keep people safe and prove people's innocence."

"I don't . . . I don't know. He'd kill me if he found out. And what about my babies?" She kissed the baby's head and looked at her toddler son. He babbled up at her.

"You don't have to do it." Hazel met Charlotte's eye. "Will you think about it?"

"Well—"

"We have to be brave. For the sake of anyone who might get hurt, for your babies, will you try?" Hazel whispered. There wasn't room or time for them to be faint of heart.

"I've never been very brave." Gilbert's gentle voice was warm and vulnerable. "I've been afraid more times than I care to admit, but life requires courage at times. Like when a man or a woman looks around, sees injustice, and decides to rise up and answer the call. This is one of those times. Be brave, please."

Charlotte stared at her children, her eyes glistening when she finally looked up. "Find your judge and, well, I might. I never liked Patrick. I always hated knowing there were still girls back there suffering 'cause of him."

Hazel exhaled. "Thank you, Charlotte."

They asked for the name of the brothel in hopes that Patrick still frequented the place. Then they promised again to keep her name safe, knowing they were either one step closer to their goal or one step closer to trouble.

CHAPTER
NINETEEN

When they were all back together that evening, Duncan gave the group some direction. "Judge Lawson thinks if we can assemble a little more evidence, the case could move forward. He also suggested we send word warning Hazel's family and asking for their discretion. If the captain of the boat does decipher who you are, then they should be on the lookout."

"My parents." Hazel's heart lurched. "I can't go back there, not yet."

"One of us could go, or you could write a letter." Duncan's serious demeanor took on a gentle softness. "The judge is supportive, and Charlotte's possible willingness to speak to him will make a big difference in the jewelry side of the case, and even with the opium. What we need is more information on Nathaniel's death."

"Charlotte will testify that Patrick was dealing in opium. But that doesn't prove that it's connected to the *Sally Belle*." Gilbert ran a hand across his jaw. "We could try to watch the boats and catch them carrying the opium off and see if the captain and Patrick ever cross paths."

"I wonder if Nathaniel's parents even know opium is being shipped on their boat. If the captain's using the boats to deliver opium without their knowing, then that's a crime, is it not?" Hazel asked, struggling to focus on the case when her heart kept going back to her parents and the siblings she'd not seen in years.

Duncan scratched his forehead. "Patrick might have middlemen who perform the transactions. I'd say it's possible to corner them, but it won't be easy. And there's a good chance we'd miss seeing them handing off the opium altogether."

"We know Patrick goes to the brothel. We might be able to catch him there," Hazel said. "But what would we do if we did discover him? We're hardly lawmen."

"I remember there being a list of trusted officers among Nathaniel's notes. We could try to contact them." Duncan put the folder on the table. "It's old information though."

Eddie grunted, scoffed, and gave them all a haughty look as though he were far superior to the others. "You're going about it wrong. Hazel has to go to Nathaniel's parents. It's smarter than us trying to corner people. They have resources we don't have."

"What?" She looked at him in disbelief.

"Get Hugo Williams involved, quietly at first so no one suspects anything. If he orders a search of his boat, no one will have to sneak around. It legitimizes our efforts. He has every right to search his own ship. We don't. Besides, he has more money, influence, and power than all of us combined, and he has a motive. His son was lost because of this. If we want to end this, we need his help."

Gilbert put a hand on Hazel's. "What do you think?"

"I think he's right. I don't want to go, but with Hugo's help, we could have solid proof." Hazel bit her bottom lip. She'd dreamed of seeing the Williamses again one day, but not like this, begging for their aid. "It won't be easy. I feel shaky all over just thinking about it."

"You don't have to," Gilbert said. "We can find another way."

"She has to go," Eddie said. "You know you have to, Hazel. Your mission to set it all right will never be complete if you don't make amends with them, and this is how you can do it. Prove to them that you're innocent, and let them help avenge their son's death."

"I'll go." She met Eddie's eyes. "You're right. So many things are beyond my ability to make restitution for, but I can offer Nathaniel's family the pieces of information we have. I'll go tomorrow."

"I'll tell you what else I learned today." Eddie seemed to enjoy holding everyone in suspense. A wicked gleam sparkled in his eyes, leaving Hazel unsettled. No matter her guilt, she'd never enjoyed being laughed at, and his eyes were full of cruel humor.

"Tell us," Hazel said.

"I went to see Arnold Prewitt. A friend from my days in Buffalo. Hazel, I'm sure you remember him."

She ducked her head, once again wishing she could flee her past. With Eddie around to pick at the scab, it'd never heal.

"What does this have to do with anything?" Gilbert's tone was defensive.

"He said Hazel's sister Mathilda is sick." Eddie sat with a cruel smirk across his face. "I think it's serious. From what he said, she's near death."

Hazel pushed back from the table, stood, and marched over to Eddie. In a flash, she slapped him across the face. Her hand stung with the contact, but she did not wince. "How dare you treat such news as though it was an exciting surprise. My sister is an angel. She's done nothing to you. And I've done nothing to you in years. Will you never even look at me long enough to realize I'm not the girl I was before? And to think I allowed myself to believe you were not the same boy. You are still just as spiteful as ever."

Gilbert reached for her hand, but she brushed it away and left.

"What will you do?" Ina asked when she entered the rented room where Hazel lay curled on her side, still in her day dress. "Will you go to them? To your family?"

"I can't." She reached for the handkerchief she had beside her and blew her nose. "I promised I wouldn't. But I don't know what to do. When I think of Mathilda, I burst into tears. She's not like me. She's wholesome and good."

"You're good too." Ina sat beside her and put a hand on her shoulder. "All of this will be over soon. Then you can go home and live there if you wish."

"What if I'm too late and something terrible happens to her? A world without Mathilda would break my heart. I can't lose her." Hazel wiped her nose again. "Will I have to live out all my days wishing things had been different?"

Ina rubbed her shoulder. "No. I think you'll always remember where you came from and what you've been through, but someday it'll be just a memory like all the others. It'll be a bump in the road but one you were carried over by the Good Master. I believe he refines us in our times of trial, even when we bring them on ourselves, if we let him."

"I pray for it daily. I keep hoping that when this is over, I'll stop hating myself so much."

"What we're doing is important and it's right, but I think the forgiveness is there already. Look at your life, Hazel. You've changed. You care about the patients at the dental office and worry over your friend's happiness, and here you are crying over your sister's well-being. Forgive yourself," Ina soothed. "Take the forgiveness that is yours. Take it even if a judge never declares you cleared."

The idea of letting go, of putting her guilt aside and accepting the past for what it was, resonated with her, but the tears and sorrow made thinking a challenge. Here in Buffalo, with Nathaniel's journal tucked in her pack, Eddie's callous demeanor, and so many reminders of her prior life all around her, she found it difficult to make sense of anything.

When Hazel's tears subsided to sniffles, Ina said, "I can feel the pieces coming together already. Soon the men who killed Nathaniel will be behind bars, and it *will* clear your name. We'll get you home to see Mathilda. And until then, you can take solace in the fact that Eddie has a very red handprint across his face."

Hazel covered her face with her hands. "My hand stung so badly."

"But didn't it feel good? He had it coming to him, and you let him have it."

"It felt very good." She groaned. "It felt great and terrible all at the same time."

"I want your help, and I want your company," Gilbert said to Eddie. Being firm with his brother had never been a strength of his, but being soft with him would not do—not now. "I missed you when you left. Nothing seemed right without my big brother around."

"But you won't put up with me mistreating Hazel," Eddie finished for him. "I don't understand what you see in her. You could have your choice of women, especially now that you know how to talk to them."

"This has nothing to do with me attaching myself to a woman. It has to do with the fact that Hazel is a person and you trample all over her. You spout off your long-held grievances, but what about how you're treating her now? From what I've been told, she has every reason to detest you." Gilbert's voice was quiet but firm. "You wronged her greatly."

"She told you I was there?"

Gilbert nodded. "She did, and she told me she doesn't hate you for it. She asked me not to mention it, but you need to see this clearly. Think of the grudge she could hold. Because of that marriage, she spent five years in prison for a crime she didn't commit. And because of that sentence, she came home to no one. Her own family was shamed and asked her to wait to return home. Parents should not have to pick between their children, but hers did. Despite it all, she forgives you. And maybe if you could forgive her, she'd be able to forgive herself." He pushed himself forcefully away from the table. "I wish you'd try to see the good in her."

Eddie rubbed the side of his face where Hazel had slapped him. "She's got an arm. Some might see that as a positive trait."

"Never mess with a redhead." Gilbert stepped away from his brother. "I've had enough for one day. Think about what I said."

CHAPTER
TWENTY

"Would you like me to come with you?" Gilbert asked.

"No, I want to go alone." Hazel rubbed her swollen red eyes. Having him nearby normally gave her a sense of strength, but this was something she had to face alone. "There's so much to explain without having to explain who you are. Where is everyone else?"

"Eddie was out all night. I don't know where he is now."

"Did something happen?" Hazel asked in a sheepish voice. "After I . . . after I left."

"After you slapped him?"

She nodded, unsure if she'd hurt Gilbert as well as his brother with her actions.

"I told him where I stood."

"He's your brother." She swallowed, thinking of her own family and her deep desire to plead with them to allow her back into their lives. "If I am coming between you and Eddie . . . if I am . . ."

"No. He needed to hear what I had to say."

"And Duncan?" she asked.

"He's spending the morning in church with Ina."

"I saw her dressing for church. I should have assumed they'd go together. I would have liked to go too."

"I'd have liked sitting beside you. May I walk with you to the Williamses' home? I respect your desire to speak with them alone, but there's no reason you should walk the streets by yourself." He offered his hand. "And while we walk, I promise not to talk about anything that has to do with the case."

She'd never imagined a man could know her so well. The case was weighing heavily on her. One moment she was elated, believing they were so close to clearing her name, and the next she was shaking with fright, afraid the past would never be set right. "I'd like that."

The streets were quieter today than they'd been yesterday, when they could barely hear one another over the noisy din. She sighed. It was not as peaceful as their hill in Amherst, but it was still fresh air and good company. There was something oddly comforting about walking the streets of her childhood.

"Is that a snowflake?" she asked with her hand out, trying to catch it.

"Looks like winter's coming."

She rubbed her arms absently. "It makes me cold thinking about winter. It was summer when I last saw my family. A long-ago summer."

"You'll be home again soon. With Mathilda and

all your family." He put an arm on her back and rubbed it. "You need a thicker coat."

"I think I'll have to put in a few more hours at the dental office so I can get one."

"I was thinking about your work, and I've decided we need to make a few changes." He looked at her with a serious expression. "It's the way it has to be."

"What changes?" Her heart beat faster. She looked for signs of his subtle humor. "I can work harder. Whatever you need me to do."

"I need you to accept a raise in pay." He fought a smile, but she saw it creeping onto his face and smacked his arm.

"You're horrible. You had me worried."

"Don't you think that's a bit harsh? Most people would say thank you."

She put her hand on his arm where she'd hit him. "I'm sorry."

"You didn't hurt me." He pulled her tight against his side. "I couldn't get rid of you. You're the best lady in attendance I've ever had."

"I'm the only one you've ever had."

"That still makes you the finest." He pulled her tighter still, and though it was only with one arm and from the side, she felt like she was being embraced. "I'm sorry about Eddie and how he handled things last night."

"I'm sorry too. I know I shouldn't have slapped him."

"I wouldn't waste too much time feeling sorry about that."

"I didn't lose much sleep over Eddie. Mostly I worried for Mathilda. I think after I speak with the Williamses, I'll write my parents a letter and have someone deliver it." The flakes were coming harder now. With the temperature hovering near freezing, they were large flakes that floated through the air like finely crafted lace. "Mathilda loves snow. When she was little, she'd stay outside until her fingers were red with cold."

"It's beautiful," he said. "I believe God's an artist, the most amazing artist there is. Perhaps he created this snow with Mathilda in mind."

"I want to see her again. I want to see all of them. Not just so I can plead my innocence but so I can love them. I didn't do enough of that before."

"You'll get to. It's out of my power to promise it, but I believe it." He pressed a kiss to her hair. "For years you wanted to put the pieces together, and now they're coming together quickly. Remember that when you feel discouraged. We've been here for a short amount of time and we're close. Providence is behind it."

She looked up at him and could feel the tears welling in her eyes. His optimism gave her reason to hope. "I've tried to make sense of the timing, all the years of heartache and pain. I want to wish them away, but without them I'd never have found such dear friends." She held on to his arm a little tighter. "I wouldn't have found you. And now, with each of you helping, I believe the impossible may become possible."

"You're being watched over." He looked up toward the snow-filled sky. "I'm certain you are."

"Do you think so?" she asked. "So many things have gone askew in my life, I wonder. And then I believe, and then I wonder all over again."

"I believe." They turned a corner and headed into a wealthy neighborhood where the houses were wide and tall, with ornate gates and manicured lawns.

"And maybe he knew I needed a not-so-quiet dentist for a friend." She brushed a stray tear aside and smiled. "You act as though all of this is nothing. But I begged so many people for help, and none of them would lift a finger. You're different."

"A redhead is hard to resist."

She stopped in her tracks and put her hands on her hips. "It's brown."

"Red! After last night, how can you even deny it?" He looked down the street. "Which house?"

"We still have a ways to go." She pointed ahead of them. "Once we go around the corner, it'll be on the right."

"Are you ready?"

"I think so. Eddie was right about Nathaniel's

parents. They are in a position to help us, and I do need to see them. What will you do while I'm there?"

"I'll stay close so I'll be able to walk you back." He pulled his arm away from her as they neared the house, leaving her colder and more afraid. "Remember that no matter what kind of welcome they offer, you've got people who care."

"You don't know what your words mean to me."

He took a deep breath and let it out slowly. "They are more than words."

"You're right. You're a man of action." She rubbed her forearms. "It's so cold. You should go to the hotel and get warm. I can walk back on my own."

He shook his head. "No. I'll be here for you. I'll wait. Don't hurry either. I'll be here no matter how long it takes."

She took a few steps past him toward the enormous house but turned back. "Gil."

He walked to her side. "Yes?"

"Thank you. I'm so afraid, and somehow having you nearby makes it all seem better."

He put a gentle hand on her face, cradling it. Their eyes locked, and for one enchanted moment it was just the two of them, standing in the snow with no cares or worries. Their gaze and touch conveyed the tender regard they had for each other.

"You thank me, but little do you know the many

ways you've rescued me." Beneath his hand, she shook her head. "You don't believe me, but you have. I was destined to live my life as a reclusive dentist until you came along. Because of you, I find myself with plans and hopes. You've changed me for the better."

With so much goodness wrapped up in one moment, Hazel was tempted to grab his hand and beg him to run away with her. They could run west together, leave all this behind and lose themselves in their love. Instead, she pulled away from his touch, pivoted toward the house of her former in-laws, and, with his words written on her heart, went to face her past.

A woman opened the massive front door. "Can I help you?"

Hazel used to know all the staff, but it had been so long since she'd been here, she wasn't surprised to see a stranger's face.

"I'm here to see Hugo and Elizabeth Williams. I'm their daughter-in-law, Hazel, or at least I was. I was married to Nathaniel."

The woman's eyes grew large as she looked her up and down. "I'll let them know," she finally said. "You may follow me to the parlor."

The furniture and paintings brought back long-suppressed memories of the hours she'd spent on Nathaniel's arm as a new bride, unsure of her place in the family.

"Wait here."

Hazel sat on a floral chaise, nervously fidgeting with the fabric covering. Above the mantel was a portrait of Nathaniel in an elaborate gold frame. His sandy hair was parted to the side in his signature style, his suit she recognized as the one he wore when they would go out about town. His eyes gave her pause. They held hers, sucked her in, and made her wonder anew if he'd been miserable with her. When they were first wed, his eyes held only anger and sadness, but with time they'd changed to acquiescence. Before he died, she'd caught glimpses of another emotion, but she was not able to identify it with any certainty, though she hoped it had been affection.

"Were you happy with me?" she whispered to the painting. "Even a little?"

"Hazel?"

She jumped, then turned to see Hugo and Elizabeth enter the parlor. Signs of age were evident in their graying hair and wrinkled faces. Her throat went dry, and she could not think of any words to say. Emotion she hadn't expected to feel made her weak in the knees.

"What are you doing here?" Elizabeth asked quietly. "It's been so long."

She swallowed, hoping to loosen the words inside her. "I . . . I need to speak to you."

Hugo sat and pulled his wife down beside him. They'd been a strong couple before, always relying on each other, and it was apparent that time had changed them physically, but emotionally they were still each other's anchors. It was a strength she had hoped to one day achieve with Nathaniel.

"We're listening," Hugo said.

In a timid voice, she said, "I was just looking at Nathaniel's portrait."

"He was a handsome man." Elizabeth's voice was uneven. "There are days we still expect to hear him come bursting through the door. I wish so often that he'd not been out that night. We'd still have him with us, and perhaps you wouldn't have—"

"I don't think he was killed on accident." Her heart rate finally slowed as she began to say what she had come to tell them. She took a seat across from them. If they'd listen, perhaps the worry and grief would ease from their faces.

"Tell us," Hugo said. "I wondered at first, but then when you . . . well . . ." he stammered. "We'll listen."

"I want to tell you everything so you can decide for yourselves. But first, I must say I'm sorry. I'm sorry I could not stop him from dying, and I'm sorry for any shame I ever brought to your family." As though a physical burden had been lifted, she sat a little straighter. They had not accepted her apology, but she'd said it. "I'd rectify it all if I could, but my sorrow is all I can offer, as well as the little information I have about Nathaniel's death."

Hugo put a tender arm around his wife, who wept softly, and nodded his head toward Hazel. "Tell us what you've come to say."

And so Hazel started at the beginning. She told about their son's visits to the docks, about his death and his last words, the jewels, and the years of her wondering.

Before she could say any more, they stopped her. "We could have saved you from your time in prison if only we'd searched for the truth." Hugo's face went pale. "We should have. We were so lost in our grief that we failed you. We blamed you when we should have rallied around you."

"No. You never failed me. I've never thought that. You welcomed me into your family despite the way I entered, and you did so much more. Please, let me tell the rest."

And so she told about trying to find help and receiving none from the authorities. She described her despair and her thoughts of running away. She spoke of her separation from her family and her search for work. "It's all been hard, I can't deny that, but I've experienced much good too. I learned to truly pray at the reformatory, and I learned that the Lord listens. And in Amherst I've found friends—one is even a lawyer. We've been here in Buffalo all weekend, and already we've found so much information I can hardly believe it. It's unfolding before our eyes as though a miracle is being bestowed."

"Do you know who did all this and why?" Hugo leaned forward in his chair, his elbows on his knees.

"I believe we do. Though we need more proof. Which is why we need you." She told him all she could. Every detail, every clue, every idea she and her friends had come up with.

"You've had a busy couple of days." He folded his arms across his chest and spoke slower but with resolve. "We must be smart and cautious, but I believe you're on to something. Jacob Grost is the captain of the *Sally Belle*, and though he never misses a delivery, he's never been the most forthright man. The idea of him having secrets is believable. If I show up unannounced, he always seems uneasy, nervous."

"We have to catch the captain transferring goods to Patrick."

"Yes, but if we find they are transporting opium and don't discover where to, then we will only have half our answer," Hugo said.

"Didn't you say some police officers may be involved?" Elizabeth asked.

"We believe some are. We have the lists that Nathaniel left, and we have Charlotte." Hazel smiled for the first time since entering the home. "I know it won't bring him back, but I think he'd be glad to know we finished what he started. He was putting the pieces together and would have wanted this stopped. We can do that."

"I agree." Hugo stood and walked to the mantel. "I'll spend this week getting to the bottom of it. I'll hire some men to keep watch. No matter the cost, I'll settle this. Can you come back again at the end of the week? Bring your friends. You can stay here when you come."

"Just a week?" Elizabeth asked.

Hugo nodded. "It might take longer, but the *Sally Belle* leaves and returns this week. If it's carrying a load of opium, we'll find out. We don't have too many more runs before the boats are docked for the winter."

"I'll come back." She wanted to jump up and down and shout out of pure relief and happiness. Their welcome was more than she'd dared to hope for. "Whatever we can do this week, you can count on us."

Elizabeth put her hand on Hazel's arm. "I don't think it'd be wise for you to come too often until this is settled. I don't like what you said about the captain possibly recognizing you. Stay in Amherst this week, but when it's over"—she looked to Hugo—"we would like to have you back in our home as often as you can come."

"You believe I'm innocent?"

"We were wrong not to ask all the questions and search for answers before. Nathaniel cared for you, and we should have looked after you in his absence. Can you ever forgive us?"

Hazel burst into tears and, somehow, she and Elizabeth fell into each other's arms. "I've never blamed you."

"Oh, you dear girl," Elizabeth said, patting her back. "You dear, sweet girl. I must confess another wrong. I could not bring myself to enter the house you shared with Nathaniel. I stayed away for a year. But then I went in. I hardly touched anything, but I found his journal and I read it. Since then I've wanted to see you, but I was a coward."

"I have the journal now. I found it when we went looking for clues," Hazel said in a whisper. "I've been afraid to read it."

"You must read it." Elizabeth wiped away the tears streaming down her face.

Countless nights Hazel had prayed to know the heart of her deceased husband. Would his journal be a nightmare or a gift? She dared not ask and simply nodded. "I'll read it."

CHAPTER
TWENTY-ONE

Gilbert walked past the Williamses' home every few minutes to ensure he did not miss Hazel. He'd thought about sitting and waiting, but the wind had picked up and the flakes were now falling in earnest. When he stopped moving, the cold seeped in.

The grandeur of the homes kept him preoccupied for some time, but they were not enough of a distraction to stop him from wondering how Hazel fared. Circling around again, he breathed easier, seeing Hazel cross the threshold and step into the blustery air. She ducked her head as a gust of wind whipped through the neighborhood, but her tread did not slow.

"Hazel!" he called, quickening his pace until they met in the street.

Her pace was fast, as though she were lighter now than when she'd gone into the house. The sight of her warmed his heart. "You're all right. It went well?"

"Yes. I'm fine. Oh, Gil, it was so good to sit across from them and tell them how I felt and what I've learned and"—he brushed a snowflake from her cheek—"to hear them tell me they don't think it's my fault, not anymore. I'd expected to plead with them, but all I had to do was tell them the truth and they listened. I suppose it could be because we've all had time to think on our losses. Or perhaps we put too many requirements on forgiveness. Today all it took was understanding and words of truth."

"I believe you're right. Forgiveness can be instant if we let it be." He took her hand and led her through the snowy streets. "We have to get back. This weather is changing quickly."

Walking warmed them but not enough to keep all their shivers away. With chattering teeth, she told him how Hugo and Elizabeth had agreed to help and that they were to come back in a week. In a softer voice, she said, "We talked of Nathaniel, and I find myself wondering how he truly felt about me. For a long time I tried not to think of him, but now I feel guilty and curious and . . . so many feelings. I'm eager now to read his journal."

Gilbert nodded but said nothing. He wasn't sure what to say or how he fit into it all. Nathaniel was a piece of Hazel's story that he'd never be a part of. A chapter he wasn't sure he'd ever fully understand.

"I'm sorry I left you in the cold for so long."

"Don't be." He quickened the pace, afraid they'd be trapped in the city if they didn't hurry.

"When we get back to the hotel, I will pen a letter to my parents letting them know all that's happened and asking if I might see them next week. Then I'll be ready to go."

He nodded. "I'll pray their hearts will be as soft as Hugo's and Elizabeth's were."

When they stepped through the hotel doors, he sighed as the heat kissed his frozen fingers and nose, sending a painful tingle through them. Moments later, they were greeted by Ina and Duncan.

"I'll make arrangements for our ride while you write your letter," Gilbert said after they gave them a brief recap of their morning. "We can discuss our plans as we travel. We need to leave as soon as we can."

"But where is Eddie?" Hazel asked. "We can't leave him."

"He came back earlier and said he was finding his own way home. We tried to stop him, but he insisted." Ina looked distraught over the confession. "We tried. Honest we did."

"I don't doubt it. Don't worry about him. The time alone might even do him good," Gilbert said despite the worry he felt. "I will run to my room and pack. I'll meet you in the lobby."

Dear Father and Mother,

I know you've requested I not write, and throughout the trying days since my release, I have obeyed your wishes. I would continue to do so, but I feel I have cause to write.

In as few lines as possible, she summarized the case, beginning with her initial fears and finishing with the help Hugo and Elizabeth promised.

> I know it is a lot to ask that you believe me innocent, but I beg you to try. I'll be back next week, and I'd like to see you and Mathilda. I've heard she is sick, and I fear I won't rest easy until I see her and tell her once again how I adore her. I must also warn you that there is a small but real chance that danger could befall you if anyone knows that I am back and working to clear my past. Be on the lookout. I'll pray for your safety, Mathilda's health, and our reunion. If you will allow me to visit next week, send word to Mrs. Northly's boardinghouse for women in Amherst. Address it to Hazel McDowell. I'll explain it all later.

Hazel looked out the window at the falling snow. She needed to hurry and leave. There was so much more to be said, but there was no time. She quickly finished the letter.

> I want you to know that I love you all. I didn't appreciate familial love like I should have, but when it was absent from my life, I felt the void. I turned to the

Lord and found peace and comfort, but I still long for another chance to be the daughter I should have been.

All my love,
Hazel

She folded and sealed the letter, then dashed downstairs, where she paid the doorman to deliver it to her parents and joined the rest of the group. They hurried into their rented ride and under the travel blankets.

"With Hugo and Elizabeth's connections and money and all the evidence we have already, it should not be a hard case to prove." Duncan sat back in his seat. "I hadn't expected everything to go this smoothly."

"I wished for it and prayed for it," Hazel said. "No matter what, I'm grateful for your efforts and kindness."

Gilbert gripped her hand then and held it as they traveled home. The journey was easy despite the snow, the goodbyes were brief but heartfelt, and then Hazel and Ina found themselves back at Mrs. Northly's. They readied for bed in the same way they always did. It felt odd to do such normal things while in the midst of so much uncertainty.

"Are you going to read Nathaniel's journal now?" Ina's eyes went to the leather book Hazel had set beside her bed.

"Yes, though I'm afraid to open it. I know what I want to find, but I'm afraid of what I will find." She flipped absently through the pages. "I *will* read it though. No matter what the entries say, it will be better to know how he felt than to always wonder."

"Will it change things with Gilbert?"

"The journal?" Hazel sighed. She'd asked herself the same thing. "I don't know. I've insisted we remain only the best of friends, and I think that's wise considering the history I share with Eddie." She ran her hand over the soft leather cover. "I think what I want is for the journal to somehow reassure me that Nathaniel did not go to his grave regretting our marriage. I'd find a measure of comfort in that, and maybe some courage too."

Ina looked up. "Courage?"

"I've been afraid for years now that I ruined a man's life, and knowing that I didn't would . . . well, it would change things. I'd like to know that I was not a wretched woman to live with, and maybe then I could be brave enough one day to remarry." She fidgeted, uncomfortable with such vulnerability. She had never voiced her fears of remarrying before, and now with her worries floating around them for Ina to interpret however she wished, Hazel felt exposed.

"You mustn't think that. Soon you'll be able to leave here if you wish and start life with a man or go back with your family. Either way, you'll be able to leave this boardinghouse. The doors to your future are opening. Life is changing. Can you feel it?"

Hazel's hand froze in midair as she processed what her friend had said, well aware that she should feel nothing but happiness. Going home with her head high, walking through her parents' front door. That was what she had wanted for such a long time. Then why did her stomach clench at the thought of leaving Amherst behind?

"What I know is that we don't return to Buffalo for another week. I have a journal to read and the very best friend living down the hall. The rest is out of my control. No, not the rest," she said. Life had taught her that she could control how she faced each day. "I could not get out of my marriage to Nathaniel, so I chose to try and find happiness there. I could not shorten my sentence, so I chose to seek reformation. And so, in whatever lies ahead, I'll try to control what I can. I shall take it one day at a time."

"It'll be a good week. You'll make it so," Ina said. "I can feel it in the air."

"That's snow you feel." Hazel smiled at her friend.

She shook her head. "No, it's not just snow. It's hope. We both have bright futures ahead."

• • •

Once alone, Hazel sat on her bed and opened
Nathaniel's old leather journal. The first entry
was from two weeks before they ever met.

> I spent the early morning down at the
> docks with Father. I thought I might not
> like working with him, but I find the days
> enjoyable, and he's a smart and good
> businessman.
>
> After our morning at the docks, we
> walked through the city together and
> I almost told Father how I felt about
> Joanna. It's hard to speak feelings out
> loud, so I didn't tell him but hope to soon.
> I've never been more comfortable around
> a woman than I am with her. I will wait
> until after her sister's wedding to ask her
> for her hand.

Hazel closed her eyes, unable to read another
word, her chest heavy, weighed down by the
reality of what she'd done. He'd been in love,
happy, and then she came into his life. Kneeling
beside her bed, she offered her heartache
and regret once again heavenward, knowing
retribution was out of reach.

"Good morning," Hazel said as she walked
through the door of the dental office the next

morning. "I thought I might blow away before I ever made it here."

"Hopefully this is just a passing storm." Gilbert took her thin coat and hung it up. "With any luck, it'll melt quickly."

"Has Eddie returned?" Hazel picked up the day's schedule and busied herself looking at it, hoping her calm demeanor would mask the worry she felt whenever she dwelt on the rift she'd caused between Gilbert and his brother.

"He was home before I arrived last night. He never told me how he got there."

She looked up from the paper she held. "Is he still upset?"

"He's angry, but I think that has to do with more than you." He stepped near her. "He said he would go back to Buffalo and try to find out more about Patrick Harper. So at least we can still count on his help."

"That is good of him." She took a deep breath. "Today will be a busy one at the office. The schedule is full."

"It's a good thing the snow didn't keep us trapped in Buffalo."

"I think half of Amherst would have been upset. This schedule is the busiest I've seen." She shrugged. "Time passes faster when it's full. We'll be back in Buffalo in no time."

"I'm eager for it—for your sake."

"Only for my sake?"

He touched a strand of her hair. "I'm a little worried for myself."

"You are?"

"I'm afraid this week may be our last together." He gestured around the dental office, and her eyes followed his movements. She'd come to love it all—the desks, the paintings, even the drill. "Me, you, patients, humming while you clean. I want you to be free. You deserve that. But I'm selfish, so I'm afraid that when you go, I'll have a hole in my life that I'm not sure I'll ever be able to fill."

"I've loved my time here." She'd found a purpose within these walls that she'd never known before.

He put a hand on her shoulder. "Well, Red, at least we have this week together. And I believe our first patient is headed this way. Let's soak it all in."

"If I find time to scrub the floors today, I promise to hum while I clean."

"I'll work extra fast so I can hear it." He went to the front door, but before he opened it, he said, "Spend extra time with me this week?"

"Yes."

That morning they pulled teeth and fitted a denture. During the first small lull of the day, Hazel filled her bucket with water and mopped the floors. She hummed as she scrubbed, and whenever she dared a glance in his direction, she saw him smiling back at her.

"I didn't realize I had a favorite sound. But now I know I do."

"Really?" she asked and then hummed a ridiculous tune that sounded more like a sick cat than something memorable and lovely. She struggled to keep a straight face. "How was that?"

"That's my favorite tune. How did you know?" Gilbert wore a playful smirk on his face.

"It is not." She stood up and threw a rag at him. "You didn't."

"Oh, I did." She reached for the rag again.

He grabbed her around the waist. "No you don't."

Laughing, she struggled to get away, giggling harder with the effort. Suddenly she froze and her eyes found his. The playfulness from moments before vanished, replaced by something stronger, deeper, and more exhilarating. Her heart beat wildly as she stood in his arms. Everything in her wanted to reach up and rest a hand on his cheek, but she held back, knowing that if all went well, she'd be at a crossroads. Toying with Gilbert would not do. She cared too much for him to sink into his embrace when she was so very uncertain about her future.

"Hazel," he whispered in a voice full of yearning, "I know you didn't steal. It makes no difference to me if the law ever acknowledges it. You've told me your past, and it does not scare me that you used to walk on railings and flirt. I see it all, and I still want you. I care about who you are now. There's no reason—"

She squirmed in his arms, torn between breaking away and melting into them.

He looked down at her, his eyes pleading. "If you're willing, we could talk about lines and how they can change."

She bit her bottom lip but held his gaze.

He moved his head closer, his lips enticing her to close the distance.

"Gil," she whispered, "I can't. Not with Mathilda sick and your brother angry and so many unknowns. And seeing Nathaniel's parents. I have so much to think about. After that . . . I can't make any promises. It'd be unfair to you."

His eyes lost their fervor, but he nodded. "I'll be content with listening to you hum all week. They are your lines to move."

"Thank you for understanding and . . ." She opened her mouth to say more but shut it again when the front door creaked. "That must be Diana Maas."

"The future can wait, but Diana will not," he said before walking away from her.

I met Joanna today by the large oak tree in the park. It is the spot I'd hoped to offer my hand in marriage, but today I met her there and broke her heart. I've never felt so cruel as I did watching her crumble into tears, knowing I could not comfort her.

And now I am back with my wife. I'm a married man. Married to a woman I did not choose and have no affection for. Everyone knows Hazel Bradshaw is a beauty with conniving ways. Men who don't know her long to be associated with her, but I never had such desires. Now I am to love and cherish her all the days of my life. I don't know that I can keep my vows, which saddens *me*.

Hazel shut the book and paced her small room. She wrung her hands together, sat back down, flipped several pages ahead, and read again.

I spent the day at the *Sally Belle*. It docked last night, and I wanted to help Father get her unloaded. I think I'll try to familiarize myself with the comings and goings so I can be an asset to the business. Things seem to run smoothly, but sometimes an eerie feeling comes over me and I believe something may be amiss. Most likely it is just nerves about being new and unfamiliar in my role there.

I've been married a month now, and each day I accept my fate a little more.

I no longer wake wondering why there's a woman in my home. Her presence has worked itself comfortably into my daily life. She is not as overbearing as I had expected, and occasionally she is thoughtful and kind. My lot is cast and mine is to be a marriage of convenience, but I find it will not be the burden I originally feared.

It was hardly a confession of love, but it offered Hazel some comfort. At least he'd found her to be a reasonable companion. She tucked the journal beneath her pillow and walked to Ina's room to see how her visit with Duncan and Amy had gone.

Ina greeted her warmly, excited to relay the evening's events. "Amy was so happy to see me, and she gave me a picture she made." Ina went to her desk and picked up a piece of paper. "See here? This is me and this is her, and she drew Duncan next to us."

"I love their little stick legs. And look, she drew you taller than Duncan!"

"It's a treasure," Ina said, returning the masterpiece to the desk. "We had a perfect evening. Amy asked Duncan when she could come and live with him, and he said soon. Then he looked at me over her head and winked, and everything inside of me melted."

Hazel gasped. "I never would have guessed that Duncan would wink. That seems so out of character for him."

"I would have agreed with you at first, but he does little things like that now. I think he feels safe enough with me that he can have a little more fun. Do you feel that way with Gilbert? That time has shown you more of his personality and character?"

"You and Duncan are courting. Everyone knows that. Gilbert and I are . . . well, we're something else. But there are moments when I feel us becoming more friendly." She thought of the rag she'd tossed at him and the way he'd held her in his strong arms and nearly kissed her. "He still holds back some."

"Probably because he's waiting for permission." Ina had a knack for simplifying things. "You told me yourself that you'd set boundaries and he'd promised to obey your every wish until you changed the rules."

"You're right. I don't deny it. I've set rules and questioned those rules and utterly confused the poor man." She paused, contemplating it all. "Do you think I could make a man happy? After Nathaniel, I worry."

"I do," Ina said with an earnest expression. "I think you could be happy too. I . . . I have to confess something. I feel silly now for not saying it at first."

"What is it?"

"Duncan spoke to me about marrying him."

"I thought the wink was good news, but this is so much better. Why didn't you tell me straightaway?"

Ina flipped the end of her hair around in her hand. "I wanted to, but I didn't know what to say. I thought you'd think me a ninny for feeling confused. I care for Duncan. I love him."

"What is it, then?"

"I'm scared of getting what I want and waking up to find it's not as wonderful as I always dreamed it would be. My whole life I've had romantic notions, and now they're coming true and I'm afraid of what it will really be like." Ina kept her head lowered. "I'm afraid I'll be disappointed or not know what to dream about next."

Hazel groaned, then giggled. "Why is it so hard for us to be happy? I worry about everything too."

"What do I do?"

"I'm not the best person to ask for advice, but I believe if you love him, and I know you do, then you choose not to worry. You wake up each day and embrace your own story. And whatever the day holds, you make it wonderful. And the bad days you laugh about and put behind you. Besides, if you only ever dream, you'll always wonder, and I can't imagine that is a better way to live." Hazel heard her own words and wondered if she'd ever be brave enough to follow them. "Love the life you're given. There will be long days and hard days and days when you both wonder how you'll ever come together and be one. But those days will only make the other days more magical."

"Was that how it was for you?"

"You have an advantage over Nathaniel and me. We didn't even know each other when we got married. I'm certain he wondered what was wrong with me some days."

"And the good days?" Ina asked.

"I think I need to finish reading his journal." She hugged her friend. "And I think if I were to marry again, I would know how to have more happy days. But you are already selfless. I was still learning to care about others when Nathaniel died. Marriage will suit you from the start." She grabbed Ina's hand and held it tightly. "Now, tell me exactly what Duncan said to you. Enough of this serious talk. I want to hear all the romantic details."

Ina's eyes brightened, and she squeezed Hazel's hand back. "It differed from how I ever expected to be asked."

"Was it beautiful though? Even if it was different?"

Her head bobbed enthusiastically. "Yes. We were eating with Amy, and Duncan took my hand. It was after the wink and after Amy told us she wanted to come live with her father. He held my hand and said he'd been thinking about it and he thought she should come home soon. She asked when, and even teared up a little. Duncan turned to me and asked me if I'd be his wife and if we could all be a family. It was simple. He said he loved me and that he felt happy when he was with me. I told him I'd be honored, and then he kissed me. Just a little kiss, but it was my first *real* kiss." Ina's cheeks turned a perfect shade of pink as she recollected it all. "It wasn't just on the cheek like before. Oh, Hazel, it made my heart soar. After that we ate cake, and everything in the world felt right. It was only later that I worried."

Hazel grinned. "You are going to marry Duncan!" She stood up and pulled her friend with her. "You're going to marry him!"

"I am! I'm going to marry him and be his wife." Ina burst into tears. "I'm getting married."

Back in her room, Hazel dressed for bed, then prayed for Mathilda and for Ina and Duncan's love and for answers to her own heart's queries. The hour was late and sleep tugged at her weary body, but she was restless and picked up Nathaniel's journal again. She read several entries about ordinary life—business and news of his friends. She pored over his words, searching for answers and wanting desperately to know what had been in his heart. She paused on an entry from three months into their marriage.

Today I returned home from work to find that Hazel had gone to visit her family. The house felt quiet. It was then I realized I enjoyed Hazel's company. She has a lively and impulsive way about her. I can tell that living here with me is trying for her, but she keeps her chin up and seems determined to make a go of it. I feel it is too early yet to decide what will become of us as we grow old, but I don't dread finding out like I once did.

When Hazel returned, we went out and ordered new furniture for the house. We had very different preferences, but in the end the house will be a strange compilation of her tastes and mine. But perhaps all homes are the reflection of two lost souls merging together.

Hazel closed her eyes, remembering the day. She'd gone to visit her little sisters. They'd snuggled up to her and asked what married life was like.

When she returned, Nathaniel was in a strange mood. He followed her around like a shadow, asking about her day and her family and all sorts of nothingness.

Finally, he asked, "Would you like to buy things for the house? We've been living in a half-furnished home long enough."

"Yes," she replied. "I'd love that."

That outing was the first comfortable one they'd shared. They had laughed together as they debated what to buy.

The happy entry led her to read further, hoping to find more pleasurable moments.

Four months of marriage, and today I woke up wondering how I ended up with a spitfire for a wife. There's something wrong with Hazel.

She snapped the journal shut, then pulled her hand back to throw it across the floor, stopping herself when she realized such an action would only confirm his horrid entry. Instead, she smiled smugly as though he were there and with exaggerated calmness opened the journal again.

I wonder if I am the only married man who wonders why women act the way they do. She seems perfectly adjusted to this new life of ours one day, and then she wakes up fuming mad the next, yelling at me about staying out late and keeping secrets. I tried to tell her I was working, but she only grew angrier. Her eyes were like nothing I'd ever seen before. I avoided them whenever possible, but then of course she had to yell that I wouldn't even look at her.

I left, uncertain about what I would come home to. To my great relief, she seemed content and good-natured upon my return. She must have overcome or tucked away whatever had been bothering her. Married life, I have come to believe, is like being on a boat in the middle of a storm. One moment the gray and livid sky is threatening, and the next it's overwhelmingly beautiful.

Hazel shut the journal and put it on her desk. She couldn't expect Nathaniel to have been happy all the time. She hadn't been. There'd been days when she was angry about her loss of freedom or frustrated by how little they knew about each other or battling with her selfish nature. Still, it would have been nice to read that he'd been blissfully happy. Was such happiness even possible?

CHAPTER
TWENTY-TWO

"It's four in the morning," Gilbert said to his brother after opening the front door and finding Eddie on the porch brushing snow from his shoulders. Eddie had insisted on heading back to Buffalo the day before, giving Gilbert no idea as to when he would return. "Where have you been?"

"Stop staring at me like I've committed a crime and I'll tell you," Eddie said, making his way into the house.

Gilbert grumbled but sat in the parlor ready to talk if Eddie was willing.

Eddie continued brushing snow off himself as he recounted his evening's escapades. "I went to the brothel. I wanted to go before the *Sally Belle* left port again. I was hoping to catch Patrick or Jacob, the captain. Or at the least ask a few questions."

"Did you?"

"Not right away. I was able to find out from one of the card dealers that they were both in often. He asked me if I was there for a delivery, so I went along with it and asked him if I could expect one today." Eddie ran a hand through his wet hair. "He said he expected it later that night.

So I played a lot of cards and looked at a lot of beautiful women."

"Eddie!" Gilbert balked. "You didn't."

"Settle down. I said that to get you riled up, but I assure you I have retained some of the moral convictions Father tried so hard to instill in me. Anyway, around eleven a couple of men came in. The dealer leaned over and told me they worked for Patrick Harper. He also told me that the *Sally Belle* was heading out soon and I ought to get what I could now because weather might slow the next shipment. You would have been impressed with my calm demeanor as I watched it all happen." Eddie leaned back, reenacting his pose from earlier in the night. "I don't think they want anyone knowing the opium all travels up the Erie Canal on the *Sally Belle*."

Eddie unlaced his wet boots and slid his feet out. Water pooled beneath the soles of his shoes, puddling up on the wood floor. Gilbert cringed but said nothing. A bit of water paled in comparison to the case. "I decided that since I was so close, I ought to go to the Williamses' home and tell them what I'd seen and heard. We sat and talked over all our theories, and Hugo told me he had found trustworthy men to watch the ship and keep an eye out for Patrick."

Gilbert slapped his brother's shoulder. "Well done."

"I didn't want you going." He smirked. "I knew

your innocence would never survive the hours at the brothel."

"Is that why you're helping? You want to protect my virtue?" Gilbert raised a brow. His brother's story didn't add up.

Eddie blew into his hands to warm them. "No. It's not just that."

"What is it?"

"You were right. I have been holding grudges for too long, but I think it's more than that. I feel guilty for so many things. I let myself believe that if Hazel was worse than I was, still lost and conniving, then I wasn't so bad." He scratched his head. "I figured I'd done some bad things, but if I could cling to the notion that what she'd done was worse, well, somehow that made me innocent."

Gilbert stood and walked the aged floors. "You're saying that you think if you can convince us all that Hazel's some sort of heathen, then that washes your sins away? I'd always believed you to be more levelheaded than that."

"The night at the park when Hazel was tricked into marrying Nathaniel to save her reputation? That was my doing. I orchestrated that. The memory haunts me. What sort of coward am I to stand back and watch?" For the first time since they'd reconnected, Eddie seemed genuinely sorry. This was the Eddie whom Gilbert had known—sincere and real. "I'd gotten better at ignoring the memories and subduing the guilt, but now here she is."

"Why not just apologize? You don't have to remain a coward. She would forgive you. She already has. Her heart is good like that."

"I was wrong to do what I did. I should have stepped out of the shadows and stopped it all. I suppose I'm trying to make up for that by helping you now." Eddie's head flew up, and his hands fisted together. "But I'm not lying when I tell you she is not someone you want to be attached to."

"You know the Hazel from before. I know the Hazel now." Frustrated by his brother's stubbornness, Gilbert walked the floor. Why couldn't Eddie see how wrong he was? Living stuck in the past robbed the future.

Eddie shook his head. "What if it's an act?"

"If you think there's no way for someone to change, then you must still be the type of man who would stand by and watch two strangers marry under false pretenses. But I don't think that's who you are anymore. You've changed. So has she." Gilbert let his pacing take him to the stairs. "I'm glad you went to the brothel. It puts us closer to solving all this." He walked up two steps, then stopped. "I care for Hazel. I don't know if there's any hope of us having a future together, but I believe with all my heart that she is a fine woman. I hope you'll try to forgive her and forgive yourself."

Eddie shifted in his seat, then he stood and walked to the mantel, where the picture of their father sat. "Do you think our father would have forgiven me? If he were here in this room, would he welcome me?"

"Yes," Gilbert said without so much as a pause. "He'd welcome you with open arms."

"You don't even know why I left."

"I don't have to. I know he would have forgiven you. You're a good man, Eddie, and Father was the sort to believe that our faults could be overcome. Whatever the indiscretion, he'd have stood by you as you wrestled through it." Gilbert walked to his brother's side. "Put it behind you. Fix it if you can, but move forward. Let's live the dreams we always talked about."

"Going to sea." Eddie smiled sadly. "I'm not sure that's my dream anymore."

"No. Not those dreams. But the dreams of living good lives near each other. You were always sweet on someone, and you used to talk about settling down. You could still do that. And I could too. We could have families and be husbands and fathers. We could honor our own father as we love our children. Doesn't that sound better than carrying around grudges?"

Eddie raised his head and looked his brother in the eyes. "You make it sound simple."

"I've watched you fight to stay angry, and from my vantage point, I'd say grudges are not simple.

They require endless feeding. Forgiving may in fact be the easier route, and there's no doubt it's the better one. Go to sleep now, but think about it."

"Have you heard?" Hazel asked Gilbert at the office the next day as soon as she entered.

"Heard what?"

"Duncan asked Ina to marry him!" She had her hands clasped near her heart. "Oh, isn't it the greatest news? When I first met Ina, she was so certain love would never find her, and now she's getting married. And it's a real marriage, a love match."

He stopped what he was doing and asked, "Do you think they'll name their firstborn after me?"

"What?" Hazel laughed. "Why?"

"Have you forgotten that I introduced them at the corn husking?"

"I will never forget the corn husking! I'll tell her you expect a child named Gilbert. Gilbert Franklin. I like it. I'm sure she'll turn crimson red at the thought of babies and namesakes." Hazel sighed. "I'm so happy for her."

"Does it make you think of love and marriage for yourself?"

"I suppose it does." Heat crept up her neck all the way to her ears. "After I see my family and when my sister is well, maybe I'll think about the possibility of marrying again. I didn't think I ever would, but perhaps—"

"I hope I'm not interrupting." Hazel jerked her head toward the voice, only to see Eddie moseying into the room. "I'd like to speak to Hazel. Can you spare her?"

"You don't have to." Gilbert closed the distance between them.

"It's fine," she said, searching Eddie for understanding. He looked different, less smug. "Would you like to go outside? I noticed the snow has stopped."

Eddie nodded and stepped through the door ahead of her.

The air was crisp and fresh, with a slight wind blowing from the east. She pulled her coat tightly around herself, trying to keep the cold from seeping into her bones as they walked along the street.

"My brother has found a new gift since meeting you," Eddie began.

"Has he?"

"He seems to have found his tongue and has decided he likes using it to speak plainly to me."

She put a hand over her mouth to mask the smile that raced to it. Eddie might not appreciate Gilbert's liberated tongue, but she loved that he was a man of words now.

"He spoke rather forcibly last night. I wrestled with myself half the night and finally decided that he spoke the truth. No need to tell him that though."

"I'm glad I didn't help him find a lying tongue."

"No, that wouldn't have fit Gilbert well at all." Eddie stopped walking and leaned against the brick wall of a little shop. "I owe you an apology."

"No you don't," she blurted.

"I do. I have little practice offering them, so try to listen and be patient with me even if I sound like a dunce."

Knowing firsthand what a battle of pride and humility felt like, she granted him an easy audience. "Very well. I'm listening."

"I should have stepped out from the trees all those years ago. I've felt sorry about it ever since." He was looking down at his feet. "I'm sorry for all the trials my actions caused you. And I'm sorry for what I said about Mathilda. I wish no ill upon her or upon you."

Matching his honesty, she said, "I should not have played games with your friend's affections. I was a foolish youth. I too have lived with the burden of regret."

"You've really changed?" he asked. "You're not going to hurt Gilbert?"

"The truth is, I never would have chosen to marry Nathaniel, but once I found myself married to him, I also found myself faced with a lot of harsh realities. I knew I'd hurt him and I couldn't walk away from his pain like I'd walked away from all the others before him. We were stuck together, so every single day I saw the hurt and the anger in his eyes. And then I learned that I could ease the pain by thinking of his needs and not just mine." Hazel folded her arms across her chest and shivered slightly. "Since then, I've never willfully hurt another soul." She darted a glance at him. "That's not entirely true. It wasn't so long ago that I slapped a man."

"That was deserved." He put his hands in his pockets, then slowly blew a puff of breath into the cold air, making a cloud above him. "I should have given you a chance. Gilbert asked me to, but I was born with a stubborn streak."

"Give me a chance now. The rest is forgotten." She smiled at him—not a forced smile but a genuine one. "I think the two of us will be great friends."

He smirked at her. "I think we will be more than friends."

Hazel took a small step back and raised an inquisitive eyebrow, unsure what he was implying. "More?"

"I think before long, you and I will be like brother and sister." He laughed, and for once she heard no malice behind it. "I'd like to know you as you are now. I hope you'll give me another chance."

"I've never had an older brother." She laughed with him, amazed by how quickly the angst between them disappeared. "It's liberating, isn't it?"

"Begging for forgiveness?"

"Letting go."

He nodded. "It is. I'm sorry it took so long."

CHAPTER
TWENTY-THREE

"There's no one else scheduled today." Gilbert put the freshly cleaned instruments back in their spots.

"I'm glad." Hazel rubbed her lower back and sighed. "I'll never know how you lean over all day without complaining of an aching back."

Gilbert held out Hazel's coat to her. "Sometimes I have to walk the pain away."

"So you are human and do hurt from time to time."

"Guilty." He watched as she slid her arms into her coat sleeves. "Will you walk to my father's grave with me?"

"To his grave? Yes, of course." She picked up her reticule. "Do you go often?"

"I go on special days and when I want to feel close to him." He led her from the office, locking the door behind her. "Today marks the anniversary of his death."

"Is it a hard day for you?"

"He was in a lot of pain before he died. I'm glad he no longer suffers, but I'd give anything for another conversation with him."

"What would you talk about?"

"I'd tell him about you and about how daring

I've been as of late." He puffed out his chest and laughed. "I think I'd tell him that I'm happy."

They walked together down the street toward the Eggert Cemetery, avoiding the patches of lingering snow. Rays of sunshine broke through the dense clouds, bathing everything in deceptive yellow light that felt like spring and not the end of fall.

"It's our lucky day. I think that's Alberta," Gilbert whispered to Hazel. "Shall we hide? I think we could both fit behind that large maple."

"I think it's too late for that. Look how quickly she's moving. I suppose you'll have to repent again tonight." She grinned at him. "For all the uncharitable thoughts you are about to have."

"I didn't know you would throw my transgressions in my face. If I'd known, I'd have let you go on thinking I was perfect," Gilbert said, loving how Hazel's presence added so much humor and laughter to his once-dull life.

"Only this one sin. The rest are safe. I'll never tell a soul about you eating half a pie without permission. That one will go to the grave with me." She squeezed his arm. "Brace yourself for attack," she whispered.

"Together outside of the office?" Alberta's voice broke into their fun. "Everywhere I go, I see couples pairing off and traipsing this city."

"We're headed to the cemetery. You have no

need to worry about our intentions." Gilbert smiled at her. "It's hardly a dark alley."

"Laughing on your way to the cemetery? That's not very reverent." She put her hands on her hips as she appraised the two of them.

"We were only laughing at a thought Gilbert had. You must ask him about it." Hazel gnawed on her bottom lip as though she were fighting a laugh even now. "I think you'll find it entertaining. He's surprisingly witty."

"Well. What was it?" Alberta questioned him.

"I was only . . . only thinking of a joke my father used to tell me." Gilbert fought to quickly recall his father's favorite joke.

Hazel seemed to cover a cough.

"You need to see a doctor," Alberta said to Hazel. "Every time I've seen you, you're coughing. Now, I have places to be. What joke did your father tell you?"

Gilbert waited while Hazel fought to suppress her "cough." Once she was again in control of her voice, she said, "Do share. Tell us the joke again."

"Well, when we'd walk near the cemetery, he'd always say, 'Did you know a man living on this side of the road can't be buried in the Eggert Cemetery?' "

"That's not a joke. Anyone who can buy a plot can be buried here. It doesn't matter where they live." Alberta scowled. "I thought your father was a brighter man than that."

"It's supposed to be funny. You see, anyone *living* can't be buried. Only dead people can be."

Alberta stared hard at him. "Over thirty for a reason. There's always a reason." She grabbed the side of her skirts and walked away.

Hazel laughed. "I'm sorry."

"You think you're so funny. I almost told her what I really was thinking." He smiled with her, and the sound of her laugh made his heart happy in a way he'd never known before. This woman, with her dancing eyes and clever wit, would be the death of his ordinary life—and he didn't mind one bit.

"That was quick thinking. And for what it's worth, I thought it was a clever joke." Hazel waited while he opened the cemetery gate for her.

"No one can please Alberta. But she's not the girl I'm worried about pleasing, anyway. The one I care most about just had a good laugh, so I'll consider this day a success." They meandered through headstones, commenting on names and dates and wondering after the lives of these men and women who had come before them. "My father's grave is over here."

"I would have liked to have known him."

"He was the best man I've ever known." He put an arm around her. Perhaps Alberta was right and couples were becoming more comfortable, but he couldn't see how leaning on a friend while

319

discussing the loss of a loved one was wrong. "I've always wanted to be like him."

"I think you are. You tell the same jokes." She turned her head and looked up at him. "What do you think he would have thought of me?"

He pulled her tighter. "He would have liked you." Gilbert tried to imagine his father alive and there beside them. He knew he would offer wisdom and advice. Gilbert played it safe though. He smirked and said, "He would have said that you ought to be proud of who you are today, and then he would have laughed and said that I was right and your hair is red."

Hazel and I spent the evening with my parents. Before leaving, they told me privately how much they've come to care for her. I think it's because she makes them laugh. She makes me laugh too. It's been almost six months, and I've laughed more in that time than ever before. The days have flown by, and they've been good days.

I heard Joanna has married, and I'm surprised to feel no remorse over it. I never thought I'd be glad I was forced to marry, but I don't think I'd have it any other way.

I am sitting here next to the bed, watching Hazel sleep. She looks peaceful and less mischievous when she's resting. I am married to a friend. One I love a little more each day.

Tears dripped from Hazel's eyes and onto the page as she read the last line over and over. Warmth radiated through her every time she read the word *love*. They never got to see what was ahead for them. They never shared children or grew old together. Theirs was not the love of sweethearts or the aged. Rather, it was an unexpected love that never got the chance to fully bloom. But even in its tender early stages, it was real.

She no longer felt like she was closing the book on Nathaniel unfinished. She was able to close it with a smile, like an author who knows the story is complete. Hazel brought the journal to her lips, pressed a kiss to it, set it aside, and made her way to the dining room for breakfast.

"Why are you so happy this morning?" Ina whispered moments later when she sat beside her. "Did something happen with Gilbert that you haven't told me?"

"No. I've told you everything. But maybe something will happen." She twirled her spoon around in her oatmeal. "You were right. I don't know how to explain it, but last night I prayed for direction and this morning I found a new sense of peace." She groaned, then laughed. "It's hard for me to explain."

"Are you telling me you're ready to forgive yourself?" Ina asked.

"I think I am. I've been thinking, and maybe romance is not a game of chess."

"More like a three-legged race. You can only win if you work together," Ina whispered with a smile on her face. "And it's full of exhilarating bursts of speed and stumbles and joy when you cross the finish line."

Hazel set her spoon down and nodded. "Yes. I like that. I've never run in a three-legged race, but I think that's got to be what real romance is like."

"All this whispering. Do the two of you have some guilty secret you are keeping from the rest of us?" Mrs. Northly asked. She set a basket of bread in the center of the table and scowled at them.

"No, of course not," Ina said. "I've already announced my news."

"That Duncan fellow."

"Yes, Duncan." Ina smiled brightly. "We will be getting married in a few short weeks. I hope you'll come."

"I may." Mrs. Northly nodded. "A wholesome marriage is a cause for celebration, even if you're rushing into it." The woman's eyes narrowed toward Hazel. "And what about you? You going to marry the dentist you are always out with?"

"He is rather nice to look at." Hazel gave her a questioning look. "Don't you think?"

"You're an impossible one. I'm not sure what he sees in you."

"I'm sorry, Mrs. Northly, but I knew you wouldn't like whatever I had to say." She gathered her dishes in her hands and headed for the kitchen. "I don't know if I'll marry him. I guess that all depends on if he ever asks me."

She waited for the sick twisting of her insides to come or a wave of nausea. But the only thing she felt was a sweet longing to enter the dental office and see Gil's handsome face. Hazel retreated to her room for a few minutes of solitude before she left for work. Half of that time was spent staring at the painting done by Gilbert, with its warm orange and red leaves and autumn sky. Each brushstroke painted meticulously. What would a future be like with such a man?

"You'll be late," Ina called from outside her door.

"I'm coming." She grabbed her flute box and lunch tin.

Once outside, they both shivered as the winter chill crept through their coats. "Did you mean it?" Ina asked while tightening her scarf around her mouth and nose. "That you'd marry Gilbert if he asked?"

"I probably should not have said that to her, especially since I'm not sure. I think I might say yes, but I'd like to have at least a good solid week of no worries before I decided."

"After this weekend, you may have just that." Ina grabbed her hand. "Imagine, we could both be married to the best of men before long."

Hazel squeezed her friend's hand in response. "Shhh, don't tell Gilbert what I said. It's merely a dream. Well, more like an idea right now—and not one I'm decided on. It may never happen, and I don't think I could ever set foot in the dental office again if he heard of our conversation."

"You may not have to work there after this weekend. I think we ought to tell him. I'd love to see the look on his face."

"Not funny," Hazel said. "For now, we still have to see if Hugo can catch the captain and Patrick. It's much too soon to decide when my time at the office will end."

They were at the crossroads where they said their farewell each morning—Ina off to the schoolhouse and Hazel to work as an attending lady. Such a small part of her day, but one she cherished.

"Duncan is taking me to dinner tonight, and we will make wedding plans. I want to hear all about your day when I get home." Ina hugged her quickly. "I'll see you later."

"Have a wonderful evening." Hazel waved and watched her friend skip off down the road. Then she turned and walked toward the dental office.

"You've brought your flute," Gilbert said when she walked through the door. His face was clean-shaven and his tie straight. Such a handsome man.

"I thought during the noon break I might play. With the weather turning cold, I don't think I'll walk. But I'm so nervous for the coming weekend. I knew I couldn't just sit."

"I hope you'll let me listen."

"I had planned to play for you." She ran her hand along the flute box. "I have a new song I want you to hear."

The day passed like a fairy tale. They stole glances over the heads of patients, she played her heart into her music when they were alone, and before she left, he offered to walk her home. Simple pleasures.

"You have a letter," Mrs. Northly said as they approached the boardinghouse.

Hazel grabbed Gilbert's hand and pulled him faster toward Mrs. Northly, who stood on the porch, waving the letter in the air. "It must be my parents."

As soon as she had the letter in her hands, she looked around for a warm place to read it with Gilbert. "May we read it in the parlor?"

"You haven't made arrangements to use the parlor," Mrs. Northly said.

"Fine. We'll sit here in the freezing cold and read it. I'll have to sit very close to him so that I don't catch my death in this weather." She inched closer to Gilbert. "You don't mind, do you, Gil?"

He cleared his throat. "I'll keep you warm."

Mrs. Northly's eyes grew large. "Stop this nonsense and go into the parlor."

"That's so kind of you." Hazel stepped past her into the house, with Gilbert at her heels. Once out of Mrs. Northly's earshot, she whispered, "Do you think I'll get a lecture later?"

"The whole house is going to hear about your behavior." He winked at her. "Let's read your letter before she decides we've shared too much time in each other's presence."

"I'm nervous. I want my family in my life. I want their love and forgiveness, and I pray this letter is an invitation home. But if it's not, that doesn't diminish my worth."

"Only God knows our true worth."

"Yes, that's what I have been reminded of." She broke the seal of the letter, looked to Gilbert once more for encouragement, and then read.

Dear Hazel,

Come home and be with us. With Mathilda so sick, we have had reason to pause and ponder what matters in our lives. Knowing you are free and living among us but not with us has weighed on our hearts as we have endured this current trial. We did not know your whereabouts to summon you home until now or we would have written sooner.

Forgive us. We are family and wish to have you near.

There is so much to write and so many questions to ask, but with your sister convalescing, we will have to wait until we are under the same roof again. We will be by the window watching for your return.

Love,
Mother and Father

PS: We have not been threatened or unsafe.

Hazel looked up from the page. "They want me to come home."

Gilbert's face had creases where she'd never seen them before. "I'm glad for you."

"Are you?"

Gilbert nodded.

"Gil, I can't make sense of it all," she said through her tears. "I want to go home. I want it so badly I hurt, but I want . . . I want other things too."

"Time to go." Mrs. Northly entered the room with a frown on her face. "Say your goodbyes."

"I'll see you tomorrow." Hazel stood and walked beside him to the door and out onto the porch, where they were once again alone. "Gil?"

"Yes."

She kept the words she wanted to say inside and simply said, "Thank you."

"For what?"

"For being you." She gripped his hand tightly, desiring a better goodbye but settling for the touch of his hand. She promised to see him the next day, then hurried to her room, where the tears flowed freely.

TWENTY-FOUR

"Did you pack everything?" Ina asked Hazel as they readied to leave for Buffalo.

She nodded.

"I'm sure your family will be glad to have you back." Ina's face reddened.

"I've sent word letting them know we'll be at the Williamses while the case is sorted out, and I'll be coming home afterward. They're to notify me if there's an urgent reason to come sooner." She'd wanted to go home straightaway but feared she would bring danger with her and in the end decided she needed to first hear the latest news about the case.

"You'll come to the wedding, won't you?" Duncan asked. "Even if you are settled back in Buffalo?"

"Nothing could keep me from it." Hazel looked out the window as soon as she was settled in for the carriage ride, afraid she'd be unable to maintain her controlled, unaffected demeanor if she met anyone's eye. The school and the church were visible out her window, and past them she saw the little hill she'd sat on next to Gilbert. It was no longer adorned with trees full of red and yellow leaves, as a dusting of snow now covered it. But it was still their hill. What would it look like in the fresh greens of spring?

As if on cue, Gilbert put his arm around her and eased her toward him. "Amherst is not so far from Buffalo." He said the words but he did not sound convinced. "We'll see you."

"Why all the down faces?" Eddie asked. "We're supposed to be celebrating. Aren't we bound for Buffalo to right wrongs and liberate the innocent? Seems we should smile and be a bit more jovial than this."

They all nodded, then sat in silence again as the driver turned down the street leading away from Amherst. Hazel tried to think of something lighthearted to say, but in the end, she looked out the window and watched the city she'd come to love fade away. The drive felt longer than normal, the tension palpable in the air as they all worried about the case—and the future.

"It's that one up ahead," Hazel said when they neared their destination and the long, awkward drive reached its conclusion.

"It's so grand. I've never been in a house so large." Ina reached up and touched her red face. "I'm not sure this is a good idea."

Duncan pulled her hand away from her chin and held it. "It'll be fine. Hazel says they're good people."

"They are. You'll see. We'll all be welcomed."

As soon as the door opened, Elizabeth was

there greeting them. Her arms found their way around Hazel first, and then she reached for the others. "I'm so glad you've all come. It's lovely seeing your young faces."

Hugo entered the room, and Hazel gasped. The right side of his face was blue and purple, swollen with a scabbed-over gash below his eye. "What happened?"

"It's been an eventful week," he said as he touched his face and winced. "Let me meet our guests, and then I'll tell you all how I bruised my face. I haven't had a story about throwing punches in a long time."

"I expect he'll be telling everyone about this for years to come." Elizabeth's eyes trailed her husband's every move. "I'd prefer we just forget it. Blood and bruises make my stomach sick."

Hugo laughed at his wife's comments while he shook hands with everyone and led them deeper into the massive home. "Tell me, how did you find yourself involved in all this?" he asked Gilbert.

"Hazel is . . . well, I'm a dentist and she was my lady in attendance. I sympathized with her cause as soon as she told me."

She crept up to his side and laced her arm in his. "I *am* his lady in attendance. That's how we became acquainted, but now Gilbert is a dear friend."

"I'm grateful beyond words that our Hazel has

found such helpful companionship. You're a good man to see past all the slander and harm done to her. I wish we'd been as clear-sighted, and perhaps this all could have been resolved years ago." Hugo frowned remorsefully. "If everyone will follow us to the dining room, we've prepared a meal."

"Let them freshen up first. I'm told the meal is not quite ready," Elizabeth said. "I'll have someone show you to your rooms. We'll meet back here."

Fifteen minutes later they were back. Hazel had repinned her hair and hung her dresses before returning.

"Won't you tell us what happened?" Hazel asked as soon as she spotted Hugo again. They were all making their way to the dining room.

"You always were a little impatient." He spoke to her in a gentle voice, like a father speaking to his child. "I promise to tell you the whole story."

Large double doors separated the dining room from the entryway. They creaked open on oversized hinges. The guests were greeted with the scent of rich foods. The table ran the full length of the room, with one end set lavishly for the party. Candlesticks, flowers, and full place settings. She breathed deeply, letting the aroma fill her lungs and the memories her heart.

"Mrs. Northly ought to take a lesson from their

chef. I've smelled nothing like this before," Ina whispered to Hazel. "It's so fancy."

When the guests were settled into their seats, Hugo stood. "I'd like to welcome you all to our home. What you've done for our late son and for our daughter-in-law will not soon be forgotten. While you eat, I'll tell you the progress we've made in the case. Enjoy your meal." He motioned for them to begin.

Forks and knives clanked against the fine plates as they all dug into the savory feast. For Hazel, each mouth-watering bite brought back memories and created new ones.

"We were able to corner the captain making an exchange with a man we later learned worked for Patrick." Hugo pointed proudly to his blackened eye. "I hired men to watch from every angle. But the more I thought about Nathaniel, the more I felt a need to be there. I sat perched in a nearby building waiting and watching. It was late in the night, well after midnight, when a group of men approached the ship. The captain, Jacob, was there, and we all witnessed an exchange of money. I grew angrier and angrier as I realized that for a pile of money, my son was dead. I left my hideout and confronted the captain."

Elizabeth, sitting beside him, sniffled. "I'm sorry. It still worries me thinking of the danger you were in. I could have lost you."

Hugo patted his wife's shoulder. "I was safe.

The other men all moved in with me. I didn't even say a thing to him. I just hit him with all the force I could muster. Before anyone could stop him, he returned the blow." He rubbed the side of his face. "We don't have to worry any longer, because he is now in jail along with the man he was dealing with. They were interrogated and gave up Patrick's name, adding to the case we've already built against him. We haven't apprehended Patrick yet, but with any luck that'll happen soon. The information all of you put together made this possible." He paused while the staff served another platter of food.

"We've also been able to bring in many of the men listed in Nathaniel's notes, and although it will take weeks for them all to testify and be found guilty, we're making good headway. It turns out we were not the only people trying to cleanse the police force of anyone crooked. When I approached the mayor for help, he sent me to several detectives who were working on cases of corruption within the police force. With our information, they were able to solve not only this case but others as well."

Hazel listened to the recounting with awed amazement. They'd captured the captain and were about to get Patrick, and that meant . . . She couldn't process the words. How could it be so? Mere weeks ago, she'd been unable to find anyone to help her and now men were behind bars.

Elizabeth rose from her seat and stood by Hugo's side. "Tomorrow," she said, "we've made arrangements to have Charlotte testify. She's nervous but determined to meet with Judge Lawson at the courthouse. And, Hazel, once she declares her former testimony false, your name will be cleared. A reporter is scheduled to interview you. We want the news to be in the paper so everyone will know you were sentenced in error. We've also been in correspondence with your family, and your sister's health is precarious but stable. They're expecting you tomorrow."

"Tomorrow I'll be cleared and I'll see my sister?" Hazel set down her fork and stared at them. "Tomorrow? It all sounds too simple."

"We've been working tirelessly all week. I had to hire my own army of men to watch the ships and brothel, and even then it wouldn't have been possible if we hadn't had all the information you gathered and that Nathaniel left." Hugo's gaze found Hazel's. "I think it was more than hard work though."

"You do?"

"I've felt closer to Nathaniel all week. More at peace. Some greater power must have his hands in it." Hugo raised his glass. "For Nathaniel," he said, and they all raised their glasses with his.

When the murmur died down, Gilbert dared to ask what they were all wondering. "Does that mean"—he cleared his throat—"that you've found the man who . . . who took your son's life?"

"We aren't sure. I've heard different accounts, but two people have said it was Jacob." Hugo reached for his wife's hand. "He betrayed us. All these years I believed he was a friend, or at the least a good captain. He was neither. But we have Hazel home, and she's been good enough to forgive us. Tonight we'll dwell on our blessings."

Eddie raised his glass.

"To Hazel," he said, and everyone joined in.

Hugo and Elizabeth smiled at her with familial love. Ina had tears trailing down her cheeks, and when she met Hazel's eyes, she said, "They're happy tears. You're getting your life back."

Duncan nodded when she looked at him. Even Eddie looked happy. "I always knew you didn't do it," he said, earning himself a glare from her. She couldn't keep it though, and soon she smiled back at him.

She looked at Gilbert, who had a smile on his face, but she saw sadness behind it.

"The future's yours now," he said. If they'd been alone, she would have put her hand on his arm and let her eyes hold his. She would have told him that this moment would never have happened without him. But they were not alone.

Hugo and Elizabeth controlled most of the dinner conversation. They discussed not only the case but also stories from the past and even expressed some of their hopes for the future. When the meal concluded, they stood and left the dishes on the table as they guided everyone to the parlor. There was a time when Hazel had not thought twice about who washed the dishes, but now leaving them felt odd. Had she been away from this world for too long to fall back in step with it?

When the conversations began to wane and the sun had long ago disappeared beyond the horizon, they bid goodnight to Hugo and Elizabeth and one by one left for their assigned guest rooms.

"Where are you going?" Hazel asked when she spotted Gilbert inching toward the door and his boots. "You'll wake everyone going out at this hour."

"I wasn't leaving, not back to Amherst anyway. I just thought I'd go for a walk."

"At eleven?" she asked, utterly confused. "Why?"

"I like to think while I walk." He set his shoes back next to the door. "I'll stay. It was just a whim."

"Let's go upstairs. Tomorrow will be a big day." She pulled him toward the stairs. "Perhaps there will be time for a walk tomorrow."

The massive house felt even larger in the dark as they made their way up the stairs to the guest rooms. Hallways, doors, and more hallways.

"My room is that way." He pointed to his left. "Second door to the left."

"And mine is that way." She pointed in the opposite direction. "Third room on the right."

"Until tomorrow, then."

Rather than go to her room, she stepped closer so she could see his face better. The corners of his mouth drooped down. "Why the long face?"

He shrugged. "Just tired, I suppose."

Hazel watched him, but his expression remained pensive, causing an ache to grow in her own heart. She pushed onto her tiptoes and kissed his scruffy cheek. "I think Clara would say you looked like a poor orphan boy tonight. Tell her I did what I could to lift your spirits."

His frown deepened.

Another kiss to his cheek, and he chuckled a little. "I didn't realize all I had to do was look a little downcast and I'd get a kiss."

"I think I must be in a particularly charitable mood. Or maybe I've always had a soft spot for lonely orphans."

"One more, then," he said, offering her an exaggerated playful frown, but he couldn't hide the twinkle in his eye. Slowly, she put a hand on one side of his face and eased him closer to her. Her heart beat faster, and she was anxious to place her lips on his face once again. This time she kissed him slower, letting her lips linger on his cheek as she savored the feel of his warm skin. The moment lost its seriousness when Hazel laughed. She put her hands over her mouth, trying to cover it.

"You're horrible," she whispered once she was back in control. "That frown could win you all sorts of affection. You're not sad at all—you're just toying with me."

"No I'm not. I'm terribly sad." He frowned even bigger. "I'm so sad and lonely. Have pity on a poor orphan boy."

She swatted his arm. "Stop, you'll make me laugh again. You know it's not right to trick someone into kissing you."

"Very well. How about one more simply because we are celebrating the freedom you will gain tomorrow when Charlotte testifies?"

She pursed her lips and looked him over, wanting to understand what was happening between them. His frown was gone, replaced by an earnest face full of longing. She swallowed, wondering if her face had the same desire written on it. Surely her heart did. She inched closer. "I'll give you one more, but not because you are sad or lonely and not because I'll be free tomorrow. I'll give you one more because you never doubted. And because you are the kindest man I've ever met. I knew it from the start. I felt safe around you. You've given me wings."

She watched his Adam's apple bob up and down as she slowly moved her hands back to his face. At her touch, he put his hands on her waist and urged her closer. She lifted herself up onto her tiptoes, and this time when she pressed her lips to his cheek, she sighed. With her face still near his, she said rather breathlessly, "No more frowns."

"Not after that." He looked into her eyes, brought a hand to her face, and ran his fingers along her cheekbone. In the darkness he whispered, "Goodnight, Red."

They parted ways, each bound for their room. Hazel walked as carefully as she could, softly padding down the hall, but still Ina heard her and poked her head out of her bedroom doorway.

"Hazel, is that you?"

"I was so quiet. How did you hear me?"

"Mrs. Northly always says your laugh could wake an entire village."

"She says that about me?" Hazel nearly laughed again.

"She says all kinds of things about you. Most of them aren't true, but you do have a rather loud laugh. Tell me what you and Gilbert were doing in the hall?"

"He was feeling a little down, and I tried to help him feel better."

"I don't think that was all that happened." Ina scrutinized her. "Why are you grinning?"

Drat that Ina and her perceptiveness. "I just . . . well . . . I might have told him that he changed my life." Hazel smiled, proud of the honest but elusive answer she gave.

"Hmm . . . I believe you did say those words.

Now tell me what else you *did?*" Ina's brow was raised like a mother who'd caught her child snitching sweets.

"Ina!"

"I knew it. You were kissing in the hall, weren't you?" Ina clapped her hands together. "Don't lie to me. But do tell me all about it."

Hazel groaned. "Just a friendly kiss. It's not what you think."

"Someday soon I hope you'll stop lying to yourself. When you do, I don't think Gilbert will have a reason to be sad any longer. You know he worries you will stay here and never come back. That's what makes him sad, but he's too good of a man to ask you to leave the world you've wanted for so long for him."

"I need to see my family, but after that, if all goes well, I do intend to come back to him."

"He worries because he cares. Did he kiss you back?" Ina asked, her voice low.

"It wasn't that sort of a kiss."

It *was* just a friendly kiss, wasn't it? She retreated to her room, hoping she'd have a reason to give more friendly kisses soon. Or perhaps, when the dust settled and her sister was well, a kiss that was more than friendly.

CHAPTER
TWENTY-FIVE

"You're telling us you never owned the jewels that were found in Hazel Williams's home?" Judge Lawson asked the shaking Charlotte the next morning at the courthouse.

"No, I never did." Charlotte rubbed her hands together, then set them in the lap of her faded blue dress. "I just said those things 'cause I didn't have no money, and Patrick said he'd give me some. He put the jewels in her house. I never knew nothing about Hazel."

"Was Patrick Harper a violent man?"

"He could be when he was in a foul mood or if he'd been drinkin'. He said he'd kill me if I ever told anyone about the jewelry and the money. I believed him too, but a man like that's got to be stopped."

Judge Lawson wrote a few notes. "You needn't worry. I expect he'll be apprehended soon enough. Do you also testify that he brought opium into the brothel and sold it from there?"

"He met people there, and they sold it all over the city. Sometimes he left some for the girls, but mostly he sold it to other people. A lot of us can swear to that. He never saw us as nobody, so he'd say all kinds of stuff with us in the room."

"I'll keep that in mind. If you think of anything else, please let us know." The judge jotted down a few more observations, then closed his book. "That will be all for today."

"What of Hazel's case?" Hugo asked.

"It's as good as official. I have plenty of evidence to reverse her verdict." Judge Lawson turned to Hazel. "On behalf of the court, I apologize to you for the pain you've suffered and the years you've lost."

Hazel stood and walked to the judge. "Thank you for helping set it straight." Then she walked to Charlotte. "Thank you for coming in. You don't know what it means to me."

"I shouldn't have told them lies."

"It's forgiven." Hazel hugged the woman. "You saved me today, and that's all that matters. You were very brave."

"The reporter says he needs to get your answers soon if he's going to get your story in tomorrow's paper," Hugo said. "Will you excuse us?" he asked Charlotte.

Hazel hugged Charlotte once more, then walked over to Mr. Oskovy, who'd sat in the back of the room all morning taking notes and listening. His spectacles were low on his nose and in his hand was a pencil with a chewed-on end.

"I've already gotten most of the details from Mr. Williams. Is it right for me to assume he is to credit with your case's reversal?"

"Hugo and Elizabeth were monumental in all that has taken place this week. I'm immensely grateful for their support and efforts. But they should not receive sole credit for all that has happened."

He looked up from his paper. "Who, then?"

"Doctor Gilbert Watts of Amherst believed me innocent from the beginning. His brother, Edward Watts, put many of the clues together. Attorney Duncan Franklin, also of Amherst, helped us navigate the old cases. His betrothed, Ina White, was with us, supporting our cause. They care little for praise, but they are due." She looked to the other end of the room, where her four friends were sitting and visiting as they waited for her. "I've been blessed."

He scribbled on his notepad before looking up and asking, "What plans do you have now that your sentence has been reversed?"

"I hope to spend time with my family. That is the only real plan I've made."

"Are you angry? You spent five years in a reformatory."

Hazel paused. Words would never capture all she'd been through, all she'd lost, and all she'd gained. "I would not have picked the trials I have endured, but there's no going back, and I've learned that being angry does no good. I refuse to carry the burden of regret and have chosen to be grateful I am where I am today and not dwell on the path that has led me here."

He looked up and studied her for a moment. "I pride myself on being an unbiased reporter, but I must say that I admire your choice." He cleared his throat. "I'll write this up and get it in the paper tomorrow. I expect it'll be the talk of the town, that *you* will be the talk of the town." He grabbed the hat that sat next to him, put it on, then stood to leave. "It'll be a good day at the presses."

"Glad I can keep them rolling." Rubbing her palms together, she pivoted toward the group and crossed the room. "I'm done," she said when she reached them. "We're free to go."

She froze as her own words sank in. It was over. A lump formed in her throat. Could this all be true?

"It's over," she said, her voice trembling.

Gilbert clapped his hands, and soon the others joined in. Their excitement grew more exuberant as they cheered and embraced one another. Hazel's eyes glistened. It was finished! When the shock wore off, the joy came in earnest.

"Duncan is going to look over a few notes with Hugo. The rest of us are planning to go back with Elizabeth," Ina said.

"I think I'll walk from here to my parents' house. I promised Gilbert we'd take a stroll today." She cocked a smile at him. "Will you walk with me?"

"Of course. But only if you promise to hold

your head extra high and look everyone straight in the eye."

"I promise. But I can't promise I won't run and skip and giggle like a schoolgirl."

He grinned. "What are we waiting for?"

They said goodbye to the rest of the group, then stepped away from the courthouse.

"How do you feel?" Gilbert asked her.

"I realized this week that no matter what happened in the courtroom, it was time to forgive myself. Not because of what the judge said but because it was the truth." She straightened her spine, not caring if anyone recognized her. Let them stare, or let them turn away if they wished. She knew her heart. "But still, there's something sweet about knowing others can now clearly see the truth."

"Tomorrow when the paper comes out, everyone will know," he said as they rounded a corner. "And today your parents will hear the good news."

"I'm anxious." She brought her hands to her mouth and blew hot breath on them. "It's gotten cold so fast this year."

"Where are your gloves?"

"I forgot them this morning. I think I was more nervous than I admitted." She blew again.

"Give me your hand. I'll warm it." He offered his hand. Hazel hesitated only a moment before accepting it and enjoying the warmth from his large hand.

"Thank you."

"It's the least I can do." He squeezed her fingers. "Eddie said he could hear you laughing in the hall last night. He interrogated me."

"Ina said she could too. I had no idea I had such a boisterous laugh. Ina cornered me and asked what happened. If it hadn't been so dark, I think she'd have seen my face burning up. I was so embarrassed."

"You do have a laugh that carries, but I like it. In fact, I like everything that happened in the hallway last night." He brought her fingers to his lips and kissed them, sending waves of happiness through her whole body. "You made me promise that I'd remain only a friend. Is that still your wish?"

She let go of his hand and moved to his other side. "This hand is cold now," she said, taking his other one in hers. "I think I may want to take back those words. First, though, I want to see my family, make sure Mathilda is all right, and just breathe the sweet air of freedom."

"I don't mean to rush you." He took a deep breath. "But you are my favorite person to walk with, and someday if you're willing, I'd love to laugh with you and feel your kisses on my cheek each night before bed. I didn't think I would ever find a woman I could be comfortable around, but now I cannot imagine life without you."

She stopped walking and looked up at him. "Gil, promise me that when I'm ready, you'll say all those things again."

He let his free hand brush her face and slowly trace the outline of her lips. "I promise you that when you're ready, this not-so-quiet dentist who can never find the right words will give you the most eloquent confession of love."

"Of love?" she whispered, still reeling from his touch. "Love?"

"Of love." He bent so near to her, she was certain he'd kiss her. "I love you, Hazel." His lips brushed her cheek lightly, like they had so long ago at the corn husking. And just like before, it sent a fire racing through her.

Stepping away, he straightened his coat and said, "Don't get any ideas. That was just a friendly kiss. When you're ready and you give me permission, I'll give you a real one."

She struggled to calm her racing heart. "Who are you? The Gil I know requires a red ear of corn to kiss the girls."

"You've changed me. Now all I need is your permission." He grabbed her hand and led her down the street again. "Let's get you home. The sooner you reconnect with your family, the sooner you'll return to Amherst and we can start our life together."

Minutes later, Hazel and Gilbert stood in front of two enormous entry doors. She picked up the knocker but didn't let it go.

"Are you going to knock?" Gilbert asked in a

gentle voice. "You read their letter. You know they want you back."

"I want them to see how I've changed." She took a deep breath, then forced her hand to release the knocker. The sound of it thudding made her body tense. She waited, listening for the sound of approaching feet. When it came, her heart threatened to leap from her chest. Time moved slower as she waited for the doors that had been closed so long to her to open.

Julia, the maid, glared at her through a crack in the door. "What are you doing here?" she hissed. "They got trouble enough with Mathilda sick. They don't need you begging at the door."

Hazel cringed as a multitude of memories flooded back to her. *You've changed,* she reminded herself. But still, a tremor raced up her spine.

"The Bradshaws are expecting her." Gilbert put his hand on the small of Hazel's back. "Please tell them she's here."

Julia looked behind her and sighed. "Wait outside."

Gilbert kept his steadying hand on Hazel's back while they waited. In a soft but strong voice, he reassured her, reminding her of her worth and importance and bolstering her resolve.

"Hazel!" She heard her father's voice before she saw him. "Hazel!" he called as he approached the door. Her heart that had been suffering from trepidation now leapt at the sound of his welcoming voice.

"Father!" she called back, and then the door opened wide and there he was standing before her. His face looked older and his hair had lost its dark luster, but her heart knew him despite any outward differences.

"You've come home!" He too looked at her intently as though he could not believe she were real. "You're back."

"Yes, and I'm so happy to be home." She stepped inside and put her hand on his arm and nearly cried. There he was, flesh and bone. "It's been so long."

"It's been too long." Creases near his eyes grew deeper as he drank in the sight of his daughter. "You're our Hazel, and you're back." He clung to her and she buried her face in his shoulder and their tears mixed together. The tears were sad, they were happy, they were a summary of the long years apart and their hope for the future. Warmth seeped deep inside her, filling her bit by bit as the embrace continued.

"I'm sorry for everything."

"None of that matters. Not anymore." His welcoming arms confirmed his words.

Remembering all that had happened, she pulled away. "How is Mathilda?"

He ran his hands through his hair. "She's frail." Her usually composed and serious father blubbered, "I'm worried. I'm so afraid for her."

"I'm sorry I haven't been here," Hazel whispered. She meant to sound strong, but seeing her father so overwhelmed increased her worry tenfold. "Let me help you care for her."

"I've been so afraid that I'd never again have all my children here." He kissed her forehead. "But you're home."

"I am here. I'll help, and it's my hope you'll see I'm a changed woman."

Her father squeezed her hand and looked to Gilbert. "Who's your friend?"

"This is Gilbert Watts. He's a dentist in Amherst, and I've been working for him as a lady in attendance. He's one of the people who helped me clear my name."

"What about the money we gave you?" Her father's brows formed a deep furrow.

"I'll tell you everything, but right now I need to see Mathilda. I've been so worried." She tried to smile, but all she felt was concern for her sister.

"I want to hear every detail." He offered her his arm, then said to Gilbert, "Come meet the rest of the family. Then we'll discuss some way I can repay you for your kindness."

"No need," Gilbert said as he followed them down the hall.

The sickroom was on the main floor beside the large master bedroom. Hazel clung to her father as they peered inside. Her first glimpses of Mathilda's thin, frail body caused her to cover her mouth to avoid crying out. She'd grown from a child to a young woman while Hazel was incarcerated. Her skin color and sunken cheeks testified to the battle she faced physically. Hazel's mother sat beside her holding one of the woman's hands, her head bent as though she were praying.

"What's wrong with Matty? I know she's sick, but what is it?" she whispered to her father.

"The doctor says she has a severe case of pneumonia. She's never had the strong constitution you have. When she got sick . . . that's when I realized how wrong I'd been to send you away. We should have been together." He stared off into the sickroom. "It hasn't looked good. Not from the start."

"Will she be all right?"

"No one knows. She seems weaker every day, but the doctor says we still have reason to hope. If she will only fight, she might regain the strength she's lost. Let me tell them you are here." He stepped into the room and quietly spoke to Hazel's mother. Hazel held her breath and waited. Maria's head jerked up, and her eyes, red-rimmed and tired, grew large. She turned toward Hazel and then a sob escaped. She leaned over and said something to Matty before standing.

"I'm sorry, Hazel." Gilbert put a hand on her back. "Forget what I said about hurrying back.

This is where you're needed now. Stay with your sister." Gilbert kissed the top of her head. "Be strong. That's what she'll need from you."

She put a hand on his forearm. "Thank you for understanding."

"My dear girl." Her mother emerged from the sickroom and grabbed Hazel's hands in her own. "You're home."

"I'm home!" It was all too easy, too perfect. So many nights she'd worried over her return, unsure if she'd be welcomed. Matty was sick, and perhaps that's what had changed everything. When life and death wrestled, everything else fell away, leaving only the most important things in their wake. "I've missed you."

They held each other at arm's length, both staring dazedly at the other as they accepted that this dream was real. She let go of her mother and nudged Gilbert forward. "I want you to meet Gilbert Watts. I'll tell you my whole story soon, but this man was there for me when I was alone." Her mother pursed her lips, then smiled. Hazel sensed her concern and added, "I've been working in his dental office. He's a good man."

"I'm grateful you had someone there for you." She patted Gilbert's arm. "Thank you for all you've done."

Two of Hazel's brothers came thumping down the stairs. They stopped in their tracks when they saw Hazel and Gilbert. Both sets of eyes looked to their mother for direction. When she nodded, giving them permission to welcome Hazel, they came closer. The hallway filled with the ruckus of reunion as Hazel accepted their welcome and she in return introduced Gilbert.

"Bernice and Fred are over at Aunt Sarah's," Maria explained. "I think they'll be back soon. Go in and see Mathilda. Lift her spirits if you can."

Hazel and Gilbert stepped into the sickroom and sat beside the bed. Hazel put a hand on her sister's thin shoulder. "Matty, it's me, Hazel."

"Hazel?" Mathilda turned her head toward her big sister. Her voice was weak, but her eyes brightened with recognition. "Are you a dream?"

"It feels like a dream to be back with you. I heard my Matty was sick, and I thought you might need your bossy older sister to come home and tell you to get well." She rubbed her sister's fragile arm. "Get well, little sister. You must. I have so many things to tell you and so many things I want to do with you."

"I missed you." Her brow glistened with sweat. Hazel reached for the rag beside the basin and wrung it out. "Who's with you?"

"This is Gilbert Watts. He's a good friend of mine and wanted to meet you." She pulled Gilbert closer. "Gil, this is Mathilda. She's my baby sister."

Mathilda tried to prop herself up on her elbow.

"I'm not a baby. I went to a social and was asked to dance five times."

Gilbert leaned forward. "Five times. I haven't even danced with Hazel that much. You must have been the belle of the ball. It's nice to finally meet you." He paused and smiled his warm, friendly smile down at her. "I heard you liked snow. Did you know it's snowing outside right now?"

Mathilda nodded her weak head. "I love snow."

"You get well, and we'll all go out in it. You and I will throw snowballs at Hazel." Gilbert elbowed Hazel, causing her to squawk involuntarily. "Do you think she'd like that?"

"She's got a wicked temper," Mathilda said weakly. "But I think it'd be fun."

"Then we'll risk her temper and do it. You get better as quick as you can." He sat up straighter and spoke to Hazel. "I'm going to go back and let the others know you are with your family. I'll have someone send your belongings here."

"Tell them I'm sorry I can't say goodbye, and tell Elizabeth I'll see her soon." She squeezed his arm, wishing there was some way to make him understand she wanted to be here and in Amherst with him.

He stood and moved away from the bed. "Get better, Matty."

"I will."

Hazel stood too. "Will you be back? Or is this goodbye?"

"I think you should have time with your family. Take care of them and enjoy being back in the fold. If you need me, send word and I'll come straightaway. No matter what, I'll come." He looked past Hazel toward Mathilda. "Take care of Matty. We've already made plans for when she is well again."

Hazel nodded and braced herself for his departure. "Gil."

"Yes." He stepped forward, closing the small distance, and cradled her face with his hand. "Take care of yourself."

"I will." She put her hand on top of his. "Take care of our patients, and make sure Clara feeds you. You know how I feel about poor orphans. Besides, I have plans that involve you."

"Plans? You aren't going to throw snow at me, are you?"

"No. Other plans."

For a long moment, they stood lost in each other's eyes, his hand warming the side of her face as he traced the curve of her cheekbone. The moment faded as she moved his hand away and immediately felt its absence.

"Get her better so I can find out. And be careful. I don't like leaving knowing Patrick is still out there."

"I'll be safe. I'm sure the police will bring him in any day now."

He nodded and with a heavy tread, turned and

walked away from her. Their comfortable days spent together were over, at least for now.

"She's staying with her family. They'll keep her safe. I'm sure they will . . ." Gilbert said to Ina through gritted teeth. Fear had been his companion as he walked away from Hazel. Fear for himself as he struggled to make peace with an uncertain future, fear for her as she nursed her sister and reconnected with the past, and fear for all of their safety as the last pieces of the case were wrapped up. "Her sister didn't look well at all. She's frail. I've never seen a girl so thin. Hazel's had so much disappointment already. I pray she doesn't lose her sister."

"How long will she stay?"

He shook his head, wishing he had an answer. If he knew for certain she was returning and when, he could count down. But there was no way of putting a time limit on illness and recovery and no guarantee she'd want to leave Buffalo now that she was back.

"I don't know. But she needs to be there." Gilbert looked away, afraid she'd see his worry. "I don't know what she'll end up doing."

"She'll come back. She loves you."

Gilbert ran his hand along his broad jaw. "Has she told you that?"

"Not exactly, but I know she does. It's only there's been so much happening. She was afraid to make any promises she couldn't keep, and for so long she doubted herself."

He tightened his grip on his bag. "She'll be welcomed back to society. She may decide she loves this life more than my quiet one. I can hardly blame her. I can't promise her a life of excitement." He moved toward the door. "I have to go."

"You did a good thing helping her."

"We all did. I don't regret that. Be sure to stop by the office sometime. I'll be there every day, same as always." But he'd be alone. No humming, no infectious laughter. He needed to go. He needed to get away from the city and back to the fresh air. Maybe then he'd be able to fight off the queasy feeling that overpowered him. "I'll be at the wedding too. You can count on that."

He went out into the cold, wintry world. Back to the life he'd known for so many years, the life that had been enough until his redheaded friend arrived and turned his world upside down.

CHAPTER
TWENTY-SIX

Many things about being at home made Hazel's heart sing with happiness. The smell of the peppermints her father was forever eating, the noise of her brothers stomping through the house, and the lump-free bed in her room. It was all so familiar, and with no effort at all she worked her way back into the everyday flow.

The newspaper featured her story on the front page. The bold headline read DAUGHTER OF WEALTHY BUSINESSMAN FOUND INNOCENT AFTER YEARS OF INJUSTICE. Within the first hour of the paper's distribution, the family began receiving invitations. Everyone wanted to befriend the now-famous spectacle and her family, or rather, they wanted to be privy to the details of her former life in exile. The invitations all felt counterfeit to Hazel, and she politely declined most of the requests, using her sister's health as her excuse for remaining home.

"I don't feel the need to dress up and put on a show for a whole slew of people who cared nothing for me just days ago," she told her mother.

"Stay in all you want. I don't like you going out too often until Patrick is apprehended." Her mother ran a hand through her daughter's hair. "I'm not sure when it happened, but you grew up on me. Not just in years but in wisdom."

"Do you think so?"

"I do. You care for your sister with tenderness, you've handled the press with finesse, and you . . . well, your heart seems to have grown a great deal. I know your road has been rocky, but you have come through it well."

Hazel loved having her mother close, feeling her love and acceptance. They'd butted heads for so many years, but now there was an easy, comfortable peace between the two of them. "I'm sorry for all the mistakes I made."

Maria sighed. "I worried over you more than I worried over any of the other children. And now here you sit, a thoughtful and kind grown woman." She kissed Hazel's forehead. "I won't insist you make any calls you don't want to make. I trust your judgment."

No remarks on her beauty or manners would ever mean so much as a genuine observation on her character. "I do wish I could have spared you so much worry."

"When you are a mother, you'll know the joy I'm feeling now. It makes no difference that it was a long time coming. Perhaps it's even a little sweeter because it took so long."

"I hope I'm as patient a mother as you." Hazel shifted in her seat, trying to ease the tension in her back from the many hours sitting hunched in a chair beside Matty.

"I hope you get a daughter exactly like you. Then you'll know just how patient I had to be." They laughed together. Then her mother's face grew serious. "I'm glad you've begun dreaming of a family."

"I had stopped believing in love. And that anyone could ever want me, especially while I was at the reformatory. I believed no one would wish to be with a woman with such a record."

Her mother searched her face. "And now you've found reason to believe again. Is that what you're telling me?"

"I have." She didn't shy away. Her love needed no approval. She knew it was a sweet and pure love, but she did hope to have her parents' blessing. "I watched my dear friend Ina find love with her Duncan. And since I've seen you with Father again, I've realized that what you have is lasting. I even saw a glimpse of it with Gilbert."

"He seemed to be a good man."

Hazel laid her head on her mother's shoulder and sighed. "I don't care that he's not wealthy . . . it seems that everything I wanted before doesn't matter now. He's not what I used to dream of, but he's all I dream of now."

"You are a good woman. I can think of no better combination."

Hazel's time at home passed quickly as she relished the love of her family. The moments with her father were just as sweet as those with her mother. They discussed the past, both eager to apologize for all that had transpired. He was not as affectionate as her mother, but he had his own ways of showing he cared. Little things such as taking her with him when he went out or asking the cook to make her favorite foods.

And of course, she never tired of being near Mathilda and her other siblings. Day after day she sat in the sickroom reading, playing her flute, and telling Mathilda about her time away. Hazel breathed easier as her sister's health continually improved.

"Once I went to a corn husking, and a man got a red ear of corn. In Amherst, a red ear of corn means the finder gets to kiss the lady of his choice," Hazel explained one afternoon.

"Did someone kiss you?" Mathilda put a hand to her chest. "Did they?"

"Yes. In front of everyone. Can you imagine?"

Mathilda gasped. "Was it terribly embarrassing?"

"No, it was terribly romantic." She laughed. When she stopped, she grew thoughtful. "But not all kisses are. Some kisses are all about taking. This man, though, has a way about him that's different."

"I hope to be kissed someday," Mathilda said, sounding very much like Ina had sounded not so long ago—clinging to romantic ideals and hoping for afternoon strolls and bouquets of flowers.

Hazel reached for her hand. "Wait to kiss someone honorable, and wait until it means something. Learn from my mistakes, and remember that kisses are not something to carelessly throw around."

"Did your kiss at the corn husking mean something?" she asked.

Putting her hand to her cheek, she could almost feel the gentle touch of Gilbert's lips. "It did. It meant a great deal."

In her room that night, she penned a letter to Gilbert. She told him about Mathilda's health and how it was slowly improving. She shared about the numerous times she'd seen Nathaniel's parents and the joy she found in their home. She rambled on about her siblings and the food the cook was making and the wintry weather.

Everyone is eager to hear my tale. Who knew I'd be so popular? I decline most of the invitations, preferring to spend my time reconnecting with my family, but my days still fill up. At first, I was afraid of going out, knowing Patrick had not been apprehended. But the police are nearly certain he's fled the city, and I am so tired of living in fear that I have chosen to carry on with life.

I think of you often. I think of the hill we walked on together. I think of the corn husking. I think of the look you have on your face when I play my flute. I wonder if you've painted anything new and what you're creating in your art room. Has Alberta come in? If she has, I'm sorry you had to treat her alone. Know you are in my thoughts, though it'd be much nicer if you were in my presence.

I don't know when I'll be free to come and see you. Soon, I hope. Until that time, I remain your friend in spirit.

Affectionately,
Hazel

PS: I played my flute today, and I thought of you.

She wanted to include other thoughts in her letter, but some things were better said in person.

"Gilbert, we've missed seeing you." Ina shook the snow from her skirts after entering the dental office. "How have you been?"

He cleared his throat. If he told Ina how he'd been practicing dentistry in mechanical motion and moping around each evening, he'd sound pathetic. Missing a woman so deeply that he felt it every moment of every day was new territory for him. "I've been busy working."

"You miss her, don't you?" Ina said. "I miss her too, and I worry about her. Patrick hasn't been apprehended yet. I hate thinking that he is out there."

"I worry too, but what else can we do? Everyone in Buffalo is looking for him." His hands clenched at his sides. "I've been giving her time to settle back in and be with her family, but it's hard being so far away."

"Have you heard from her?"

"She sent a letter, and she sounds busy and happy. Her family and the entire city seem to be thrilled she is back."

"I am glad she is happy there, but that does not mean she doesn't miss you."

He looked around the office, his jaw flexed. Every corner of it was full of memories of her. "It was simpler before. Now I don't know what to do or to think. I take care of my patients, go home alone, and wait."

"You've got to let her know you miss her. She told me when we first met that she did not believe in romance. But later she confessed she did. You are the only one I can think of who could have changed her stance. You should be honest and tell her how you feel."

"I have not kept my feelings a secret."

"You could . . . you could offer a grand gesture."

Ina, who could do no wrong, had a mischievous look on her face. "There must be something you could do. Something that would shout your love for her in a way only she would understand."

"Has Duncan ever performed a grand gesture? Is that how he won your affection?"

"He has consistently done the most perfect small acts of love, but there also have been grand gestures." She put her hand on her heart. "When he takes me on his arm, he holds his head high. I know he's not ashamed to be seen with me. That was the first grand gesture he gave me. The next was when he let me share his daughter. But for Hazel, it would have to be something different. Something that shows her what's in your heart and tells her you will love her always. A gift, an act of service . . . only you know what."

Gilbert rubbed his forehead. "I'll have to think on it. I haven't much experience with grand gestures. Or with romance. Or even with women. The fact that I am smitten still scares me."

Ina laughed. "I think romance scares us all, at least a little. But don't be so scared that you can't open up your heart and let her see what's inside. Whatever you do, don't think too long. Just act. I want my friend to come home for your sake— and for mine." She grabbed the door handle. "I have to go. I'm meeting Duncan this afternoon. We're going to pick out fabric for a dress for

Amy to wear to the wedding. But I couldn't walk past and not say hello."

Gilbert said goodbye and watched her go, then he sat back in his chair and contemplated grand gestures, hearts, and bold proclamations of love.

CHAPTER
TWENTY-SEVEN

Hazel set her flute back in its case and made her way from the music room toward the stairs. It was getting late, yet she was in no rush to go to her room. But with everyone else in bed, she had no reason to stall. She peered into the sickroom before making her way toward her own bedchamber. Matty rested easily, still not fully recovered but past the worst of her convalescing. It wouldn't be long, and the doctor no doubt would declare her in good health.

A pounding sounded at the front door. Loud and persistent, then softer and weaker. Hazel rushed from Matty's room as quickly as she could. Two paces from the door, she froze. Her heart raced as her breath came shallowly and rapidly. Something was wrong. She backed away from the door and tried to yell for help, but her voice wouldn't obey.

Her father rushed past her toward the door, joined by an older male servant who was dressed in his nightclothes. She pressed her back against the wall, leaning on it for support. Memories assaulted her from all sides as she remembered the night Nathaniel was brought to her injured. She tried to keep the memories at bay, but they battered her.

Her father flung open the door. Hazel pressed her eyes shut, wrapped her arms around her middle, and held her breath while she waited.

"Hazel, help us." Her father's voice roused her senses. "Quickly."

She forced her eyes open, only to see a woman collapsed in the entryway. Her father and their servant knelt beside her. Hazel regained her strength as she rushed to their side to offer assistance. The woman wore nothing but tattered clothing. Her hair was a mess of wet tangles—from the snow perhaps. Her disheveled appearance was certainly cause for alarm, but it was the blood on her face and arms that Hazel found most shocking.

"What happened?" her father asked while lifting the woman and making his way toward the parlor with the woman weak in his arms. Hazel shivered as they walked by her.

"Patrick Harper. Charlotte told me to come here." The woman rallied, her arms coming around Hazel's father and grasping him tightly around the neck as though she feared uttering his name would somehow bring the man himself.

Hazel and her father shared a startled glance. Who was this woman?

"Lock the doors," Hazel said, now fully engaged. "Someone must fetch the police and a doctor."

"Do as she says," her father snapped at their

servant. "I'm sorry," he said, correcting himself. "It's important."

Hazel followed after the servant. "Quick as you can, go out the back door and tell the police to come. Send for a doctor, then send word to Gilbert Watts in Amherst. Pay whatever you must to get the message out quickly. Tell him I need him."

"Yes, miss. I'll send word right away. Don't you worry." He left, and she prayed he would go quickly.

Sending for Gilbert was hasty and impulsive, but with each beat of her heart, she felt certain his presence would somehow soothe her nerves and do her heart a world of good. She'd missed him. Every day her heart had ached for him, but now with a threat looming, she needed him.

Her mother came down the stairs, wide-eyed and afraid. "What's going on? I heard commotion."

Hazel told her all that had occurred. "You should sit with Mathilda. The police have already been sent for."

"Yes, I'll sit with her. But you must tell me if anything changes."

"I will."

Her mother went back toward the stairs. "I will tell your brother to keep everyone upstairs. I don't want them in the way."

Over the next hour, Hazel bathed and saw to

the unexpected guest's wounds. The doctor sent word that he would come soon and apologized for being unable to make it right away. The poor girl slipped in and out of consciousness, limiting their ability to question her and giving them reason to fear for her life. She was weak, terribly injured, and obviously malnourished. Eventually, she drifted into a deep slumber. While she slept, Hazel's father asked, "Do you suppose she's . . . that she's a fallen woman?"

"I don't know." Hazel pulled the blanket up tighter around the sickly woman's shoulder. "She may be. When I look at her, I see a girl with a story. Like my friends at the reformatory."

"Hazel—"

"Father, I lived with girls like this for five years. Girls who were desperate or abused or who'd been misled." She looked at the face of the young woman. It was hard to gauge her age, but Hazel guessed she was sixteen or seventeen. So young and still with her whole future ahead if only she could escape the past. What horrors had she seen? "I won't judge her even if she is a woman of the night. No one is unredeemable." She hadn't meant to say the last bit with so much force, but she'd come to believe it in such a personal and powerful way that the passion in her voice could not be helped. "I'll sit with her if you want to go to bed."

"I'll wait up for the police and the doctor to

arrive." He stared at her for a long moment. "Bless you, child. Your vision is clearer than mine."

He left a moment later when the police announced themselves through the door. Hazel was alone with the poor sleeping waif. She could think of no other ways to ease the girl's suffering, so she leaned back in her chair, but then the girl moaned.

"It's all right," Hazel cooed. "You're safe now. Can you speak?"

"Where am I?"

"You're at the Bradshaw home. I'm Hazel, and we're caring for you the best we can. A doctor will be here soon." Hazel kept her voice soft. "Will you tell me your name and what's brought you here?"

"Lizzy," she whispered through cracked lips. Hazel brought a cup of water to Lizzy's mouth and helped her drink. "Patrick came to the brothel all raging mad a week or so back. He was yellin' and screamin' about how everything was ruined. We all knew to stay away from him when he got like that, but this time was different. There was no avoiding him."

"What happened?"

"He kicked over tables and acted like a man out of his head." She paused and caught her breath. "He grabbed me by my hair and drug me out of there with him. I fought him, but he was so strong."

"Did no one try to stop him?"

Lizzy shook her head. Her scared eyes turned sad. "No one cared. Some of the girls might have, but they couldn't do nothin'."

During her time at the reformatory Hazel had heard many tragic stories. Tales of women fighting to survive and struggling to feed themselves and painful stories of neglect and violence. She'd heard hundreds of stories but still she felt the sting of Lizzy's.

"How did you come to find me?"

"He kept me with him for a week, beatin' on me and doing whatever he liked. He was always yellin' about Hazel Bradshaw and how he's gonna kill you. Says you ruined everything and are gonna pay for it. Says he should have killed you before." Lizzy pushed herself up in bed and winced. "He drank so much, he passed out before tying me up tonight. I ran away and went to Charlotte's, but she was too scared that Patrick would come there. She said for me to get help from you. She told me where you lived, said you told her she could come by if she ever needed something."

"I did say that. I meant it too. Where is Patrick now?"

"He's out of his head. I ain't seen nothing like it. I think when he wakes up, he'll come here and do everything he said he would. I think he'll kill you if he can. He'll kill me too. I didn't know where else to go." Lizzy started breathing hard and heavy. Hazel feared she'd go unconscious again. "He's gonna kill us," she said over and over, trembling with fear.

"Hush." Hazel rubbed her arm. "Try to calm yourself. We'll guard the house, and you'll be safe. I'm glad you came here. We'll take care of you. You needn't worry now."

With Hazel's calm assurance, Lizzy settled and soon drifted back to sleep. Hazel went to find her father, who was with the policemen, discussing the predicament. She told them what Lizzy had told her.

"Did she say where Patrick was located?" a tall officer asked.

"No. She's quite despondent and overwhelmed right now. I don't think I'd be able to get an answer from her. But she's certain Patrick is going to try and kill me. By tomorrow she may be able to think with a clear mind."

The officer nodded. His eyes were intense but sympathetic. "Capturing Patrick Harper is high on the department's list right now. They want him brought in before he can get away. His list of crimes is nearly endless. Don't you worry, miss, we will put an end to your troubles."

"We could guard this house tonight, and tomorrow we can get Patrick's location from the girl. The chief can determine the best course of action then," the shorter, less animated officer said. "We shouldn't be hasty. Besides, the girl says he's drunk and unconscious. I don't think he'll come anytime soon."

"No! I want my family safe." Hazel stood and paced the floor. "I could go somewhere else."

"Stay here. It's easier for us to guard one house than several. And I'd imagine he knows you are here, so your family is in danger already," the first officer chimed in. "But he might be all talk and never come. I wouldn't be surprised if he leaves and we never see him again."

"I just sat next to a girl he beat. And that happened while we all thought he was gone. We can't be too careful." Hazel let out a puff of air. "I wouldn't assume anything of him. He's clearly mad."

"That woman's a—"

"I don't care what you think she is. Any man who would lay hands on a woman is a monster." There wasn't time to set these men straight on everything, not with a criminal looming close by. "I was afraid of this."

"Of what?" her father asked.

"That somehow my presence would make others unsafe."

"This isn't your doing." Her father came to her side and put a hand on her shoulder. "We didn't stand beside you before, but now, this time we will. No matter what, we'll be here for you and we want you here."

She put a tired hand to her forehead. "He's a smart man—at least he must have been before he lost his mind. If this house is surrounded by officers, he'll wait. He'll wait until I'm alone."

"We're smarter than Patrick, don't you worry," the shorter officer said.

"Is that why he's evaded you so far?" She covered her mouth. "I'm sorry. I know you're working hard. I've no doubt you'll do all you can. I think I'll go sit by Lizzy."

The night was ever so long. Each minute dragged by as she fought to stay in control of her nerves. Every half hour or so, she peered out the window and assured herself the officers were still present and awake and, to her relief, walking laps around the house.

At four in the morning, long before the sun rose for the day, she heard a ruckus and ran to the window. The two officers were across the street and had a man pinned to the ground.

Relief, sweet and real, poured over her. Could it be so simple? Patrick had come to her house and the officers got him right away? She sighed. Her eye darted back to the man on the ground, and the sick tension returned. She pressed her face to the glass, then shrieked and sprang to action, racing away from her charge and out the front door.

"Let him go!" she shouted at the officers. "That's not Patrick. Let him go! That's Gil."

The officers' heads shot up, and their eyes

found hers. Gilbert was still pressed to the ground with his arm twisted behind his back.

"Let him go." She said each word loud and slow. "Now."

The officers released Gilbert and backed away.

"Hazel!" Gil shouted back as he struggled to his feet. "I came as quick as I could."

She stepped down the stairs, not worrying about her slippered feet and thinking only of rushing into his arms and burying her head in his strong shoulder.

"Go inside. It's not safe out here," she said as he crossed the street toward her. The police officers stayed back, looking away sheepishly. "I shouldn't have asked you to come. It's not safe. Patrick is somewhere."

"This is where I want to be." He was almost to her, and Hazel's heart cried out in anticipation. Gilbert, her Gil, was there!

"I forgot." He turned back and crossed the street, bending down to pick up a package that lay in the snow. Hazel grinned. It was foolish to feel giddy considering the situation, but she couldn't suppress it.

A noise to her left drew her attention away from Gilbert and the package in his hands. In the dim early morning light, she saw a man approaching. He staggered but moved quickly. Hazel screamed, alerting the others. The two officers quickly approached from across the street, and Gilbert dropped the package again and raced toward her.

They were too slow.

A hand came around her waist. She screamed again, and for one second her eyes locked with Gil's before the edge of something sharp came against her throat. The two officers and Gilbert moved together but didn't advance toward Hazel.

"Let her go, Patrick," Gilbert said. His quiet demeanor changed into something fierce she'd never seen before. His fists were clenched, his jaw was tight, and his eyes were on fire.

"No!" Patrick sneered, his foul breath striking her. "She ruined everything." He pushed the knife against her neck enough that it pierced her skin. A warm stream of blood trickled down her neck. She flinched, but with his arm so tight around her waist, pressing her back against his chest, and the knife at her neck, she had no way to flee. "And now she'll die," he said. Hazel could feel his head turn toward the officers. "Drop your guns."

They bent and placed their pistols on the ground. Hazel's thin nightdress and slippers offered little protection from the cold, but she barely noticed. Patrick spit, then pulled her with him as he walked backward away from the others. "You're coming with me. I'm going to destroy you just like you destroyed me."

With the blade at her throat, she couldn't utter a sound of protest. Death was near, looming and sure. Would all the years of struggle be for naught? She did her best to walk without stumbling, but going backward with an unsteady man was not easy. Gilbert and the officers inched along with them, always keeping their distance but never losing sight of her.

Hazel tapped Patrick's hand. He loosened his grip just enough so that she could speak. "Not that way." The words burned her sore throat.

"You don't get to tell me where I can go."

He walked faster in the direction she'd advised against. Her years of relentless stubbornness helped her understand this wicked man. She tapped his arm again.

"What?" he growled. "What now?"

"Not this way," she said again, leading him to the iciest patch of road around. It was so slick that if temperatures dropped, locals knew to avoid it at all costs. Hazel prayed the knife would fall when Patrick did and not injure her further. It was the only idea she had.

"Shut your mouth." He tightened the knife at her throat, making her wince. Patrick stepped onto the icy road, swaying before he even hit the worst of it. His feet jutted out, causing the knife to nick her neck again. As Patrick fought to keep his footing and steady himself with his arms, he let go of her. With no knife at her throat, Hazel turned and shoved him with all the force she could muster, then darted away, falling once on the ice herself. Gilbert ran by at full speed toward Patrick, the two officers at his heels. There was no time to pause and marvel at the sight of him—his long, lean frame not missing a step, a protective rage written across his tight features.

Like a cougar, Gilbert leapt onto the still-struggling Patrick. His force knocked Patrick to the ground, and his fists kept him there. Gil unleashed one blow after another, his breath hard and heavy, his voice fierce and threatening. The officers retrieved the knife, which Patrick had dropped at his side. Patrick tried to get up and cursed between blows, managing to hit Gilbert only once. Threatening, vile words escaped Patrick's bloody mouth. Gilbert pulled back his fist and let it land squarely on Patrick's face, finally subduing the criminal. Gil got to his feet as the officers leapt in and put Patrick in cuffs.

Gilbert wiped a hand across his face, never taking his eyes off Patrick.

"Are you hurt?" Hazel rushed to his side. "Tell me where, and I'll help you."

He shook his head, then looked at his bloodied hands. "I don't know. Hazel, I—"

"Come back to the house and I'll clean you up." She grabbed his hand and led him away.

Gilbert looked back and forth between Patrick and her, his eyes finally focusing on her neck. "You're bleeding! Your neck! Oh, Red, your neck."

Hazel ran a finger across her neck, and it came

away damp and red. He pulled a handkerchief from his pocket and pressed it against her injuries. "I'm sorry. When he was holding you—"

"It's nothing. It doesn't even hurt."

He put his other hand on the back of her neck and brought her to him, then he pressed his lips against her forehead.

"I've never hit a man," he said, letting her go and looking back toward Patrick.

"He was going to kill me." She pulled on his arm, urging him away from the scene. "Gil, he was going to kill me, and I would have never—"

"I wouldn't have let him. I would have done anything to keep you safe." Gil studied his bloodstained hands. "I've never acted like that before. Are you afraid?"

"Afraid of you?" She shook her head. "No, not at all. You came when I needed you. You risked your life. Gilbert Watts, I have never felt safer in anyone's presence than I do in yours—and not just because of what you did this morning."

They were near the house now. She pointed toward the package on the ground. "Is that yours?"

"It's a gift for you. I made it a few days ago and had planned to mail it. Ina mentioned a grand gesture . . . that's, well, that's my attempt." He looked away. "Save it and open it another time. Right now hardly seems the right time."

"Very well." Hazel picked it up, then opened the door for him. She'd planned to wash him up, look over his injuries, and fall into his arms in a pile of tears, but it was not to be. She barely had time to change her clothes. The house was soon alive and full of commotion. Police officers, doctors, and reporters trickled in, all needing to talk to Hazel and Gilbert.

Gilbert cleaned himself up and sat beside her when she was free, but they had very little time alone. The day stretched on in much the same fashion until Gilbert said, "I promised a patient I'd get them their dentures tomorrow. It's not a life-and-death thing, but I gave them my word."

"You're leaving?" Her heart sank. "I had hoped . . ."

"I'm sorry, Hazel." And she knew from his expression that he truly was, but that did not change the fact that she wanted him there with her. "But you are coming to the wedding, are you not?"

"I'll be there." She touched his cheek gently. "Your poor face."

"It'll heal." He covered her hand with his. "Will you go to the wedding with me?"

"Yes."

"I wish it didn't have to wait." He stood to leave. "I'll count down the days."

"As will I."

Lizzy moaned, and duty called. She kissed him quickly on the cheek, then, fighting tears, answered the cry of need.

CHAPTER
TWENTY-EIGHT

It was late into the night before the commotion of the day died down. The officers had left, the reporters had all been turned away, and Mathilda and Lizzy were both resting peacefully. Hazel sat at the dining room table and tipped her head back, resting it against the chair. She was tired, but she knew the wild feeling pumping through her veins would keep her from falling asleep. Over and over again she saw the wild, protective passion burning in Gilbert's eyes as he leapt across the icy street and knocked Patrick down. He'd once confessed to often being afraid, and perhaps he was fearful in that moment too, but he acted like a man who had no doubts he would succeed. Butterflies danced in her heart each time she relived the moment and saw his face. He'd been gone only a couple of hours and she'd see him soon, but she missed him.

Hazel's mother entered the room with Gilbert's box in hand. "Are you curious what he brought you?"

"I am." She took the package and hugged it tightly to herself. "He said he made this several days ago."

"It's sweet of him to think of you. You should open it."

Hazel tore the brown paper from the package

and found a note tucked inside. She opened it and read quietly to herself.

Dear Hazel,

Time has moved slowly since I last saw you. I know it's only been weeks since we were in Buffalo, but it feels much longer. I thought you'd like knowing Alberta was in again. I nearly died. I think I need you to come back and take care of me after the tongue-lashing she gave *me*.

Bianca Carluccio has learned a few English words. Not enough to easily communicate, but she's trying hard. I watched her eyes when she came in. I think she was looking for you. If I'd been able to speak Italian, I would have told her I am always watching for you too. On the street when the door opens and even in my dreams, I look for your red hair and beautiful face.

I miss my attending and her humming. I miss my friend. I understand they need you where you are. But know you are deeply missed.

I told you once that I paint my heart into pictures. So today I give you my heart.

Lovingly yours,
Gil

"Is it a nice letter?" Hazel's mother asked.

"Yes. Some of our favorite patients have been in."

"Oh, is that all?"

"No," she said slowly, enjoying the way her heart raced when she thought of Gilbert's bold words and sweet confessions. "He said more than that."

Her mother didn't press for details. Instead, she said, "Don't you want to see what he brought?"

She opened the gift, savoring the simple pleasure of discovering what was beneath the paper. Inside she found a painting unlike any other she'd ever seen. In the right corner was the profile of a face—her face. The features matched hers so well—her nose with its tiny curve and her eyes with their flecks of green. Little details that most would overlook. The rest of the painting was a mosaic of other items all blended together in an unusually artistic way. A flute, an autumn leaf, a stalk of corn, a fallen tree, and so much more.

"It's lovely but very unusual," her mother commented. "Why do you suppose he put all that together?"

"It's me. All of it is. It's my flute and my favorite season and my first corn husking and our hill. It's all me, and it's him. It's us together." She hugged the painting, wishing she were hugging the painter instead. "He paints his heart into his work. It's a grand gesture of sorts, his way of telling me that I am his heart. And he is mine."

Her mother put her hands on her daughter's cheeks. "I'll forever be grateful he protected his heart today."

Hazel filled the remaining days before the wedding caring for Lizzy and Mathilda. Both were improving daily, causing a sense of relief to fill the house. The tense atmosphere turned light and jovial. Her anticipation grew with each passing moment until the day of the long-awaited wedding arrived.

"I'll be back soon." Hazel kissed her sister's cheek. "I'd stay by your side and read to you all afternoon, but Ina would never understand if I missed her wedding."

"You have to go." A wistful look filled Mathilda's face like a child staring into the windows of the candy shop. "Will you tell me all about it?"

"I will. Every detail. What the dress looked like, what we ate, and even who I danced with." Hazel pushed a rebellious pin deeper into her hair. "How do I look?"

"Beautiful. I think Gilbert will be even more lost to you when he sees you. Mother always says you look fetching in lavender."

Hazel smiled at her reflection, loving how her new dress fit each curve of her body. "I do hope so." A noise drew her attention to the window. She peered out. "The driver's here. I have to go."

"Tell me if he sweeps you off your feet." Mathilda sat upright in her bed, a forgotten book beside her. "I hope he does."

"He can be a little quiet. I might have to take the lead." She winked at her sister. "Does that make me very modern? Or a complete heathen?"

Mathilda pulled her mouth to one side. "Depends who you ask. Mother might say you're a heathen, but I think it's romantic letting a man know you care for him."

"Since I like your judgment, you are the one I will whisper my secrets to when I come home." Her heart danced with excitement, amazed and humbled that after such a long stretch of heartache she'd found herself at the center of so much good.

Hazel kissed her sister's cheek, grabbed the little paper bundle that sat on the table, and rushed to meet her ride. She fiddled with the gift in her hands during the entire ride to Amherst. The crinkle of paper made her heart soar one moment and panic the next. Perhaps this was too soon, too presumptuous. But so much time had already been lost, and she didn't want to wait just for the sake of waiting when she knew what she wanted.

"Please drop me off here," Hazel requested when she was near her destination. "I want to walk the rest of the way."

She stood on the side of the street, closed her eyes, and breathed deeply. How great and marvelous to be back! Everything looked how she remembered, only now the snow was deeper and she was freer. She quickened her pace, lifting her skirts a little in a feckless attempt at keeping her hem dry for the wedding. Ina was a practical friend who she had no doubt would welcome her no matter how disheveled she was. It was Gilbert's reaction she cared most about.

Hazel stopped in front of his house only long enough to catch her breath, then she walked to the front door, knocked confidently, and waited.

"Well, well. If it isn't the long-lost Hazel." Eddie opened the door wide, letting her in. "I'm glad you've come. Gilbert's been moping around since his return from Buffalo. I'll go get him and let you two say your hellos. Or your I-love-yous or whatever it is you plan to say to him."

"I . . . well . . . I wasn't going to—"

"Save it for Gilbert." He dashed up the stairs, taking them two at a time.

She fidgeted with her skirts, trying to knock the snow off the bottom and smooth the riding creases. Her head popped up when she heard her name and the sound of footsteps on the stairs.

"Gil!"

"You're here!" He crossed the entryway to her. His face still showed signs of the fight with Patrick, but his arms were outstretched. She was certain she'd never seen a more welcoming sight. "You're really here. You look beautiful."

"Thank you."

"I can hardly believe you're real."

She reached out and took his hand and guided it to her face. "Flesh and bones. The real thing."

He stepped away, the smile still on his face. "I'm going to tell Eddie we're leaving. Wait here."

"Does he want to come with us?"

"He doesn't get to. He's a grown man and can find his own way there." Gilbert dashed back up the stairs, returning only seconds later. "Are you ready?"

"Yes." She took his arm and sighed. Holding on to him felt so natural and perfect.

His eyes kept finding hers, and his smile never left his face. "Tell me how Matty is and all the others."

"There's been a lot of activity since Patrick was arrested, but it's been good. He's behind bars, and I feel much more at ease knowing it. Matty and Lizzy are both doing well, and everyone else is glad life is going back to normal, though I'm not sure there is such a thing."

"Life with you is never dull, that much I know."

She walked so close to him that her shoulder pressed against his. "I loved my painting. I hung it in my room and look at it every day."

"I'd hoped you'd like it." They neared the

church. "It's only three thirty. We've still got time before the wedding."

She looked past the church toward the hill. "Do we have time to walk on our hill?"

"I think we do."

They made their way to the top in comfortable silence. Hazel no longer cared about snow on her hem or her hair. They were together, and that was all that mattered. At the top they looked out at the serene landscape, admiring their favorite view blanketed under a quilt of snow.

"I've walked up here a few times since you've been gone, but I like it better with you by my side." In his tentative way, he studied her. "I have so many things I want to say, but I don't know how or if you—"

"Open this. It's for you." Hazel straightened her shoulders and held out her gift. She gnawed on her lip while she waited, eager and nervous for his reaction.

He took it and shook it. "What is it?"

"Open it before I change my mind." She wavered between fear and readiness. "Hurry."

He shot her one quizzical look before he untied the string and pulled the paper away. Not a second later he was laughing, and Hazel felt her face flush and her heart skip a beat.

"It's a red ear of corn," he said, staring down at it, making it difficult for her to gauge his reaction.

"You found it," she said, giving him a sideways glance. "You have to use it. It's tradition."

He let the corn fall to the ground, put his hands on her waist, and, with gentle pressure, pulled her toward him. Her arms went around his shoulders and her hands found their way to the hair at the nape of his neck. "It's one of my favorite traditions, but I can't kiss you without your permission," he said near her ear. His breath tickled her skin. "Tell me I can and I will. Give me permission to be more than your friend."

She looked up at his handsome, freshly shaven face, stopping when their eyes met and she could feel the pleading in his gaze. "Kiss me. Not because it's tradition but because you want to, and then hold me because I've been aching for it since you rescued me," she whispered in a barely audible voice. "You have my permission."

He bent his head, and their lips met for the first time. A brush of his lips on hers, enough to make her long for more. He must have felt the same desire, because he kissed her again, more slowly this time. It was gentle and sweet and everything she'd never felt from a kiss before. "That one wasn't because of tradition." He kept his face near hers and said, "It was because I love you."

"It's all so hard to believe."

He smiled like a child on Christmas who woke to find their dreams fulfilled. "I do love you. I love the way you light up a room when you enter it. I love the sound of your laughter and the way your smile is a little crooked and screams of mischief. I love that you bite your fingernails when you're nervous and hum when you clean. I love that you have red hair and a fiery disposition to match it. I love that you pepper me with questions and make me think about things in a new way. I love that you think my paintings are beautiful and that you play the flute."

She inhaled quickly. His touch, his words, and the look of love in his eyes. It was all too good to be true, and yet it was. He was real. This perfect moment was real.

"We both know I'm not good with words. And even if I were, there would be no way for me to say what is in my heart. But I hope you believe me when I say I love you. I love everything about you. When I thought I might lose you . . ." He wiped a tear from his cheek. "I was so afraid, because a world without you would be incomplete. I love you, Hazel."

She wiped at a second tear that slid down his smooth cheek. "I love everything you say. I'll never tire of listening to you."

"It is my wish to tell you daily how much I care. How much I love and adore you." He kissed her again. Slower and longer this time. The quiet man, growing bolder with each touch. "Hazel, will you marry me? Be my wife. That first day I was wrong. I do not want to remain unattached.

I want nothing more than to be linked with you always."

"I remember you saying you needed a wife who played the flute and had red hair." Smiling up at him, she asked, "But are you sure you can handle a wife like me?"

"You are the only one for me."

"What about my past?" She looked away. It was a question she had to ask. An answer she had to hear. "Doesn't it change things? My reckless youth. A tragic marriage and a history of incarceration all come with me."

He put a hand under her chin and tilted her head toward him. "Your past led you to me. I love the woman you are today and who you'll be tomorrow. That woman is born from who you were yesterday. I want it all." He kissed her again, his lips meeting hers, confirming his love. "I want to marry you. Say yes."

"My answer is yes! I love you, Gil." She rested her head against his chest and listened to the gentle thumping of his heart. Each beat filled her heart with warmth and joy so sweet she felt ready to burst. "I'll love you forever."

DISCUSSION QUESTIONS

1. Hazel's past at the reformatory makes finding a job difficult. Was she wrong to give Gilbert a false name? Do you think he would have hired her if she'd told the truth?
2. Gilbert has led a solitary life for several years prior to meeting Hazel. Once they meet, his former life loses its appeal. Have you ever had a person or incident change the way you look at life?
3. Ina is often judged because of her outward appearance. Why was Duncan able to see her beauty when so many others could not?
4. Hazel realizes she has to tell Gilbert the truth about her past. Have you ever had to divulge a secret, knowing the consequences could be significant?
5. Gilbert is willing to help Hazel set her past right. Why is he willing to help even when there is no solid proof of her innocence?
6. Eddie's return presents a challenge for Hazel and causes her to feel unworthy of being with someone like Gilbert. Have your past and present ever collided in an uncomfortable way?
7. Hazel is able to read Nathaniel's old journals and find some peace through his words. If

you could go back and talk to someone who has died, who would it be? How could it affect your life now?

8. Forgiveness for others and for oneself is a theme throughout the second half of this book. Have you ever struggled to forgive yourself?

9. Gilbert worries that Hazel will want to stay in Buffalo once her name is cleared. Was he right to leave her and let her make up her own mind?

10. Hazel suffered injustice and false accusations. In the end, did her circumstances work together for her good?

AUTHOR'S NOTE

The inspiration for this story came in several ways. First was when I was with my husband at the dental school in Buffalo, New York, and we were looking at their displays of antique dental instruments. I realized that dental assisting (as we call it today) was a field that women were involved in but I'd never seen featured in a historical novel. I also really wanted to write a dentist as my leading man who was not evil or a bumbling fool. Books and movies rarely show dentists in a good light, and I decided I wanted to! It became my mission to write about a terribly romantic dentist that readers would enjoy (I hope you loved Gilbert as much as I did).

When I began diving into Hazel's backstory and trying to discover what made her journey unique, I came across the reformatory movement. In a sense, reformatories were the first juvenile facilities (although the age limits were different). The details were beyond fascinating, but sadly this story did not have room for all of them (perhaps another book someday). If you have spare time, read up on reformatories of the late-nineteenth century and learn about the forerunners in this movement—you will find some new heroes.

While writing this book, I truly came to love both Hazel and Gilbert and enjoyed every moment I shared with them as they came together, learned to forgive, and discovered how truly right they were for one another. I hope the reading journey for you was as sweet as the writing journey was for me.

This book was written years ago, set aside, reworked, and finally published. Due to its long path to publication, I am unable to properly thank everyone who helped me. I hope all my early readers know how grateful I am for your feedback. I apologize that I can't thank you all by name.

I would like to quickly thank my editors, Rachel McRae and Amy Ballor. I also want to thank the rest of the amazing team at Revell, who put up with my emails and crazy ideas, and my agent, Emily Sylvan Kim. What amazing people I have cheering me on!

I also have a whole fan club living under my roof (the joys of a big family). My husband and kids are a gift from a loving God. I feel truly blessed not only when they encourage my writing but during each day we share together. It's a loud and wonderful life!

Thank you, dear readers, for picking up my books, giving them a chance, and asking for more. Thank you for reading, for messaging me, and for all the little ways you help others find my stories. I truly appreciate you.

Rachel Fordham is the author of *The Hope of Azure Springs*, *Yours Truly, Thomas*, and *A Life Once Dreamed*. She started writing when her children began begging her for stories at night. She'd pull a book from the shelf, but they'd insist she make one up. Finally, she paired her love of good stories with her love of writing and hasn't stopped since. She lives with her husband and children on an island in the state of Washington.

Books are produced in the United States using U.S.-based materials

Books are printed using a revolutionary new process called THINKtech™ that lowers energy usage by 70% and increases overall quality

Books are durable and flexible because of Smyth-sewing

Paper is sourced using environmentally responsible foresting methods and the paper is acid-free

Center Point Large Print
600 Brooks Road / PO Box 1
Thorndike, ME 04986-0001 USA

(207) 568-3717

US & Canada:
1 800 929-9108
www.centerpointlargeprint.com